Tales of the Collapse

by Christine D. Shuck

Introduction

Stories swirl around each of my characters begging to be told. Sometimes a song lyric will get me started, as it did in *99 Problems*. Or I imagine where this character came from and what happened to them after their lives intersected, even for the briefest moment with another. Jacob's story, for instance, in *All Roads Lead to Austin* was an example of that momentary exchange that meant so much.

In others, I wanted to tell more of the backstory of how a character came to be where they were, or why they were who they were.

A societal collapse, even a civil war, does not happen overnight. Instead it is the slow and insidious undoing. It consists of multiple facets coming together to create chaos, fire, and destruction.

When I imagined *War's End* - that is what I thought of. Not one single problem, but a slow, yet growing cascade of them.

Viruses growing out of control and wreaking havoc, killing hundreds and even thousands.

Social unrest that leads to a rise in factions, including white supremacists.

Terrorist acts on American soil.

An economy in ruins.

If this is sounding eerily familiar, well, call me Cassandra. But by all means, read on. The Collapse is coming. In fact, it might be just around the corner.

Leave Now

"It's coming. You have been warned."

    Sarah could hear the news reporter on the television in the living room talking about the Hong Kong H1N5 virus. Deaths from the particularly virulent strain of flu had grown to over several hundred now and the news anchor was advising people to wear masks and stay home if they showed signs of the illness. Sarah sighed; the television was something she tried not to be bothered by. Gina kept it on all day, even when she was gone from the bungalow. Sarah, on the other hand, had grown up with a television relegated to just a few hours of use a day. The idea of keeping it on constantly had been irritating at first, but now it usually served as background noise. It wasn't much different from the hum of cars from the freeway now.

She stared at the ocean and sipped from the tall, slender coffee cup in her hands, wincing as the liquid scalded her tongue. The Santa Ana winds were warm, and she could smell the brine of the ocean, hear the gulls scream as they dove into the surf. Hunting, she supposed, for their next meal.

Gina Abernathy stretched out with a sigh on the chaise lounge to Sarah's left, "My God, Sarah, you are up at the crack of dawn. Just like your Pops, God rest his soul." Her hair was already styled, stiff with what had to be a half of a can of Aqua Net holding it in place, and her fingers encrusted with several large, gaudy rings. Sarah smiled at her friend. Gina had been a longtime live-in girlfriend of Scotty Abernathy, Daddy's literary agent, and now was his widow for the past five years. A month after Sarah's husband Theo had passed of pancreatic cancer, Gina had rousted Sarah out of her gray haze of grief, shoved her on a plane and taken her to Fiji. That had been two years ago, and Gina had been a constant companion ever since.

"I have to be at Cedars-Sinai by ten to meet with Dr. Carlson, and you know traffic is far more difficult here than in Kansas City."

"Oh Honey, you don't know the half of it. It takes an hour to go twenty miles! It's worse than New York, and that's saying a lot." Gina flapped her hands as she spoke, her East coast accent creeping through. "I just don't know what you hope to do there, girl. You do know they're all crazy, right?" She turned and stared at Sarah as if the thought had just occurred to her. Despite the early hour, Gina was made up, thick foundation caked on her face, blush, eyeliner, and mascara - the works. Gina Abernathy contributed to the livelihood of the cosmetics industry and single-handedly propped up several, by Sarah's estimation, something that was both awe-inspiring and slightly terrifying.

Sarah's mother, June, had tolerated the younger woman's presence with patience, graciously including her whenever she invited Scotty to visit her and Dad while they had both been alive. She had known and been close friends with Lucinda, Scotty's first wife. Gina had been such a sharp departure from the mousy woman that Mom had once confided to Sarah that she couldn't imagine what Scotty had seen in Gina, "Unless it is simply that he knew Lucinda could not and should not be replaced, so he found her exact opposite."

Gina would have been a pain in the ass, what with her clownish makeup, gaudy decor and garish clothing - except that she was also one of the warmest, kindest human beings Sarah had ever met. She was the type who would do anything for a friend, especially in the aftermath of the worst possible loss. Theo's illness had not only taken them by surprise, but it had robbed them of any time to enjoy a retirement or indulge in the bucket list of dreams they had slowly accumulated over the decades.

They had fallen in love in college, and for Sarah, there had never been any other man she could imagine sharing her life with. Theo had matched her - intellectually, emotionally. Being with him, spending more than thirty years together, it had been a comfort. While many of her girlfriends from high school had gotten married at the same time as her, most had divorced, at least once, and Sarah knew they had envied the close, steady relationship that she and Theo had shared.

His abdominal pain, weight loss, and repeated bouts of nausea had all tied in so neatly to a particularly nasty round of flu that had been going around. Sarah's heart panged at the thought of the six long weeks in which he had gotten progressively worse until she had insisted on getting him in to a doctor for tests. Two weeks after that, they had learned the truth, and just six weeks later, Theo was gone. There had been no time to mount a defense, no time to try any alternative treatments or aggressive chemo. The man she had thought she would spend her golden years with was gone, and Sarah had descended into a miasma of grief and loneliness that no number of visits from friends and family could shake. That is until Gina had come around and forced her back into the world again.

She was lucky she had Gina. Very lucky.

Gina waved her jewel-bedecked fingers in Sarah's face. "Earth to Sarah. You still there, Honey?"

Sarah shook herself, tried to shake off the memories, to turn her focus to the present. "Sorry, Gina, I was miles away."

"I'm just saying, girl, some of those people they have in there are crazy and violent."

"Not the one I'm seeing today. She wouldn't harm a fly."

Gina snorted. "That's what they say right before the patient tries to claw your eyes out. I just don't know *why* this was your choice of writing career. Honey, you could be a travel writer. My friend Blanche, she traveled to China, stayed in the finest hotels, saw the Great Wall, all on Conde Nast's dime. And her writing is shit compared to yours. With the genetics you got from your Pops, you might as well have been born with a pen in your hand." Gina whistled, "But you decide to write an expose on mental health care in America. Who the hell is gonna read that, Sarah? Especially when it is gonna be thicker than a textbook by the time you are done?"

She took a slurp of her coffee and shook her head, the scent of Aqua Net pouring off of her in a cloud.

Sarah's nose twitched, and she fought off a sneeze. The older woman made her smile, something that seemed a rare thing now that Theo was gone. The only other things that made her happy were her rather grim writing subject, and her two grandchildren, Chris and Jess. Sarah had spent two weeks visiting them during the summer, staying at their house in Belton, Missouri. They were teenagers now, which seemed impossible, because she distinctly remembered holding each of them in the hospital, exclaiming over their tiny little hands and wrinkled, red faces. Michael and his wife, Julie, had raised them right, however, and despite being teenagers, they were as kind as ever. Every morning, Jess had brought two large mugs of tea, Earl Grey with milk and sugar just the way Sarah liked it, down to the basement guest bedroom and sat with her grandmother planning what they could go and do that day. Chris had made it a point to introduce her to his friends, a unique combination of jocks and gangly nerds who were polite and said "yes ma'am" with regularity. One of them, Allen, who was slightly thicker around the middle, loved reading. He had spent hours talking with Sarah about their shared love of books. Good kids, all of them.

Sarah sighed. Michael kept asking her if she would consider moving in. "We could even build a mother-in-law cottage in the back if you would prefer your privacy, Mom. I just wish you were closer. You would get to see the kids more often."

She hadn't been able to stay in the house she and Theo had shared for more than 35 years. It had felt so empty. Instead, she had rented it out and, after Gina had shoved her on a plane, ended up traveling for more than a year before settling down in the spare bedroom at Gina's -first in New York and later at her beach house in Southern California. A week's stay had turned into a month, and except for visiting Michael's family, she had found a sense of peace here in this small bungalow with a view of the Pacific Ocean. It was a sharp departure from the low, rolling hills of flyover country. Even the clouds in the sky were different. They were long and thin and wispy, compared to the fat cumulonimbus in Missouri. Everything moved faster here, people, automobiles, the public transit - all frantic to get from one point to another. And it was here that she had gone back and re-examined the paperwork from her parents' files, the order to commit her father in 1954 that had been begun but never finalized, and the remaining mystery surrounding his death decades later.

Fifteen years had passed since then, but the answers had never come.

She thought about it now as she took another sip of coffee. The question of what had happened to Dad, what had *really* happened to him, remained a mystery. What do near-death experiences and psychotic breaks do to people? Dad had always seemed fine, he'd just been Dad to her, but her sister Betty had often described Dad as being very different when she was young - angry, indifferent, and resentful.

"That all changed after the accident, though." She had mused when Sarah pressed her. "He took an interest in us, and that's also when he started writing, sold the company, and soon after that, you were born." She had shrugged, "You know, they say that head injuries change people. Maybe it changed Dad for the better."

Those words had haunted her. Had the accident truly affected Dad for the *better*? If so, he was one of few. Head injuries like his, and she had examined the x-rays and spoken with numerous doctors on the subject, tended to change a person, but not for the better. And then there was his letter, one that spoke with certainty of this other life he was sure he had experienced with Mom, Betty and Danny dead, and he remarried to a nurse, Theo's mom no less! And a child born after, with her own name, Sarah Magdalene. That had been the other woman's name, Magdalene or Maggie. And it wasn't as if she could ask Maggie, for Maggie had died, just nine years after Mom and Dad's accident, in 1962. Theo had been orphaned by it. His father had never been in the picture and he had ended up being raised by relatives in a large rambling brick farmhouse in Raymore, Missouri, just a few miles south of Kansas City, where she had grown up. Their shared geography had been the first connection when they met in college - something that brought them closer and given them something to talk about.

It was mysterious to say the least, but even now she struggled to find a realistic explanation. One that was grounded in facts, not fantasy. It was this quest that had led Sarah down a somewhat winding path to where it was now. A focus on mental health in America and with it, the unique and odd interpretations of reality from the mentally ill's perspective.

   She had spoken to individuals who were involved in intense psychotherapy, under the care of psychiatrists and therapists. She had spoken to several who were incarcerated in the penal system because the mental hospitals were now the last bastion for only the luckiest of the mentally ill.

   Today, she was meeting with Dr. Carlson, who was treating a young woman who claimed to know the future. Dr. Carlson had reached out to Sarah after reading one of her articles, noted that she was writing a book, and asked if she was looking for more patients to interview. Their schedules had been full of conflicts for nearly two months, but now, today, she would finally get a chance to meet him, and his patient, for the first time.

Gina's voice interrupted her thoughts, "Sure you don't want to go shopping with me? I've just got to stop by Prada and see their new handbag line. And besides, right around the corner is Jimmy Choo, and there is a young man there that is a ridiculous flirt." Gina laughed, "The things he promises an old lady like me are, well, who knows, he might just jump start this dead as a doornail libido of mine, you never know."

Sarah suppressed a smile. Gina was loud, over the top, and full of chutzpah. She gave off an air of rich widow and that had plenty of strapping, young, pretty-faced boys drooling after her wherever she went. Whether it was over her money or her still-voluptuous body, Sarah couldn't say for sure, but Gina strung them along like puppets, never indulging, just teasing them and flirting outrageously. She had done it when Scotty was still alive, and he had pretended to be out of sorts over it, but really wasn't. Gina, despite appearances, hadn't wanted anyone but Scotty. Even *after* Scotty, for that matter. It was obvious to Sarah that the older woman had loved her husband, body and soul. There was no one who could replace him.

"Maybe next week, Gina. But I've been trying for over two months to get this appointment and as a bonus, I'll get a read on the future. Who knows, maybe she'll have some good stock tips or tell me who is slated to win at the races." Gina was an avid horse racing fan and hadn't missed a race at the Kentucky Derby in over ten years.

Gina snorted, shook her head, and drained the last of her coffee. "Sarah, honey, you are missing out. That fine, strapping lad is just the jolt to a woman's ego that every one of us fifty-something's need." Gina was in her mid-sixties, but far be it from Sarah to correct her.

"But make sure and ask her if Black Shadow has a chance of winning. Best to hedge our bets, after all." Gina had been hitting the horse races more often since one of her major investments had tanked. She still had enough money, and she was actually fairly good at judging winners, so recently her betting had been a boon instead of a bust.

There were whispers in the wind that the American economy was not what it had been. Sarah had moved most of her portfolio into steady, low-interest-bearing bonds as the Dow alternately tanked and then exploded. The rapid seesawing made her nervous, and Michael had recently sent her a text again asking for her to come home to Missouri and stay with his family. "It's not looking good, Mom, I've been reading that we are heading for the mother of all depressions," he had written, "the likes of which will make the Great Depression look like a walk in the park in comparison."

His concern was sweet, and she knew that his wife, Julie, was very involved in producing their own food and believed in self-sufficient living.

She had turned their suburban yard outside of Kansas City into a food-producing paradise filled with fruit and nut trees and bushes, as well as raised beds that grew everything from asparagus to zucchini. Sarah loved walking through the raised beds and gathering herbs and fresh vegetables when she visited. It felt like a miniature garden of Eden.

Gina interrupted Sarah's thoughts again, "There's also Shenanigans, check on that one as well. I've got a good feeling about that horse."

Sarah laughed, finished her coffee, and stood up. She leaned over and hugged her friend, holding her breath so she didn't pass out from the hairspray fumes still off-gassing and polluting the air. It was enough to give Sarah a thumping headache if she took a big enough whiff. She couldn't understand how Gina managed to stop herself from passing out.

"I'll catch lunch out, but let's make plans for dinner, okay?"

Gina gave her a fierce squeeze back, "I'll make some cannoli."

"Sounds wonderful!" Sarah had put on five pounds since she had quasi-moved in to Gina's guest room. Her friend's cooking remained out of this world and she specialized in delectable, albeit fattening, Italian cuisine.

The drive into the city was hair-raising and frantic for the first twenty minutes and then slowed to a maddening stop and go as Sarah encountered two different fender benders. She was relieved she had left a half hour earlier than planned because she had a long hike to the entrance of the hospital. All the nearby parking lots were full, and she had to park several hundred yards away. The last fifteen minutes before her appointment with Dr. Carlson were eaten up going through security, a necessary precaution for the locked psychiatric unit she would be walking through.

At just two minutes to ten, she sat down in a hard, plastic chair to wait for Dr. Carlson to respond to the page announcing she was here. She didn't have long to wait. He strode over to her and shook her hand. "Mrs. Aaronson, it's a pleasure. Please, let's meet in my office."

His office was small and held a desk, filing cabinet, and two chairs. She looked around it and realized that he must see patients elsewhere. Papers were in haphazard heaps here, there, and everywhere. Pictures of his family were half-buried by them, showing only tantalizing glimpses of a trio of tow-headed children laughing in a park.

"Thank you for taking the time to see me, Dr. Carlson."

He nodded. "I found your article on the high percentage of incarcerated mentally ill to be rather fascinating, Mrs. Aaronson. Truly, the pleasure is all mine." The psychiatrist was slim, with a receding hairline and thick coke-bottle spectacles. He wore a rather plain plaid shirt and khaki-colored pants. She had caught him sucking in his gut and smothered a smile. Even after all these years, her own frame was slim, her hair only now beginning to show white and gray hairs intermingled with blond. She still found men turning their heads when she passed. It was a lovely feeling, one that she appreciated but felt no desire to act upon. Theo had been the love of her life, but that part of her life, the one that hoped for a partner to walk through the world with, that was gone, buried with Theo.

"Can I get you anything? Coffee? Tea? Water?" he asked.

"No, thank you, I'm fine." Now that she was here, Sarah was eager to meet the patient Dr. Carlson had spoken about in his email.

"Well then," he settled into his seat and reached for a rather thin folder, "I don't have as much detail as we normally would have at this stage. Usually, by the time someone is committed, the medical history is quite complicated, and there are multiple incidents. In Cibil's case, however…"

Sarah blinked. "Her name is Sybil? As in Sybil Dorsett?" Sybil Dorsett had been the pseudonym for a woman plagued with multiple personality disorder. At the time the book had come out in the early 1970s, it had led to a movie starring Sally Field as Sybil.

"No, no, her name has a different spelling. Cibil Zradce is her full name," he pronounced it "zuh-rad-chee" as he pushed the thin file folder towards Sarah. "She was found on Rodeo Drive, screaming at the top of her lungs that her child was missing and that there was no time, that everyone needed to leave now." He shook his head, "She alternated between telling anyone who would listen that the collapse was coming, whatever that is, and that her baby is gone, that she had been taken by someone."

"So, she hadn't done anything illegal, and she wasn't placed in custody?" Sarah asked, her eyes focused on the photograph of a disheveled, raven-haired woman with piercing green eyes staring up at her.

"Initially, yes, because she ran out into traffic, screaming that her child was in the road, in a car seat, no less. Swore up and down she could see her there in the road."

"But there was no child?"

"No." He tapped the report attached to the other side, "No drugs in her system, and an examination here at Sinai determined she *had* given birth recently, but we have no records of a child's birth, no records of a Cibil Zradce for that matter, and no fingerprints in the system. Cibil Zradce had no identification, could tell us nothing about where she had grown up, where she had lived. Hell, it was as if she had appeared, freshly made, with no history, family, or records."

Sarah stared at the file and then back at Dr. Carlson, "That's..."

"Impossible?" He smiled then, and she was struck by a sense of longing. It reminded her of Theo's smile in some strange way. "Tell me about it." His smile disappeared, replaced by a more hopeful look. "That's why I contacted you. I was hoping that perhaps you could write about her, and that we could find her family, perhaps this child is in danger, we could find them and see if they could help provide the background that we need to shake her out of this muddled state. She's calmed down, somewhat, but I think that if we could just find out more about her, I could create a more effective treatment plan."

Sarah nodded, finally understanding why he had contacted her. His voice said it all. He gave a damn, and that was rare. She looked again at the photos on his desk and he followed her glance, reaching out with his left hand to fish the photo out of the tall stack of papers and handed it to her. It showed him surrounded by two boys and a girl, all tow-headed to his dark-brown hair. The children were obviously related to each other, but they looked nothing like him.

"Roger, Amelia, and Landon," he said, "I guess you could say I inherited them. My stepsister and her husband died four years ago, auto accident, and our parents were too old to take on three kids." He smiled wryly, "In a way, the kids are the best thing that ever happened to me." His grin faded. "Cibil has had a child within the last few months. The doctor who examined her was sure of it. And maybe that baby is in danger, somewhere out there." He looked back at the photograph. "There are all kinds of hair-raising stories I hear in this line of work. Abuse, neglect, drugs, even human trafficking. The situations some of my patients have endured, the worst possible of childhood and even adult trauma." He stared at the photo, his eyes betraying his devotion to the children. "I just want to make sure Cibil's baby is safe. I spoke with one of the psychologists on staff at New Jersey State Prison and he told me that you got more information out of Charles Cullen than he had in five years of therapy."

Sarah smiled and shook her head, "I got lucky."

Dr. Carlson leaned back in his chair. "No, I think it's your demeanor, the way you carry yourself, the sound of your voice - everything. Heck, I never talk about my kids. If I do, I just say they're my sister's kids and leave it at that. You've got something, Mrs. Aaronson, a gift if you will. And that's why I contacted you. I could see it in your articles, the way you have managed to interact with the people you write about. They trust you. I wanted to see if you would be able to get some details out of Cibil. Something, anything, that would help us track down that baby."

He set the picture down on his desk, gently moving the stacks of papers away from the frame, giving it a few inches of space in each direction, and stared at the photo again before turning his attention to Sarah. "The police terrify her; she clams up and won't say a word. And with me? She cries. When she isn't crying, she's telling me stories of another world, one filled with magic that hovers in another dimension in the same space as Earth. She says it fits over Earth 'Like the skin of an onion' and she insists she needs to return to that world soon, before the coming collapse. Perhaps she will talk to you, give you some details you can share with us. If not," he glanced back at the photo of his children, "then I fear for that baby."

Half an hour later, Sarah found herself face-to-face with a frail version of the disheveled woman in the photograph. According to Dr. Carlson, Cibil had been in their locked ward for nearly ten weeks. From the look of it, she had lost weight, a lot of it, in a rather short amount of time. Her raven hair was limp and stringy. Her green eyes were lackluster and half-closed. She didn't acknowledge Sarah as they sat her down in the chair on the opposite side of the table.

The door shut quietly behind the two orderlies who had escorted Cibil Zradce into the room, but Sarah knew they were right outside in the hall, in case anything went wrong during the interview.

"Good morning, Cibil, my name is Sarah."

Cibil blinked slowly, and then raised her head and stared at Sarah without speaking.

Sarah began her standard introduction, "I'm not with the police, I'm not a psychologist, I'm a journalist and, if you would like to share it, I would very much like to hear your story."

"My story?" The woman stared at her, her eyes held dark shadows under them and her skin sallow, tinged with a hint of gray. She looked haunted, and Sarah couldn't help wondering if perhaps this woman had killed her baby. It wouldn't be the first time she had spoken with a woman who had.

"Yes, your story, or whatever you want to share with me. I'm a journalist," Sarah repeated, "My job is to listen to people."

Cibil gave a strange sound, dry, like the leaves in winter, and Sarah realized the woman was laughing. "No one listens. I tell them what I see and they never listen."

"I will."

Sarah watched as Cibil looked at her then, the disheveled woman's strong psyche pushing through the haze of sedatives and anti-psychotics the staff had been feeding her and sneered, "You might listen, but you can't understand, you can never understand, and I see your death, along with others, so many others. You will be the first of many, so many."

Sarah felt a small chill crawl down her neck at Cibil's words. It lasted but a moment. She was far less afraid of death with Theo gone. It wasn't that she wanted to die, quite the opposite, but seeing it happen had changed the way she thought of life. She persisted, "Tell it to me, anyway."

Cibil's lips trembled, and Sarah could see her wrestling with a decision, "You're a journalist? Yes?"

"Yes."

"You will write down what I say?"

"Yes." Sarah fumbled to open the recording function on her cell phone. "I record the conversations. That way

I don't misremember any details. Would that be okay?"

Cibil twitched, then twitched again, more obvious this time, and Sarah realized the woman was nodding. She pressed the button, "It's recording now."

Cibil sat for a moment, unmoving and silent, before she said softly, "They say I'm confused, that I'm showing signs of postpartum psychosis. They think I killed my child."

Sarah pushed the phone closer towards Cibil, hoping that it was able to pick up her words. Cibil, in turn, leaned towards it. "I didn't kill her. Natalia is alive and well. I've seen it. I know she is safe, but she doesn't belong there, and neither do I."

"Here at the hospital?" Sarah asked.

"No, here in this world." Cibil replied, an edge creeping into her voice.

Sarah nodded. The key to dealing with the mentally ill was to affirm what they said and to provide a listening ear. "Where would you go with Natalia if not here in this world?"

"To Fyrsta Heim." Cibil replied, a dreamy look on her face, "Where my people come from."

"Tell me more about your people, and Fear... Fear..."

"Fyrsta Heim," Cibil said, her eyes sharp on Sarah's. "It means First World. It is where I and the rest of my people come from."

Sarah kept her face serene. "Another world? Is it in a different solar system?"

Cibil glared, "You mock me." She pulled back and let her dark, stringy hair fall across her face. Sarah's heart skipped a beat as she was reminded of that awful horror movie, The Ring. She had happened across it when she had been laid up with a broken ankle several years ago, long before Theo had died. She had watched the entire movie, pillows clutched in her lap. It had given her nightmares.

"I'm sorry, Cibil. I did not intend for you to feel disbelieved or mocked." Sarah kept her voice steady and calm, but Cibil turned away from her, averting her gaze. "Cibil? I am very sorry. Please, will you tell me if Natalia is on Fear... Fyrsta Heim?" The memory of Dr. Carlson's face, his earnest concern for this missing baby, it filled Sarah's heart with fear as well. The baby was innocent, and if she could just get Cibil to speak, they had a chance of finding it, no, *her*, alive.

A tear slid down Cibil's nose. "You don't believe me. No one does." Her voice was even quieter now, a cracked whisper as she fought emotion, struggled to stop the tears that had followed the first. They dripped off of her chin, a splat of liquid on the battered Formica table. "I wish I knew where Natalia was," she said, her voice rising ever so slightly. "I know she isn't in Fyrsta Heim. None of the Njerez know of her. I didn't tell them. The Arbre Genealogic controls who breeds and when, and Natalia, she wasn't planned by them. It was a chance encounter." She turned, her eyes agonized, desperate, "If he hadn't had died, I would have told them. Perhaps it would have been excused. But most have moved beyond the World Walls. I was…” she hiccupped, the tears falling faster, “I was supposed to go through them too. I was told to travel to the East Coast, to board a private plane had been chartered, to join the others heading for a thin spot in Germany. But on the way to meet the others I had a vision.”

Cibil wiped her tears away, a trail of tears and snot combining together into a stringy mess. She wiped again, smearing her hospital-issued sweatshirt with a glob of sticky goo. Sarah swallowed hard, doing her best to ignore her queasy stomach and not react. The woman was talking, and that was a big step.

“Tell me what happens when you have a vision, Cibil.”

The younger woman shook her

head. "It hurts, a lot. I black out. When I came to, I was in a hospital. They thought I had been mugged." She stopped, stared off into space, staring with a confused look at the opposite wall.

Sarah sighed to herself. Inside of locked wards like this one, the use of sedatives and anti-psychotics was liberal and often heavy-handed. Communicating with Cibil was going to be difficult if they kept her dosage at this high level.

"But instead, you had a vision? Is that right?"

"Yes." Cibil answered but did not elaborate, once again her concentration slipping away.

"What was in your vision, Cibil?"

Cibil's eyes blinked and re-focused on Sarah. "Hm?"

"You said you had a vision on your way to meet the others. What was your vision about?"

"A train bombing. In New York."

"A train bombing? Not the Twin Towers?"

"No. It was underground, fire, explosion, and the blood." Cibil stared past Sarah's shoulder, a thousand-yard stare that did not see what was in this room, but somewhere far away instead.

"What happened then, Cibil?"

At the sound of her name, her head swiveled back towards Sarah and Cibil stared at her as if seeing her for the first time. "Hm?"

"When you woke up in the hospital and they thought you had been mugged. What happened then?" Sarah prodded gently.

Cibil smiled. "I knew better than to say anything. Humans never listen. They can't imagine a world where there is no science, only magic. If you say that you can see the future, then obviously you are mad. I said nothing, only that I couldn't remember what happened, and they let me go."

"Were you pregnant then?" Sarah asked, hoping to establish a timeline and possibly pinpoint Cibil's hospital stay for Dr. Carlson to follow up.

"No, no," Cibil said, shaking her head.

"Okay. Would you like to tell me what happened next?"

"He found me."

"Who found you, Cibil?"

"Why, Conor, of course." Cibil gave her a sideways look, as if Sarah should have known the answer.

"Does Conor have a last name? Is he Natalia's father?"

The tears welled up in Cibil's eyes. "Yes. But when she quickened in me, he told me I wasn't her. I wasn't Maggie. He said that I meant nothing to him. That no one existed but Maggie and his son, Theo."

The small chill Sarah had felt at the beginning of the conversation returned when Cibil spoke Theo's name out loud. And at that moment, Cibil nodded, her green eyes intense. She held up a thin, bony finger. The fingernail had been chewed to the quick.

"You know now. Brother in one timeline, husband in the other, as if fate couldn't keep you apart. Fate's highway, it has many twists and turns." She smiled then, her teeth yellowed and stained, madness rising in her eyes. "Your father knew it, the moment you took Theo home to meet your family, to tell them of your future child." She leaned forward, her eyes sparking with interest. "Your father told you about it, didn't he? He did, I just know it. I can see it in your eyes."

Sarah stood, her chair knocking back and falling to the floor. She pressed the stop button on her recording app. "Cibil, I…" The chill hadn't left her. If anything, it had grown. Who was this woman? Who was she really? "I need to take a bathroom break, if you don't mind," she said. The words came fast, spitting out as she backpedaled, phone in hand toward the door, knocking on it briskly.

An orderly opened it and she slid

through, suddenly out of breath, as her heart raced and stuttered. The burly man, dressed in the standard blue scrubs that all the workers there wore, coughed wetly, and she could feel and see the fever racing through him. He asked, "Are you done speaking to the patient, ma'am?"

Before she could answer, Dr. Carlson entered the hallway, walking briskly out of the observation room. "Mrs. Aaronson? Are you feeling alright? You looked as if you had seen a ghost."

Sarah plastered a smile on her face. "I'm fine, Dr. Carlson. Just surprised. If I may ask, what did you share with Cibil about me prior to my meeting her?"

His concerned expression faded slightly, replaced by a confused frown, "Nothing really, just that a female journalist wanted to speak with her. I didn't follow that last bit, something about brother and husband, and..." His voice petered out as Sarah backed away.

"I'm sorry, I," she looked around, "I need to visit the Ladies Room, if you don't mind."

"Oh certainly, it's just down the hall. Through the security doors. I'll have them buzz you through."

She nodded her thanks and walked briskly towards the doors, hearing the tinny buzz as she strode over to them and pushed her way through. She found the restrooms on the left and slipped inside, her heart hammering. How had Cibil known? About Theo? About Theo's mother, Maggie?

Maggie had died in a car accident

when Theo was barely twelve years old. Her loss had left him orphaned, his father… *My God, she just told me that her child and my Theo have the same father.* But it was impossible. It had to be impossible. A gap of, what, sixty years between the two siblings? Sarah felt lightheaded, as if she had entered this alien world Cibil had spoken of, this Fyrsta Heim. *She called it First World.* But referring to the letter, something only she and Theo had read, no one else, not even Betty, God rest her soul, her older sister had gone to her grave never having read that letter that Dad had left Sarah. In the end, after reading it, and re-reading it, Sarah couldn't make sense of it. It had frightened her in many ways, as if this other world had reached out and taken some of her family with it.

She stared at her reflection in the mirror, clutching the sink, her knuckles white, her reflection pale in the cheap fluorescent light that flickered from the ceiling above.

Of all the parts of the letter from her father that she had read and re-read until the words were memorized, Cibil's comments brought one back with full force.

Of all the emotions or fears this letter might stir in you, reading that Theo is, in my memories, both your brother and your husband might be disturbing to you. Believe me, it took me by surprise, and yet it also made absolute sense. It felt as if the world was put right again in some way by Theo's return to our lives. Perhaps your souls sought each other out, reuniting that which had been lost.

"Occam's Razor. The simplest explanation is usually the correct one." Sarah whispered as she stared into the mirror. "So, what, magic and time travel and other worlds really do exist? Sarah Magdalene Edmonds Aaronson, do you realize how insane that sounds?"

A knock sounded at the door. "Mrs. Aaronson? Is everything all right in there?" Dr. Carlson's voice was muffled, yet his concern carried through the thick metal door.

She looked down at her hands. Her wedding band was set firmly on the right hand, a clear sign of widowhood. Her hands showed her age more than her face, which had only a handful of wrinkles to betray the fact that she was edging out of her fifties and would soon celebrate six decades on Earth. Or would she? Cibil had said, "I see your death, along with others, so many others."

"Mrs. Aaronson?" The muffled murmur of a second voice. A woman, possibly one of the unit nurses, joined Dr. Carlson's. It was followed by a brisk knock at the door.

Sarah stared at her hands for a second longer, reached into the stall to flush the toilet, and called out loudly, "Just a minute." She ran the water, splashed it on her hands and dried them, her ring catching and tearing the paper towel.

She marched out the door, a professional smile on her face, "My apologies, Dr. Carlson, my friend took me out to a new Thai restaurant last night and I think it must have upset my stomach. Let's get back to it, shall we?" She ignored the curious stare of the young unit nurse standing beside the doctor.

His face was full of concern, and a flash of confusion. "Oh, I thought perhaps Cibil had said something that bothered you. Are you sure you are feeling well enough to continue?"

"I'm fine, really, just a bit of stomach upset at the worst possible time." She smiled wider, perhaps too brightly, because Dr. Carlson cocked his head and looked as if he were about to object.

A commotion from beyond the locked doors distracted him, however. One orderly shouted for help, another ran from the nearby nurse's station towards the room where Sarah had spoken with Cibil. Dr. Carlson turned and hustled down the corridor, Sarah on his heels as he used his key card to buzz through the doors, his legs moving in a fast trot that Sarah was challenged to keep up with.

At the doorway, her way was blocked by Dr. Carlson and another duty nurse, but she could see inside it quite clearly. Cibil had fallen from her chair, her body locked in what appeared to be a grand mal seizure. Her back arched, impossibly far, and her hands and legs contorted into impossible angles. The carotid artery bulged out of her neck and she seemed to be drooling and choking at the same time. It was her eyes that Sarah couldn't stop staring at. The vivid green eyes that had locked onto hers just moments before were black. And not just the iris, but the entire sclera, which was normally white with the odd blood vessel twisting through - all the eye, was black. Sarah wasn't the only one who noticed. The duty nurse on the floor stood next to her. She gave a small gasp and muttered, "Her eyes, my God, what in the world?"

Cibil's slight body shook violently and Sarah winced at the sharp crack of the woman's head on the floor. Dr. Carlson pulled his white lab coat off and handed it to the orderly who shoved it under Cibil's head as her spine arched again, impossibly high, rigid, and her head lifted off the ground, only to slam back down again. Dr. Carlson shoved the table and chairs out of the way and knelt beside his patient, his hand light on her wrist. He spared a cursory glance in Sarah's direction and spoke softly to the orderly holding Cibil's head, cushioning her skull with his hand and lab coat as he looked up at Sarah.

"Mrs. Aaronson, my apologies, but it looks as if we are done for the day. It will take a few hours for Cibil to recover from her seizure. If you could return tomorrow at the same time, I would be happy to arrange access to her again at that time."

"Yes, of course," Sarah responded, backing away from the doorway. In truth, she was taken aback by the ferocity of the woman's seizure. In high school, she had once witnessed a friend of hers have an epileptic seizure. It had been terrifying for her. This one, however, had been far more violent. And it was still happening. Her spine arched repeatedly, her limbs shook, and her head slammed up and down against the orderly's hand and Dr. Carlson's folded up lab coat.

Sarah turned, the duty nurse still by her side, and walked down the hall, her mind spinning.

"Those eyes," the duty nurse murmured, "I've never seen anything like it before."

Sarah said nothing until they arrived at the locked doors. The other woman produced a key card and, seconds later, escorted Sarah through them, down the hall to the elevators. They slowed to a stop, and the woman sneezed violently twice. "Ugh, sorry. I've been fighting the flu bug all week!"

"I hope you feel better soon. And that it isn't that Hong Kong variant that is going around." Sarah said.

"Me too. My nephew's family were felled with it last week. It was touch and go with their two-year-old for a few days there." The woman produced a worn Kleenex from her pocket and blew her nose into it.

"Oh goodness, I hope everything has turned out for the best."

"It did, Tommy is back to running his parents ragged. Damned if they don't recover fast!"

"Well, thank you, Ellen," Sarah said, noting the name tag on the woman's uniform, "I know the way from here."

The woman nodded, flapped her hand at Sarah before she turned and began walking back the way she came.

Sarah pushed the down button at the elevator, her mind occupied with

Cibil. She kept replaying the words over and over, returning to the woman's claims, the people she shouldn't even know about, even the train bombing, the one in New York she mentioned. Try as she might, Sarah couldn't remember hearing of any train bombing. She clung to this fact, desperate to cast any kind of doubt on the woman's words, because if she didn't, well...

The long drive home flew by as Sarah reviewed, and reviewed again, Cibil's words, her mannerisms and reactions. She drove in the slow lane, knowing it was the safest option for her since she was used to the less frenetic Midwestern drivers. Despite maintaining the speed limit, other cars passed her on the left, honking in frustration. She ignored them as she listened to the conversation play from the voice recorder.

Sarah had listened to the recording with Cibil so many times she had lost count. Finally, she had just sat there in the stark white living room, Gina's latest minimalist obsession had been a sharp departure from her Liberace days. She stared out at the sky, filled with orange and red hues from the setting sun. Gina bustled in, shopping bags in one hand, and what smelled like Thai takeout in the other.

"Girl, you would not believe what I found! The most delicious flats you have ever seen in a cherry red!" Gina crowed, "They have them in your size, honey, and I insist we go back there tomorrow. They..." Gina took in Sarah sitting in the dark and stopped and set the bags down on the counter.

"Sarah, honey? What's wrong?"

Sarah managed a smile. "It's nothing, Gina, really."

Gina, far more empathic than anyone past Sarah or the long-departed Scotty knew, shook her head. "Right, and I'm Genghis Khan." She dumped her bags in the corner of the living room and set the Thai takeout on the counter. "I'll fix you cannoli tomorrow night."

She pulled two plates out of the cabinet, opened the myriad of boxes and beckoned Sarah over. "Food, even takeout, makes everything better."

The edges of Sarah's mouth twitched. There was no such thing as secrets when it came to Gina. And despite the older woman's flamboyant ways and addiction to shopping,

Sarah had found her friend to be intensely loyal and rather grounded. She reached for the plate and began poking through the boxes.

"Try the pad krapow moo, it's delish." Gina flapped a hand at another box, "And you haven't lived until you've tried the yum nua. It'll light you up, but it's worth it." She leaned over her plate and sucked in a large mouthful of noodles, her eyes closing in pleasure as she chewed.

Sarah dug into the food heaped on the plate. She hadn't eaten breakfast or lunch. After leaving the hospital and seeing Cibil's body contorting, her eyes as black as coal, any appetite Sarah might have had for lunch had deserted her. She had driven back to Gina's beach house on auto-pilot, her mind turning and turning again on the interview with Cibil Zradce.

There was silence for a few minutes as both of them attacked the takeout with zeal. Sarah sighed as she ate a mouthful of the yum nua. Gina was right, it was better than any Thai food she had ever tasted before.

As soon as the last bite of food had disappeared from her plate, Gina stood up, "I'm making us decaf, and then you are going to tell me what happened today." There was no question in her words, more a statement of fact. Gina was used to getting her way after all, and after she set the steaming cup of decaf down in front of Sarah, she plopped down in the chair opposite and barked, "Spill it, sister."

Sarah pressed play on her cell phone and Gina listened in silence until it was done. "Where's the rest of it?"

"When I returned from the bathroom, she was in a grand mal seizure the likes of which I had never seen before." Sarah answered quietly, "Her doctor said I could return tomorrow."

Gina stared at the phone and then back up to Sarah, "Honey, she's crazy. All that talk of another world and some guy and a train bombing. You realize she's completely off her rocker, right?"

"There was just something about her, Gina. I can't explain it. The way she looked at me, the things she said, and she knew things. Things she couldn't have known."

"Sarah honey, a broken clock is right twice a day. I figure it can't be far off from that." She took Sarah's hand,

"Listen, you need to relax, and stop thinking about this for tonight. Go back tomorrow if you must, but meanwhile, sit down and watch Dancing with the Stars with me, will ya? What's his name is so hot! I hear their ratings have skyrocketed since Mr. Hot Pants has been shaking his patoot off for all to see. Sit down for a few minutes, take your mind off the crazy people for a while, and I guarantee you will fall in lust with him right along with me."

Sarah giggled. Gina was an unstoppable force and she let the older woman pull her over to the plush white sofa and click on the large flatscreen television on the far wall.

"We missed the first few minutes, but that's okay, Mr. Hot Pants isn't on until later. He and his partner are performing nearly halfway through the hour."

As the screen jumped to life, Gina frowned and stared at the display, "What is this?"

Sarah stared, too horrified to answer as the television showed blood and gurneys and fire trucks instead of scantily clad women and their dance partners. The headline across the bottom of the screen said it all - Terrorists Strike at the Heart of the Atlantic Railway During Morning Commute.

"Oh my God," Gina whispered, "I've traveled through that station more times than I can count." Her normally ebullient self was muted in shock as she read the words trailing across the screen. "Multiple incendiary devices, fire, and…" her voice petered out.

"Over 5,000 people reported dead or missing." Sarah breathed beside her. "Cibil saw this in a vision."

The two women stared in shocked silence, occasional gasps from each of them as they watched the images rolling across the screen. The commentators themselves looked haggard and raw.

"How did we miss this?" Sarah asked.

"I had Sirius on all day," Gina replied, her perfectly applied makeup streaked with tears, "Oh God, Sarah, all of those people!"

It brought back the memories of 9/11 hard and fast, and both continued to watch the screen, Gina's hand creeping over to hold on to Sarah's, seeking the reassurance of another. Gina reached her for her phone a dozen times, only to set it down again.

"I don't think I'm ready to know," she said quietly when Sarah asked. "I just, I just *can't*, you know?"

Most of Gina's life had been spent on the East coast, around the very area affected. The dark closed in outside and the two women watched the television without speaking until nearly midnight. Sarah stood up finally and pressed the Off button and turned to Gina.

"Enough, we can't do anything tonight, but if you need to go home tomorrow, I can help you find a flight."

"No." Gina's reply was quiet, almost inaudible. "I'd only be a burden. Look at me, I'm good for shopping and makeup tips, Sarah." She flapped her fingers, the rings flashing in the dim light of the room, mascara streaking her cheeks. "I have no place there."

Sarah had never heard her friend sound so alone, so bereft. She sat back down on the couch and took Gina's hands.

"That's not true, Gina. You make the best damn cannoli I've ever tasted. Go home, volunteer to help with meals for the rescue crews, but wear flats, for crying out loud. Those Jimmy Choo's will kill your arches."

Gina snorted, stifling laughter, and then met Sarah's gaze, "Do you really think I could make a difference?"

"Gina, love, go home. Go cook up a storm. I *know* it will help."

"Did you get a lick of sleep?" Sarah asked blearily a handful of hours later as Gina bustled about the small house, packing, it appeared, for a small army to descend on New York. There were three large suitcases in addition to her carry-on and voluminous purse. Sarah sat on the edge of the sofa and tried to order her thoughts, but the lack of sleep, combined with the horror of the previous evening's news, had left her foggy-brained and slow.

"I'll sleep on the plane. Believe it or not, I get the *best* sleep on planes." Gina's face was excited as well as determined. It had taken a little more convincing last night from Sarah, but by the time Sarah headed for bed, Gina had been on line searching for flights. Her steps were fast, purposeful, as she strode from one end of the house to the next. "The cab should be here in five minutes and my flight isn't for three hours. That's more than enough time to get to LAX, go through security and have a coffee before takeoff."

Sarah nodded, and the motion made her head and stomach spin. Perhaps it was more than just lack of sleep. Was she coming down with something? She swallowed, noting a painful patch in her throat. *Now is not the time to be sick!*

Gina's voice intruded, "Sarah, honey, are you okay? You don't look as perky as you normally do."

Sarah glanced up at her friend, whose expression had turned from barely contained excitement and nervousness, to concern.

"I'm fine, Gina, probably just the beginnings of some stupid head cold. Absolutely nothing to worry about."

Gina walked over and held one cool hand up to Sarah's forehead, "You're a little warm. Perhaps some Tylenol would help." She bustled away to the bathroom and returned, pills in hand, frowning slightly. "Perhaps I should stay here."

Sarah laughed, ignoring her symptoms, pushing past the haziness she felt, "Don't be silly, Gina. I'm a grown woman and can take care of myself. I'll be fine, don't you worry about a thing."

The doorbell buzzed at that moment, which was perfect timing to keep Gina on track. Sarah bent down and lifted one of the smaller suitcases, her muscles aching as she did, and walked to the door to meet the cabbie. As he loaded the suitcases in the trunk, Sarah hugged Gina, "Go see your family, Gina. Cook for them, hug them close. Call me when you land."

"You'll be okay? Call me if you need me to come back and I'll make it happen," the older woman snapped her fingers, "lickety-split."

Sarah nodded and hugged her friend again. The last thing she would do would be to ask Gina to come back. Sometimes her friend could lose herself helping others. Most of Gina's family was the same way. They were brassy, affectionate, and loud. Sarah had met Gina's sisters and brothers, of which there were six in total, on several occasions and knew that Gina's presence in their midst would help.

By the time Sarah had woken up in the morning, Gina had received a text telling her that two of her nephews were among the missing. According to Gina's brother-in-law, Gina's sister, just two years younger than Gina, was in hysterics not knowing where her two sons were.

Sarah couldn't help but smile as she saw her friend out the door. Gina was a true friend, but Sarah was relieved to see her off. Her friend needed her family just as much as they needed her, especially in this time of crisis.

She waved goodbye until the taxi rounded the bend before shutting the door on the pre-dawn darkness. She hadn't slept well, not at all, and her throat was sore, her eyes ached, and Sarah wondered again if she might be coming down with something.

A little more rest, and I'm sure I'll be fine.

The large, comfortable bed swallowed her up, and she pulled the covers over her, slipping into a deep sleep in seconds, despite her mind's best efforts to dwell on yesterday's interview with Cibil, and the massive seizure that followed, or the terrible scenes from the train bombing. When her eyes slowly opened hours later, it felt as if she hadn't rested at all. The sun shone bright, and she struggled to focus on the clock on the bedside table. She groaned when the numbers slowly resolved to a more readable blur. It was after ten in the morning. And she felt worse than when she had first laid down.

Her phone blinked with messages.

How did I miss it ringing? It had been less than two feet away from my head on the nightstand!

Blearily she placed her glasses on her nose and peered at the screen. Two missed calls from Dr. Carlson and two texts from Gina. She read the texts first, one from her friend saying she was at the airport and the plane was late, another as the plane taxied down the runway ready for takeoff. Her head thumped in pain as Sarah tried to estimate how long the flight would take her. "Still in the air, I imagine." Her voice sounded rough, congested.

She closed her messages app and stared at the phone. There was a voicemail. She pressed the speaker button and played the message.

"Sarah, er, Mrs. Aaronson," she smiled, hearing Dr. Carlson's voice as he stumbled over her name, "John Carlson here. I wanted to let you know that Cibil has, erm, gone missing overnight. We are making all efforts to locate her, but we are unsure of her location at this time. Please feel free to call me if you have questions. I wanted to pass along to you some other information as well. Perhaps you could join me for lunch?" His voice wavered again, "I mean, if you wanted to, that is. Uh, well, anyway, call me back when you get this."

Gone missing? From a locked unit? How was that even possible?

She pressed the button and listened to the phone ring once, twice, before John Carlson's voice answered. "Dr. Carlson speaking."

"Dr. Carlson, it's Sarah Aaronson."

"Sarah, er, Mrs. Aaronson, so good to hear from you. I trust you received my voicemail."

"I did, and I am free for lunch if the offer is still open." She pushed past the exhaustion and body aches, curious to learn what other information he had. It was worth pushing her body a little, just to learn how a woman as frail as Cibil had managed to escape a locked psychiatric unit. Flu be damned, she wanted to know more!

Dr. Carlson's voice had an ebullient tone to it as he gave her directions on how to avoid a majority of the traffic and meet him at a local taqueria that he promised had the best burritos in all of L.A.

"Great, I'll see you in two hours," she said, doing her best to sound spunky. As soon as the call disconnected, Sarah's hand fell to her side, heavy, aching. Her entire body felt as if she had just run a marathon, instead of sleeping past ten in the morning. She couldn't remember the last time that had happened.

Two cups of the strongest coffee she could manage, along with a hot shower, relieved some of her malaise, enough for her to convince herself she was fine. Following the doctor's directions, she made decent time, and it was half past the hour when she arrived. The small, nondescript restaurant was packed. Dr. Carlson had waited outside for her, his face lighting up when he saw her. He waved and as she approached, the tense lines in his face smoothed, and he reached for the door. "Believe it or not, we have a table waiting."

Sarah raised her eyebrows, the

restaurant didn't seem the type to have reservations, and it was standing room only when they entered. He waved at the hostess and walked to a small table in one corner. He pulled out a chair for her, waited until she was seated and then sat down.

"Okay, I really need to know the story behind this," she said, laughing after the hostess brought her a menu and gave Dr. Carlson a kiss on the cheek.

He looked embarrassed. "I wish they wouldn't do it, but I know better than to argue. Once, I came in and didn't say anything and Ramon, he's in the kitchen, chewed out their new hostess for not seating me immediately ahead of the others."

"Go on."

"I was in the emergency room with

Landon. He had twisted his ankle falling out of a tree and it wasn't supporting his weight, so he was having it x-rayed and I saw the signs of a myocardial infarction in Ramon's grandmother who was also there in the waiting room. He's a widower, with five young children, and Abuela Vasquez," he stopped and looked sheepish, "yes, that's what I call her. Anyway, she was there with Jacinta who had a high fever." He shrugged, "She was so concerned with little Jacinta, that she was ignoring her own health. I called a nurse over. I mean, Abuela was obviously in distress, and they admitted her immediately. She underwent a quadruple bypass the next day."

"Oh, my goodness!" Sarah gasped; her hand was over her mouth.

"In any case, the family was very grateful. I was visiting her a couple of days later and Ramon came up to me and introduced himself and told me to come to the restaurant. I didn't, not for months, but finally I went by and the second he saw me, he ran out of the kitchen and gave me a huge hug." He smiled, "I was invited to Lola's quinceanara last month. She's the oldest, and my kids get along with the others so well, it just feels like family."

"That's beautiful, Dr. Carlson."

"Please, call me John."

Sarah nodded, "Only if you call me Sarah."

"Fair enough."

He looked as if he wanted to say more, but a pretty young girl arrived at that moment, "Tito John! You brought a friend!" She was small and looked far too young to be working in a restaurant during what had to be a school day.

Ben's eyes lit up, "Teresa! It must be spring break for me to see you here. How are you?" He gave her a gentle hug.

She grinned, "I'm good. Papa says he will come by later, it's very busy right now, but could Amelia come to my birthday party?"

"Of course. This weekend?"

"Yes."

Sarah felt a surge of heat, not unlike a hot flash, and then a wave of exhaustion crashed over her. She was definitely ill.

Why in the world did I think going out for lunch was a good idea?

She stared at the menu while they

chatted and when there was a pause, she glanced up and found them staring at her expectantly.

"Oh dear, what did I miss?" she asked, slightly flustered.

John frowned, a look of concern on his face, "Are you feeling okay? You look exhausted."

"I'm just tired." She forced a bright smile on her face and turned to Teresa, "I understand that your father makes the best burritos around. What do you suggest I try?"

The girl smiled, her brown eyes lighting up with pride and she said, "My favorite is the chorizo, but it has a bit of heat."

"That sounds fabulous," Sarah smiled, "I don't mind a bit of heat." She handed the menu back to Teresa.

"And I'll have the usual," John said,

smiling at the girl. She nodded and slipped away to the kitchen.

"What is the usual?" Sarah asked, her interest piqued.

"It changes," John answered, shrugging, "The first time I came here I said, 'Surprise me,' and they do, every time. Everything is amazing, by the way. Truly the best in the valley." He cocked his head and stared at her, "Are you sure you're okay?"

Sarah waved her hand distracted, "I'm mostly just tired. My friend Gina, her two nephews are missing in the train bombing, and she flew out on a red-eye this morning. Between watching the news late and Gina leaving early, it's been hard. And I might be coming down with something, I'm not sure. God, I hope not, I don't want to get you ill."

"Don't worry about me, I've got the constitution of a goat. I'm never ill," John assured her.

Sarah sipped her water and nibbled at the chips and salsa, "Enough about me, though. I'm dying to hear how Cibil has gone missing. When did it happen? Was there anything on the security video?" She had noticed the cameras throughout the hospital, their dark, round black eyes in most of the hallways as well as the room she had interviewed Cibil in.

John sighed, setting his water down and fiddling with his napkin, "Let me start with what happened after the seizure."

Sarah settled back, "Yes, please do. I had never seen a grand mal seizure that was as violent as that."

Carlson shook his head, "Nor have I.

To tell you the truth, I was shocked at the severity of it. And typically, the stronger the seizure the longer it takes to recover from, but less than an hour later, she was screaming - I could hear her down the hall." He rubbed his forehead, his hair thin. Sarah could see where his hairline had originally begun.

"In any case, she was lucid enough to tell me about a highway, a Highway 49 and a sign for a town, one called Beldon or possibly Belton? I have my secretary looking into it. She believes that is where her baby is at."

Sarah's mouth flew open in surprise, "I know exactly where that is!"

John cocked his head, "What?"

"Highway 49 runs through Belton, Missouri, just south of my hometown of Kansas City."

"Seriously?"

"Yes! My son and his family live in Belton. I'm quite familiar with the area." She pulled out her phone and typed a quick message to Michael, groaning with frustration as it refused to send. "Another service failure, these are getting more and more frequent, and not just with Connect Now."

John had his phone out, shaking his head over the connection icon. "Same here. Between the outages and the rolling blackouts, it sometimes feels like we heading back to the dark ages."

"Hey now," Sarah managed to smile at him, "I grew up in the Dark Ages!"

He had the good grace to blush, and began to stutter an apology when

Teresa returned, balancing two plates, each loaded with a burrito, Pico sauce and more. They smelled amazing. Despite feeling an ever-increasing sensation of weariness, Sarah's stomach growled in anticipation. She was thankful for the full restaurant and its ambient noise.

"Papa said you will like this one, Tito, it is a mix of barbacoa and carnitas with extra hot sauce."

John grinned at the girl, "Thank you, Teresa. And thanks to your papa, I've been looking forward to this all week!"

Sarah's burrito was deliciously spicy, but she could only manage a few bites before her body, now thoroughly convinced it needed to be in bed, rebelled. She set it down and drank some water instead, "It would truly be amazing if Cibil's baby is found in Missouri. I must admit, the thought of a baby out there, somewhere, missing and perhaps injured or worse, it keeps cycling around in my head. I can only hope we manage to get a happy ending to this."

"Indeed." Carlson said, wiping a bit of sauce from his mouth.

Sarah leaned forward, in part so she could rest her body on her two elbows and hopefully hide her malaise a little longer. "I'm dying to know how Cibil escaped from a locked ward, however."

John shook his head, "We are still trying to figure that out. Truly, I'm stumped. I'll tell you what I know, but this is off the record. Insurance and public relations are both an issue, you understand."

"Of course. I completely understand."

He took another large bite of the burrito, finished chewing and swallowing and sighed in contentment. "I wasn't kidding, I look forward to my lunch here every week. If I ate here every day, I'd end up too wide to fit in the door!" He frowned slightly at Sarah's burrito, "Was yours too spicy?"

"What? Oh God no, I just can't manage to stuff myself with any more of it right now." She waved her hand, "Too much coffee, perhaps."

"You might be catching that virus that is going around. We're operating on a skeleton crew today, two more of my staff called in sick."

"I really hope I'm not, but I'll be honest, I feel worse than I did before

I left. I'm so sorry, the last thing you need is to get some nasty virus." She leaned back in her chair, hyper-aware now, feeling warmer than she had earlier.

"Like I said, I am rarely ill, no worries, seriously." He wiped his fingers, "Back to Cibil, however."

"Yes, please."

"All we know at this point is that she was in her locked room last evening, that the orderlies logged her as present up until five a.m. when there was a shift change. The incoming staff performed a routine check of the corridor and found Cibil's door unlocked and open and her bed empty."

"Well, surely the security cameras show something. Perhaps the orderlies skipped a walk-through or

two, it's been known to happen."
Sarah asked, frowning as Dr. Carlson
shook his head.

"That's the weird part. The cameras
show nothing. Not only that, but there
is no lapse or lost time. I went
through them myself. No one can
explain it. It's as if she vanished from
her room."

"Through a window?"

He laughed, "Through the bars? Six
stories off of the ground?"

Sarah flushed in embarrassment,
"Oh." She looked up at the doctor,
met his eyes, "Then how?"

"Believe me, I'm flummoxed. I've
got nothing."

"What about external cameras?"

He frowned, "I haven't checked
them."

"Well, perhaps you should." Sarah

shrugged, "I am as befuddled as you, but I'd double-check the exterior cameras just to be sure."

"That's not a bad idea. I'll do that when I return to work." He caught the eye of the waitress and asked for two takeout boxes and dug into his wallet. "Now is when I get to be sneaky. You ready for it?" He pulled two twenty-dollar bills out.

Sarah looked around "Sneaky? Um, why?"

"They won't accept payment. No matter how often I return, so I have to get inventive. Help me out?"

"What do you need me to do?"

"I'll distract her, you slip the money into her apron pocket." He grinned at her and Sarah was struck by his open, kind smile. It reminded her of Theo, despite Dr. Carlson being at least twenty years younger. Theo had brought out the best in her and everyone around him. She missed having that in her day-to-day life.

Sarah found herself smiling back and taking the money from his hand. When Teresa returned with the takeout boxes, John distracted her by asking for her help and winked at Sarah as she managed to slip the bills into the girl's pocket.

"You make a fine co-conspirator, Sarah, thank you for that." John took her arm gently and guided her out of the restaurant after Teresa moved on to the next table.

"That was the highlight of my day. Intrigue, conspiracy, and…" Sarah's body finally rebelled, and she stopped abruptly, dizziness and fatigue now fighting with nausea. She swayed and

John's grip on her tightened.

"You aren't well at all!" John exclaimed, there was concern in his voice.

"I really thought I would be fine, but," she swayed again and she could feel sweat beading on her forehead, her cheeks flushing. "I am so sorry, John, I..."

"Here, my car is right here, let's sit you down until you can get your bearings." He guided her to the passenger side and helped her slide into the seat. The car was warm from the sun and Sarah was hit with a wave of dizziness. At that moment, all she wanted to do was curl up and sleep. She put her right hand on the dashboard and leaned forward, waited for the world to stop spinning all around her.

John's voice held concern, "I really think I should take you to the Emergency Room, or would you rather see your primary doctor?"

"I don't, oh," another wave of dizziness, "would you believe I don't have a doctor here in L.A.? It sounds so stupid now, but honestly, I've been so healthy that I haven't bothered finding one. I do my annual when I go to visit my son and his family in Missouri each summer. And, oh, I don't want to be sick in your car." She tried to stand up, but Carlson wasn't having it.

"Sarah, I'm happy to take you to the ER. I'll get a bag in case you feel nauseous, but you have no business driving right now. Especially not with some of the drivers I see loose on the road!"

She knew he was right. "Okay, but honestly, I just need to go home and rest."

"Are you sure?" He handed her a thick, insulated bag. "I'm worried about you."

"Really, I'll be fine. I'm sure it's just a nasty virus. A couple of days and I'll be right as rain."

The ride back to Gina's beach house was subdued. John had assured her that her car would be safe there in the parking lot and had double-checked that it was locked. Sarah concentrated on not throwing up, her stomach was spinning and she felt sweaty and feverish. When they arrived, John parked the car in the drive, got out, and opened Sarah's door. Everything was moving faster around her, while she sloshed through a thick mire, her brain fogged and her body miserable.

Why did I ever think I was okay to leave the house this morning?

She was dimly aware of the doctor's hands steadying her as they walked together to the front door. All she wanted was to be in bed. If she could just lay still, surely the nausea would pass.

"I am so sorry," she mumbled, "I had no idea I would feel this ill." She kicked off her shoes and tried to smile up at John. Two or three copies of his face swam in front of her.

"Please let me take you to the ER, Sarah." There was such deep concern in his face, and despite him being at least ten years younger than her, she was reminded again of Theo.

She reached up, her hand hot

against his cheek, "Really. I'll be fine. I just need to lie down and rest. You'll keep me updated if you hear anything? If they find the baby? Or if they locate Cibil?"

"Of course. May I check in on you later today and see how you are doing?"

She nodded, and he backed down the hall towards the door, "And if you need anything, anything at all, you will call me?"

"Yes, of course." She managed to smile. He was a kind man and for the first time in years, she felt a spark of desire. More for the companionship than anything else. The steadfast presence of another person in your life. She felt Gina's absence, and Theo's, keenly at that moment. "Once I have a rest, I'll feel much better. I'm sure of it."

She fought to stand steady on her feet until he left, the door closed and locked behind him, before she tottered to her bed, and collapsed.

Nightmares, and bouts of semi-conscious wakefulness stole any real rest from her sleep for the next several hours. At some point of it, the nausea finally gave way to a panicked run to the toilet where she managed to get most of the contents of her stomach into the bowl. Unlike most bouts of nausea, she felt worse after, not better. The room spun as she levered her way into a standing position and rinsed her face, hair and shirt. She felt ridiculously guilty for not keeping the tasty burrito down, even though she knew it wasn't her fault. Also, it had burned worse coming up.

   As the afternoon sun sent the rays of light sliding around to the west, her room cooled. A relief from her fever at first, but she was soon shivering uncontrollably. Her phone buzzed intermittently. Gina would have landed by now and Sarah's thoughts landed in a murky gray half consciousness that kept needling her to answer the phone. She couldn't though. Her body was stripped of energy for any other activity than running to the bathroom and laying on her rumpled bed. She closed her eyes, ignoring the phone, the cold descending over her limbs, and lost herself to the darkness.

   "Sarah? Sarah!" A voice intruded on the dark oblivion. Theo's voice was calling to her. What was he doing here, anyway? She tried to open her eyes, but it seemed like too much effort.

Maybe in a little while, once I've had more sleep.

She sank back into the darkness, a part of her noting that the voice couldn't be Theo's, but sounded familiar. He was talking to someone else now too.

"Right this way, she's in here."

"Sir? If you could please give us some room." An unfamiliar voice. A cool hand on her wrist, hands gently rolling her onto her back. She was too tired to respond. As she cracked an eye open, a blinding light caused her to flinch. "Are you her husband, sir?"

"No, no, I'm a friend." He sounded distraught, "I should have taken her to the emergency room earlier, but she said she just wanted to go home."

"Don't beat yourself up, we've been seeing this a lot in the past week. The virus hits fast and hard, especially in the very young and the elderly."

Gentle hands, a gloved finger opening one eye. She flinched again and then, without her normal ten second warning, found herself retching up a dark green bile. It dribbled down the side of the bed and onto the white carpet.

"Okay, Mrs. Aaronson, okay. I think it's time for a quick ride to the hospital." The man turned away, speaking to his partner, "Let's get an IV hooked up with a saline drip. She's dehydrated and her temp is at 104.2. Also, call ahead and let them know we have one for potential admit to the ICU."

Sarah heard Theo, no, not Theo, it was John, John Carlson pacing at the far end of the room. "I should have taken her straight to the ER," he muttered. A young woman's voice then, "You couldn't have known, Uncle John. And besides, you got help for her. Come on, we can drive ahead to the hospital."

She felt hands lift her, then she was settled onto a hard surface before Sarah slipped back into the abyss.

Hours later, as the sun's rays turned the skyline from a midnight blue to a rosy pink, John pulled out his phone and dialed home. It rang twice before Amelia answered, her voice husky with sleep, "Still at the hospital, Uncle J?"

He looked out of the window. To the

east he could see the sky lighting up with salmon, pink, contrasting sharply against the low foothills in the distance. His chest felt heavy, constricted. "I am. I just wanted to check in and see if Mrs. Almeida could take you to practice. I'll be home by noon, and I don't want you to be late with the championship coming up."

"Okay, I'll ask her in a bit, after I take a shower."

"Are the boys okay?"

"They're still sound asleep. They watched some horror flick and Landon curled up in my bed." She sounded annoyed. John smiled briefly, Amelia was the oldest, and at fourteen, was full of the typical teenage angst.

"Is your friend any better?"

John's smile dropped away. "No."

Amelia's tone changed, "Oh. I'm

sorry, Uncle J."

"Yeah, I have to finish making calls now."

"Okay. I'll make sure and make breakfast for everyone." She paused, "And Uncle J?"

"Yes?"

"It was really good of you to stay with her, you know? She wasn't alone."

John nodded, even though his niece couldn't see it, "I'll see you after practice, Am."

The bed they had placed her in was empty, Sarah's body had already been transported down to the morgue. The sheets had been stripped, and the room cleaned with speed. There were more ill patients being brought in. He had been downstairs, the ER and the halls near the admissions desk were clogged with scores more who had arrived sick with the flu.

He had sat there, next to her bed, against the rules and held her hand and talked to her. He told her that the baby had been found. The story seemed impossible, the infant had been strapped into a baby seat, still spinning in the middle of the road when a couple had very nearly hit her. She was in care now, with the very people who had discovered her.

"The craziest part of it, Sarah?" he had said, her hand limp in his, "The baby was found on the same day as Cibil was taken into custody."

There had been no response. She hadn't stirred, not once, never gaining consciousness, never learning the news that had compelled him to first call and then come to her door the night before.

He had been too late to save her, and he felt wretched at the thought of her passing from the world without anyone but him by her side. They had been practically strangers. Despite this, he had felt a connection with her, one that ached with loss, grief, as he imagined what could have been if they had just had more time.

He glanced down at his watch, noted the time and headed for the door. Her son's plane would be touching down soon. He had found Michael's name in the contact info on Sarah's phone and called him near midnight as her breathing became uneven and the doctor had shaken his head, the look on his face betraying the truth. Michael had been first suspicious, who wouldn't with a call from a stranger in the middle of the night? But once John had explained the connection, and the dire situation, Sarah's son had made reservations on a red-eye and headed for the airport, calling John from the runway before departure to give him the flight information.

It would be close to two hours before he landed, just enough time in rush hour to make it to the airport.

John parked his car and as he oriented himself to the correct terminal, Sarah's phone buzzed in his pocket. He thought of letting it ring. Who was he to answer a dead woman's phone? He saw the number was local, however, and pressed the green button.

The woman on the other end was already talking, "Sarah honey, I've been trying to reach you since I landed yesterday. Where have you been? Oh girl, you were so right, aren't you always?" This had to be Gina, Sarah's roommate. Sarah had described Gina as someone who could talk a mile a minute without taking a breath. "Coming here was the best thing I could have done. My sister was losing her ever-loving mind and everyone was coming over and just standing around. I mean, really, just working themselves up something fierce while we waited for word and so I fixed that cannoli like you suggested and Carmelina and Lucina went from crying and screaming to calm in nothing flat. And the best news, Sarah, honey! They found both the boys. I mean, they're not boys any longer, Mario's pushing forty, and

Silvio's not far behind, but they are both okay. Beat to hell, Mario's got a broken leg, ribs, and missing a pinky for the love of God, but Silvio walked out with scratches. He was helping get others out and both of them lost their phones in the confusion.

By the time the cannoli were out of the oven, we got word he was alive and fine. Though I'm pretty sure Carmelina is gonna kill him for not calling home. And I'm running on fumes, the pull-out in the front room is lumpier than my auntie's mashed potatoes..."

"I'm so sorry, but..." John interjected.

Gina gasped, "Who is this? What have you done with Sarah?"

"My name is John Carlson, I'm the department psychiatrist at Cedar-

Sinai. Sarah fell ill with a bad strain of flu, Gina."

There was silence from Gina's end, just a whoosh of air, then a door closed, and Gina didn't say anything for a long moment. When she did, her ebullient tone gone. "Is Sarah all right?"

"I'm sorry... she's... not. We met for lunch yesterday. She was obviously ill, but insisted she would be fine. Later in the evening she wasn't answering her phone. I came by and found her very ill. I called for an ambulance. They admitted her to the hospital, but unfortunately, she worsened. I am so sorry to tell you this, but she passed away early this morning."

"Oh God." Gina began to sob, "Oh, I should have been there for her. That woman, that patient of yours, she told

Sarah she would die. I never should have left. Never. She was right. About the bombing, about Sarah dying, everything."

As he stood there, he could see the plane taxi up, nestling against the gate. He watched as the first passengers appeared from the long hallway. John's fingers felt numb. He hadn't thought of it until now, what Cibil had said in the observation room. How could he have forgotten it? He'd written it off, certain of her mental instability, that he'd barely given the words credence save for any mentions of her child. How had she known?

Gina was still talking, "Cibil was right. She was right about the bombing; she was right about the flu. What else is she right about?"

A group of three women appeared first, behind them a short, older man, a sour expression on his face.

"I'm so sorry, Gina. I wish I knew what to say." John told her. "I, I have to go, her son flew in and his plane just landed." Whatever she said next, he missed it, his eyes fixed on a taller man who had appeared, a backpack in one hand. He looked anxious as his eyes searching the crowd waiting for the passengers to disembark. John could see a strong resemblance to Sarah in him.

"Michael?" He stepped forward and the younger man zeroed his attention on John.

"Dr. Carlson?" He asked, his brilliant blue eyes laser-focused, "How is my mother?"

John shook his head. "I cannot tell

you how sorry I am, Michael. Sarah passed away two hours ago."

The younger man, shook his head, his mouth opened and closed in shock and grief.

Hours later, John returned to his house. It was empty, Amelia was at practice and the boys had left a note that they were at a friend's house and would be back after they ate dinner.

John peeled off the clothes he had worn for more than 24 hours and stepped into the shower.

The baby had been found, even if her mother was now missing. And the world had lost a talented, kind woman. John Carlson closed his eyes as the water ran in rivulets, washing his body clean, the steam billowing over the top of the shower doors.

A storm was coming. He could feel it

building.

Reek of Bone

"Not with a bang, but a whimper."

"Hi Dad, it's me, Isaac. Did I wake you up?"

The man's voice pulled Camelia from the depths of the paperback she had been reading. *A Life Relived* was a sharp digression from Dean Edmonds other books, which she had enjoyed immensely. This one, however different, was enthralling. She was nearly done, just a handful of pages left, and she found herself re-reading the pages, unwilling for it to end.

She peeked up and took in his blond hair and dark brown eyes. Their eyes met momentarily. He gave her a small smile and nod, and kept talking, eyes flitting elsewhere.

His accent was definitely not East coast. *Hm, possibly a Southerner, maybe from Georgia?* He had smiled as well, something that New Yorkers rarely did when making eye contact with a stranger. Camelia had dated a guy from Georgia right before her mom was diagnosed. He had been obsessed with her skin.

I've never felt anything so silky smooth.

He would touch her endlessly, his hands almost obsessive in their need to connect with her. Whether it was to slip his arm around her waist, even touch her hand or press his lips against her hair, he had been attentive and kind. Too bad his family had been such racist pricks. They had threatened to cut off his funding and him with no job and a full-time student.

She had been the one to break it off.

Her eyes traveled up to his face, admiring the fine stubble, the few stray white hairs interspersed in the blond. She had always had an attraction to older guys.

Hm, handsome.

"No? Oh good. I... no, no, nothing's wrong. Everyone is great, actually. I have some exciting news and I wanted you to be the first to hear."

Her gaze traveled to his left hand, which was clutching the seat in front of her.

Married. Damn.

"We will be adding a new Perdue to the family! Yes, you heard me right.

And Dad, we just learned it is a boy."

The tall blond man laughed, his warm brown eyes sparkling with excitement. "I knew you would be happy to hear that. Who knows, he might just take over for you there on the farm!"

He laughed again, "Well, you will just have to hang in there another twenty years. That shouldn't be a problem, right?"

He glanced out of the window.

"Hey Dad, look sorry, but I have to go. We are almost at the tunnel and the connection will cut off in a few more seconds. I just wanted to tell you the good news and I promise we will head down there soon. Next month, for sure, during Thanksgiving break. Yeah, I promise. Yeah, I love you too."

Fumbling with his cell phone, the man accidentally stepped on Camelia's toes, "Oh, I'm so sorry, ma'am, my apologies!" His smile was replaced with an embarrassed look of apology as he reached out and grabbed the back of a seat to steady himself again. The train swayed and continued to rumble down the track. Outside, the concrete walls were rising as the tracks angled down towards the tunnel.

"No worries." Camelia said, smiling up at him. "Congratulations, by the way." she added. "I couldn't help overhearing. How many children do you have?"

He grinned happily, "Baby boy will make three. I have two girls, ages ten and thirteen."

He was dressed in a suit, an

expensive leather briefcase wedged between his feet. His right hand tucked the cell phone into his pocket while he steadied himself with the left. The train was crowded, unusually so. A bridge shutdown, along with several road repair projects, had impacted the entire area, and the passenger trains, normally with seats still available, were now full to capacity, with standing room only.

"How wonderful for you."

The train slipped into the East River tunnel and darkness enfolded them. The interior lights blinked twice and brightened.

His smile stretched wider. "Thank you! It's been a long time coming, I'll tell you! We have been trying for just one more for over three years. My wife, she's forty-one, and, well, it isn't as easy now as it was with the girls. We didn't want to say anything, at least not until we were in the second trimester and the baby was doing well."

"I did a rotation in Obstetrics. I miss it. There's nothing that beats catching babies. But Sinai had an opening in Oncology and it meant better hours, so I had to say yes. Having a regular schedule, well, for the most part, is rare in the medical field."

"Are you a doctor?" He asked, his gaze slipping to her scrubs.

"No, I'm an RN, but I hope to begin studying for my MSN next semester, after I've got a good feel for the department."

"Well, you are definitely in a growing field. Especially with all of these aging baby boomers."

"When is your wife due?"

"The last week of February. The first two went over, so it might end up being the first week of March."

Camelia laughed. "Babies seem to have a mind of their own. You never know, this one might surprise you."

"Indeed, he might." He grimaced then. "It means moving, though. We have a two bedroom in Auburndale, and my wife is campaigning for a brownstone in Brooklyn. She wants the girls to go to Berkeley Carroll."

"I've heard of it. It's K through twelve, if I remember right. Very expensive, but worth it."

"Tell me about it, I might have to take on a second job just to pay for tuition!"

"There's nothing better than a good

start, though. Berkeley Carroll is a great choice. A girlfriend of mine has her daughter enrolled there. The scholastics are far and above other schools in the area." Camelia smiled. "Someday I'll find Mr. Right and make a family of my own. Kids are our piece of immortality, after all."

"Indeed." He nodded at her book. "Dean Edmonds, eh? My favorite book of his is *Fate's Highway.* What about you?"

"I'm really enjoying this one. It's completely different from anything he ever wrote before and it almost feels like memoir instead of his tried and true speculative fiction, but my hands-down favorite is *Touched by Light.*"

"Oh wow, I remember that one! It was good. I saw an interview with his daughter back in 2002, at the release of the 20-year anniversary edition. She said it was her favorite book."

Camelia opened her mouth, but before either of them could say anything more, a tremendous roar and concussive blast hit the train. On its heels came darkness, pain, and screams. A blackness descended, but there was no silence. Instead, the screams of passengers blending with the high screech of twisting metal, the floor of the car bending and gravity shifting around them.

The blast knocked the breath out of Camelia's lungs, and she felt as if her entire body was being thrown—legs and arms pinwheeling, before she crashed back into place. The train car itself twisted, screaming in metallic agony as the skin of it tore and the train, what was left of it, ground to an agonized stop.

There was a strong crack as something hard connected with the side of her face.

And then blackness descended.

How long it lasted—whether it was seconds, minutes or even hours—waking to darkness was unnerving.

What happened? How long was I out? Where am I?

Camelia took a breath, and instantly her throat closed, choking on the grit, dust, hair, and more. She coughed, spit it out, and tried to remember where she was.

Above all, rational thought was a grinding, overwhelming pain. It felt as if it were consuming her whole body in electric jolts of agony.

In the distance, a shower of sparks elicited weak screams and moans.

She could hear coughing, the sound
of a woman, or possibly a man,
wailing, their words rapid fire and
foreign. New York was a melting pot,
in this train alone they could have a
hundred nationalities. Nearby, at her
elbow, she could hear choking and
coughing, labored breathing.

The world felt off center, unsteady.
In the nearly consuming black, there
was no reference to up, down,
forward or back.

*I was on the train. Going to work.
Going to Sinai.*

Camelia felt around her. The padded
seat she had been sitting in was
tilted, crumpled from the feel of it.
Sharp metal stuck through the
padding and there was a wet
stickiness everywhere. She could
smell smoke. It had a greasy, oily

taste to it.

The darkness was not as absolute as she had first perceived. There was a light, in the distance, in the direction of the front of the train. At least, she thought it was the front of the train.

If her skin and bones could speak, they would have been screaming curses, not unlike the others in the distance. Her training kicked in.

Assess the situation. Possibly cracked, even broken ribs?

Her right arm wasn't moving, and the right shoulder hurt like hell. She dragged her left one out from under her and flexed it experimentally. She bent the elbow, and although all the arm felt bruised, she could move it. The fingers of her left hand gently explored her chest and ribs. The pressure of her fingers generated new agony.

Cracked, probably not broken.

What the hell had happened? The train must have jumped the tracks.

She had been talking to the man about his kids.

Where was he? What was his name?

The massive sound, an explosion perhaps? It had obliterated his words, turned the lights into showers of sharp, shards of glass, and lifted the train from its tracks.

The dampness was spreading. She could feel it everywhere now. The fingers of her left hand traveled, probing her right arm and stopping at a response of white-hot agony. She was curled on her side, in a half ball, as if her body had known what to do even if her mind had not. It had sought to protect itself, to gather in, but was prevented by something. Her traveling fingers found a head of hair. It had to be him under her fingers. He was warm, still breathing, but with a choked liquidity to it.

Not good.

"Hey,"

Damn it, what was his name? Wait. He had called himself Isaac on the phone.

"Isaac?"

God, it hurt to talk. My face feels wrong, somehow.

He moaned, moved slightly, and gasped. His head was near her stomach and her hands explored his blood-soaked hair and face, tapping him lightly with her fingers. "Hey Isaac, can you hear me?"

Her words sounded garbled, just like they had after a visit to the dentist and several fillings, her cheeks numb and tongue heavy.

"Christ, what happened?" he mumbled, rising slightly only to collapse again with a pained groan. "I can't move."

"Don't try to get up."

The smoke was increasing and now she was sure there was a fire.

Was it the train engine? Is that what had caused whatever this was?

Isaac coughed, and Camelia felt a spray of wetness on her arm. "I couldn't move if I tried. My legs, they're pinned."

"I'm sure there will be someone here soon. Just try to stay still."

"We are about midway through the tunnel; it's going to take them a while." He coughed again and Camelia felt another shower of droplets.

   She reached for her purse, fingers reaching in the darkness until she found it. In the destruction it had upended and she ran her fingers over surfaces, sharp edges, and under a limp, obviously dead hand before she found her keys. A flashlight was attached to the chain. She pressed the small button on the side and the light revealed a scene out of hell.

   Blood and bodies, parts of bodies, interspersed with twisted metal, the remains of seats, and wreckage surrounded them. A shoe without a foot in it, another with just a foot inside, grisly bone and meat, shocked her into letting go of the tiny button. Darkness descended, and Isaac coughed again. It sounded wet, and his breathing bubbled in and out, his head cradled against her stomach.

She pushed the button again, and he winced as the light filled his eyes. He was twisted, his body bent. *He shouldn't look like that. A human body doesn't turn that way.*

His head was against her, his body caught in an impossible grip of metal and the remains of chairs. Near where his feet should be was a twisted conglomeration of body parts, blood, and metal. Blood covered his face. She winced and wondered what she should do. More likely, what *could* she do? He had internal bleeding. He needed to be in the ER.

The train no longer resembled the sleek, gleaming machine she had boarded in Long Island. Instead, it was sharp, bloodied, and broken, just like the bodies it held within its bowels.

In the distance, she could see that the fire was growing, expanding, and beginning to move slowly towards them. It was yards away, but still, they couldn't stay here.

"I smell smoke." Isaac wheezed.

Forget the fire. The smoke will kill us first.

"Yeah, something up at the front is burning. Maybe that's what caused this."

He shook his head slightly, which was enough to induce yet another coughing fit. "No, that was no accident. That was a bomb." He said it with certainty. "We have to get out of here. *Now.*"

Camelia nodded, "Yeah. I know." She took a breath, which felt like she was breathing in broken glass and motor oil, and shifted. Isaac's head rolled to the right, and he hissed in pain and began coughing again. It burbled out of him, wet and thick.

Camelia wiggled while her ribs and right shoulder screamed objections, and slowly pushed herself to a seated position. The fire was gathering strength, and the flames lit up patches of the twisted train car, illuminating gore and death in every corner. No one else in the car was moving except for her and Isaac, but she needed to check on them, try to provide assistance if she could. She coughed and tried to breathe shallow. It hurt less when she did.

"Your arm doesn't look so good." Isaac noted, staring at her right arm hanging limp.

"I'm pretty sure it's dislocated. I

can't move it." She stared at him, "Don't worry about me, I'll be fine."

They were both silent for a moment, and Camelia used her flashlight to assess the situation. The train car had been full, with some of the passengers, like Isaac, standing.

"I need to check on the others." Her legs were shaking, and she was dizzy.

He nodded and coughed again.

The car was crushed beyond recognition. She tried to get her bearings. They had been in the front of the last set of three cars, hadn't they? There were two more cars behind them, with the rest of the train on the other side of the fire, deep within the tunnel.

As she looked around, it was obvious that, at least in this car, they were the only two who had survived.

Was it really a bomb?

Her face pulsed in pain, especially on the right side. She set the flashlight down and touched her face. She quickly pulled her hand away when her fingers touched teeth and bone where her cheek was supposed to have been.

She made her way back to Isaac.

"You need to get out of here." He said, his voice already sounded tired, defeated.

"Don't you mean *we* need to get out of here?" she fired back. As if she would leave a patient who needed her.

"What's your name?" He asked, then coughed again, another gout of blood escaping and dribbling down his cheek. "You know mine, but I don't know yours."

"It's Camelia. Camelia Garcia. I work at Mount Sinai Beth Israel."

He smiled and then winced as he tried to shift his hand. She realized he was trying to reach out and shake her hand. His right arm was badly broken from the looks of it.

"I'd say that it was a pleasure to meet you, Miz Garcia, but circumstances being what they are." He coughed again. He managed to pull his head back enough to see the blood. "This isn't looking good."

Camelia's ears strained to hear sounds of any kind of rescue effort, but she couldn't hear anyone other than the handful of survivors screaming, crying, and the sound of the fire crackling and spitting.

She could smell it then. There was nothing quite like the smell of burning flesh. She had learned that after a stint in the ER and a bus crash. Most of the passengers had been trapped as the fuel line had ignited and began to burn them alive. The horror of that experience had stayed with her for weeks and Camelia had sworn there and then to find a field that would take her far from burn units or ER work. It was the smell that was the worst. The distinctive greasy reek of flesh and bone that stayed in her nose long after she had finished her shift, stripped off her scrubs, and showered.

Her fingers rested on his wrist and took his pulse. It was thready and irregular. Combine that with internal bleeding and the lower half of him trapped, if not crushed, in the twisted remains of the train car, and Isaac was right, it didn't look good at all.

She tried to reassure him again. "We just need to wait for the rescue team. Hang in there."

"Tell me what you see, Camelia," Isaac gasped, coughing again.

"About as much as you see. Darkness, twisted metal, and a fire that is spreading."

"Any others alive? There had been a woman and her child who boarded after me. I let them have my seat."

She could see a tiny limp and bloody hand beneath a section of collapsed concrete. "There's no one else alive in this car."

"What about me?"

"What about you, Isaac?"

"Why can't I move?"

"You're pinned. The rescuers, they'll be here soon." She took a breath and cued the professional voice, the one that had calmed scores of stressed patients. "They will have tools and equipment. They'll be able to get you out."

"My body, it doesn't feel right. Like it is turned wrong. What do you see?" He asked again, stopping every third word to cough and choke. More blood seeped out of his mouth, dark red, mottled with black clots.

Camelia stared into the darkness. The opening to the tunnel was far behind them, around several bends. There wasn't even a spot of light to betray its presence. Her ears strained for any sound of voices or movement from that direction. But there was nothing.

"Camelia?"

She settled back next to him. "I wish

I knew what to say, Isaac."

"Tell me the truth."

Had she ever been this honest with a patient? "You are seriously injured. Spinal injuries, internal bleeding. The rescuers must be on their way, but they aren't here yet. Just hang in there, okay?"

"Listen, I need you to do something for me." His skin held a sheen of sweat. "I need you to find my wife. Her name is Amy Perdue. I need you to tell her how much I love her. How much I love our life and tell my girls…" He coughed again, the thick blood choking him, his words mixed with bubbles of red escaping from his lips, "Tell them that," the rest of his sentence was obliterated by a fresh gout of blood.

Camelia shined her light on the

man's legs and where they disappeared into the twisted metal. It would take hours to get him out, and Isaac didn't have hours. He had minutes.

"Shh, Isaac, you can tell them all of this, just…"

"Please, don't. Let us have truth between us. I'm dying, I can feel it." His fingers closed on hers. The act of moving the badly damaged arm had to be excruciating. She could feel his eyes on hers, the flickering of the flames growing closer. "Tell my girls to be strong and love their brother and their mother. Tell them to leave New York and get out of this death trap."

He gasped and choked on more blood. It was bright red. "You need to go, Camelia. There are others who need your help."

She knew he was right. Camelia could see the man's death approaching. It couldn't have been clearer if the angel of death had appeared before them.

The flames were beginning to crackle, and the heat was building as it inched closer. More screams and moans now from other cars. In their own ruined train car, there were only the two of them and this moment.

Her chest hurt. Not from the cracked ribs, but from the thought of the handsome man lying half in and half out of her lap. She imagined the family he was leaving behind. His wife, her belly swelling with a boy who would grow up knowing his father only through pictures and stories. His daughters. Girls needed strong, kind fathers like this one.

Camelia reached for the cross around her neck, praying silently for the dying man.

"You'll find them?" he asked, choking out the words.

"Yes. I promise I will."

"Go now." The fire edged closer. "You must go. So that my children and wife know. I don't want them left without answers."

She couldn't just leave him. Not like this. "May I pray with you, Isaac?"

"I'm not, I mean, I haven't," he faltered and coughed again, choking on the blood, "I haven't prayed in a long time."

She took his hand in hers. She wondered if it was for her more than it was for him that she was praying. Did it matter?

"Hail Mary, full of grace. The Lord is with thee. Blessed art thou amongst women, and blessed is the fruit of thy womb, Jesus. Holy Mary, Mother of God, pray for us sinners, now and at the hour of our death. Amen."

"Amen," he choked in response, blood bubbling past his lips. He squeezed her hand.

The fire was inching closer, the reek of burning flesh and bone a now omnipresent smell, the sulfurous odor of burning hair mixed with the coppery metallic smell that was both nauseating and sweet.

Camelia pulled her way upright, her eyes never leaving Isaac's. As she stood, shaking from the effort, he managed to smile at her, and then he sighed. One last bubble of red, and his eyes fixed and staring. He was gone.

She sucked in an agonized breath, her body reminding her in a thousand ways that she was alive but in desperate need of medical treatment if she wanted to stay that way.

She reached down, closed his eyes, crossed herself and whispered, "Vaya con Dios," before crawling away. She had to get out. The fire was growing, and the air was now thick with the choking smoke.

The train was shredded. Strips of metal littered the concrete and track and there was a steady wind coming from behind, feeding the ever-expanding fire. Crawling out of the wreckage, Camelia had glanced back to see only a handful of others heading her way. The train cars behind were just as damaged as hers had been and she wondered how it was possible she had survived the initial explosion, if that was what it really was.

Her face, ribs, and right arm were all agonized points of heat and pain. She could hear a steady hissing, the fire flaring and burning hotter with every passing moment.

"There's no one back there alive." An older man said, reaching for her right arm. She bit back a scream of agony.

"Your arm," he winced, his hand falling away, "I'm sorry, I was trying to help."

She clenched her teeth, focusing her energy on staying upright. "It's dislocated. Are you sure there is no one else back there?"

He shook his head in the orange-hued gloom, coughing as some of the oily black smoke rolled past them.

"Only the dead."

One of the others, a guy with a buzz cut and Carhart pants and coat, flapped a hand at her. "Come on lady, we gotta go."

"I'm a nurse, I should check."

Buzz Cut shook his head, "Look lady, unless you are Jesus Christ himself, come to raise Lazarus, you ain't gonna be able to help them. Everyone is fucking *dead*. Whatever that was, it cut the train in half and capsized parts of the tunnel. We gotta head back to Astoria before this fire catches up to us."

Camelia knew he was right. And as hurt as she was, there was little that she could do for the other victims. As they trudged through the dark, she tried to calculate how many passengers had been on the train.

Each car could hold, what, fifty seated, plus those standing, so maybe sixty-five, seventy tops? And there were, what, fifteen passenger cars?

Her brain struggled to complete the math.

Somewhere around nine hundred, maybe more, maybe less.

She shook her head and lurched dizzily to the side, leaning against the concrete wall as she struggled to comprehend it. She had been in the last set of cars. Perhaps the front of the train, on the other side, hadn't been as devastated.

Camelia stumbled and fell against the older man, her feet refusing to cooperate.

Shock is setting in.

Blood caked her neck on the right side of her face. She must look bad. Both the old man and the younger one had avoided looking at her. Their gazes sliding away from her face, concentrating on anywhere but there.

Buzz Cut pulled her up, and they kept going. Behind them, the fire was turning the tunnel, and the ruined train into a hellscape of death and destruction. No one was screaming, not anymore.

Each step seemed harder than the last. No matter how hard she concentrated, her knees kept buckling. As they made their way slowly, painfully, down the tunnel, they were joined by two more. An older woman and a young girl, both had been sitting on the tracks, staring in blank-eyed shock as the others approached.

The tunnel was narrow, barely three feet wider than the train that was now fully engulfed in flames, the hissing growing louder and louder. Chest high on each side, the walls were lined with a concrete ledge. Camelia stared at them, wondering if she and the others were supposed to be walking on them instead of down below on the track.

The older woman, her scalp torn and bloody, her business suit in ruins, put Camelia's fears to words, "What if another train comes?" Camelia noticed the woman was missing one of her shoes and limping badly on the other.

"Just keep moving, we should see the end soon," came the clipped response from Buzz Cut. He stopped occasionally; his face contorted with pain. The piece of jagged metal protruding from his left elbow had rendered the limb useless. They shambled, all of them, lurching through the tunnel, guided only by the dim, intermittent lights of cell phones and Camelia's keychain flashlight.

Far ahead in the distance, a dim sliver of daylight could be seen. The lights that normally lit this length of tunnel were dark, and glass from the broken bulbs crunched under their feet. The woman without a shoe said nothing more, only occasionally hitching her bare foot reflexively as she encountered more broken glass or rocks.

"Walk in the middle, as far from the glass as you can," Camelia mumbled, her cheek now swollen, her teeth aching. Her injuries were affecting her speech.

In the far distance, Camelia could see the dim light momentarily blocked and the sound of voices.

"Oh, thank you, Jesus," the older man said, "We're here!" His voice ricocheted against the tunnel walls, and Camelia heard one of them shout back. Lights and movement were headed towards them. The hissing behind them had turned into a low roar that was growing. The fire was now something else entirely, a white-hot light behind them that lit up the track, the tunnel, and even the rescuers, still hundreds of feet away.

"We gotta go, the train's gonna blow up." Buzz Cut grabbed her arm and Camelia bit back a shriek of pain.

"The train already blew up!"

"Nah, that was a bomb, this is something else. Come on, we gotta move!"

The rescuers were running faster, and within moments, they reached the small group of survivors. By this time the whine, turned roar, turned white hot light, had completely engulfed the tunnel behind them. Camelia's legs collapsed under her just as two sets of hands lifted her and everyone ran from the inferno. If she had looked back at that moment, she would have been temporarily blinded by it.

But by then, Camelia had already passed out.

Two days later...

"The terrible events of the past forty-eight hours have shaken New

York and the East coast to its core. Once again, our nation has found itself attacked by the lowest of the low. These cowardly, vicious individuals have sought to strike at the core of our hard-working community."

Camelia heard the newscaster first, recognizing her without needing to see her. She was a stunning blond with a perfect body. She had stridden into the ER a few years back on the heels of a hot story. Her stiletto heels had clicked on the hospital floor tiles like gunshots. Camelia had found her revolting.

She opened her eyes and stared at the television. The thick white bandages on the right side of her face obscured her vision.

"Due to the nature of the blasts, all

apparently timed to go off at the peak rush hour when the LIRR and Amtrak trains were deep within tunnels, and…" the reporter paused, intently listening to her discreet Bluetooth headset.

A brief flash of giddiness crossed her face before it morphed into a mask of fake concern. "Oh my, it seems that we are now receiving confirmation of a series of bombings on the BART train systems in the San Francisco Bay Area. One of which may have damaged the tunnels that run under the San Francisco Bay. There are reports of capsized tunnels and flooding."

Camelia could hear a hum of voices rise outside of her room and someone say, "And thousands already dead in the New York train bombings, by God, somebody's gonna pay."

"Why look who is awake!" Camelia turned to see a portly, red-haired nurse beaming at her. "You are in Sinai—Queens, and I'm Jackie." Her hands were warm. "We have been waiting for you to wake up and tell us your name, Miss..."

"Camelia Garcia." Her mouth felt full of cotton, her words still garbled. "I'm a nurse, at Sinai Beth Israel."

"Well, Camelia, you are lucky to be alive. Not many made it out of those tunnels after the bombs went off. The fire afterward, well, I'm sure you remember that."

Camelia nodded. "I do."

"You have been through so much Camelia; I can't even imagine how you must be feeling. I'll let the doctor know you have woken up, and there's a team of trauma counselors who will be adding you to their rotation, but who else can I call for you? A friend? A family member?"

Camelia thought about it. Work would need to be notified, but more importantly, "I need to find Amy Perdue. Can you help me with that?"

"Sure, what's her phone number?"

"I'm sorry, I don't know her number."

The nurse nodded and picked up Camelia's chart. "You were brought in along with four others. They are all still here and I can check and see if there is an Amy listed."

"No, she wasn't on the train. Her husband was, and, well…" She could picture those last moments, the life fading from his eyes, "He didn't make it."

"Ah, I see." The woman set down the chart. "I can ask around. Is there anyone else I can contact for you? Family? Friends?"

Camelia thought of her mother, Esperanza, in a nursing home upstate. She had begun to show signs of Alzheimers when Camelia was in middle school. And there had just been the two of them since Dad had died in a highway crash shortly after Camelia's fourth birthday. She barely remembered him.

The Alzheimer's had intensified by the end of high school and if it hadn't been for Camelia's excellent grades and the chance at a scholarship, she would have had no way to go to college. Mom no longer recognized her and the decision to place her in a home had been a hard, but necessary one.

The tenuous friendships made in high school washed away in the bustle of everyday life. The city had swallowed her up, and she fell into a routine of school, work, and then back home to the tiny efficiency apartment. One day didn't much differ from the next.

"No, there's no one."

Jackie clucked her tongue sympathetically, "Well then, let me see if I can find this Amy Perdue and we will go from there. Now you rest, Camelia, and I'll let Sinai know you are here."

Camelia thanked her, and the woman bustled away, moving quickly.

Hours later, after meeting with the doctor who informed her, she would need several surgeries to repair the injuries to her face, and being told how lucky she was to have survived when over 800 passengers had not, Camelia closed her eyes in exhaustion.

There had been a total of fifteen survivors—ten emerged on the Manhattan side, and the five in her group in Astoria. The train had not only been blown to hell and back by the bomb, which had capsized several sections of the tunnel, but it had also contained thermite, which burned so hot, that it had immolated the passengers trapped inside. The fire had turned the twisted remains of the train car into slag and made identifying the bodies impossible.

And it hadn't been the only one. Three other trains and two subway lines had been targeted and the simultaneous attacks had been carried out with precision. The news reports were still trying to put a total on the number of dead, but it was threatening to exceed the World Trade Center bombings, possibly even double that grim number.

"Excuse me, Miz Garcia?" A soft voice at the foot of her bed woke her from her half-doze. She opened her eyes to see a pretty blond woman clutching her purse. Behind the purse, Camelia could see the woman's rounded, protruding belly. Her eyes were red and swollen, and they had dark circles under them. This had to be Isaac's wife.

"Are you Amy?" Camelia asked in return, "Isaac's wife?"

The woman's chin trembled, "Yes, I am. I understand you were on the train that was in the East River tunnel. Is that right?"

"Yes. I was sitting near your husband at the time of the explosion."

Tears filled the woman's eyes then, and Amy's shoulders began to shake. "He's gone, isn't he?"

"I'm so sorry. Yes, I was there with him when he died. He asked me to find you."

The woman began to sob uncontrollably. Camelia reached out her hand, and Amy took it, squeezing hard.

"Please, tell me everything."

And Camelia did. The two women shared stories and tears and Amy hugged her and cried again.

Hours later, after the sun had slid behind the buildings, its orange glow lighting up a sky still tainted with the black smoke of death and loss, Camelia thought about Isaac's words.

"Tell them to leave New York and get out of this death trap."

Camelia had lived in New York her entire life. But there had been something in his words, in the fear in his voice. Camelia wondered if, standing there on the edge of this world, looking into the next, he had seen something she couldn't. And ever since the train tunnel, no matter how many times she scrubbed at her skin with her favorite lavender vanilla soap, her nose remained filled with the reek of burning bone.

Perhaps it was time to leave New York.

And the following week, after visiting one last time with her mother, that is just what Camelia did.

Other Mother

"Sometimes, you can't hide, no matter how hard you try."

Enid hid in the tall grass at the edge of the field and watched a column of ants move past her outstretched bare toes. It was late summer and everything was dry and crackling. Most of the insects, so numerous in the wet spring and early summer, were now hidden from view. Except for the solitary line of ants. Where were they going? Perhaps to the shade of the forest? She watched them pick their way around a large clod of earth, all marching in the same direction. Heading, it seemed, towards the trees.

She was far away from the

farmhouse, too far to hear Other Mother, and that was as it should be. Mom was gone, replaced by Other Mother and Enid didn't know how long it would be until she returned. She had watched the change happen this time. Mom had stiffened when Enid handed her the scissors. A coldness had replaced the warmth and love that her mother opened each day with.

Mom would fling open the curtains, "Wake up, sleepyhead! It is a new day and full of possibilities!" And Enid would stretch and smile and be caught up in a warm hug.

When Other Mother made an appearance, the best possible option was to leave, to hide. It was safer that way. She sat at the edge of the cornfield in the tall, dry grass and watched the ants march and tried to ignore the heat of the sun beating down on her neck and arms. She would have a sunburn for sure.

Enid tried to imagine what it would be like to be Dorothy from The Wizard of Oz. Mom had read the book to her a few months ago, during a calm spell. As she read it, she had run her hand down Enid's long, dark hair, stroking it, her fingers occasionally catching on the smallest of tangles, working the hair with her fingers until the knot disappeared. Enid marveled at how Mom could read for so long without stopping, her fingers working at Enid's hair, her voice almost hypnotic in its ability to act out the various characters' voices. Enid would find herself lost in the story.

What would it be like to be picked

up, sucked into a maelstrom of wind and rain and noise before finding yourself in a magical, far away land? Enid had her very own ruby slippers. Well, they were a pair of house slippers decorated with sparkling red sequins. They had been purchased on a road trip to Kansas City when they stopped off in Wamego and visited the Oz Museum. She would slip them on at night and pretend she was walking down the Yellow Brick Road. She wished she could be Dorothy. Instead, she was simply Enid Walters, aged seven years, on a farm near Atchison, Kansas.

A rustling caught her attention. Someone was moving through the cornstalks corn. Someone tall. The stalks had grown high, far above her head. The deeply tanned neck and face of her dad appeared. His face held concern. "I came looking for you, Half Pint. You weren't at supper."

Daddy had taken to calling Enid Half Pint, just like Laura Ingalls. Pa had called her Half-Pint in the Little House on the Prairie books that Mom had read her last year. He had listened to the stories right along with Enid, although sometimes he had dozed off. Enid couldn't help but giggle when he began to snore softly.

He handed her a sandwich, and she took it.

"You all right?"

Enid shook her head and looked away from him, trying not to cry.

"I didn't mean to make her mad, Daddy."

"Sure, and I know that, Half Pint. You haven't got a bad bone in your

body. So, what did you say this time?"
He asked, slowly easing his body
down next to hers. His boot crossed
the line of ants, disrupting the dirt,
and with it the chemical trail they had
laid. The back of the line scattered,
and the ants began milling about in
panic.

"I just handed her the scissors.
That's all."

"Had she asked you for them?"

"No."

"Then why..."

Enid's eyes filled with tears. She had
known Mom needed the scissors. She
knew that she was going to reach for
them in her sewing bag and that they
wouldn't be in the right place. She
knew, just as sure as if it had already
happened, that Mom would reach too
deep and find a stray pin instead. It

would have stuck in her finger; it would have bled. She had seen it. But she had done it too soon. When the vision had hit her, she'd just got up and went to the sewing box and pulled out the scissors. She had placed them in Mom's hand, and returned to playing, like she normally would. But Mom wasn't sewing. Not then, at least. If Enid had been paying attention, she would have remembered that in the vision the short clock hand had pointed to the one and the long one to the twelve. If she hadn't been busy thinking of a story she had read in school on Friday, she would have avoided giving Mom the scissors until after supper, not at the moment she was layering the sandwich meat onto the homemade bread.

She told her dad the whole long explanation, just as she had Mom when Mom asked why she handed her the scissors.

"I think that I scared Mom and so she went away and Other Mother came out."

"Other Mother." He said it slowly, letting it roll off his tongue. "That's what you call it when Mom gets a little off?"

Daddy didn't understand. He didn't see what it was like when Mom went away and Other Mother came out. She hid it well. Mom did. She waited until he left a room, was out of the house, and then Other Mother came out and those same arms that could hug Enid could also grab, twist, slap, and more. It was a physical transformation. She walked harder;

her step heavy on the floor. Her touch was iron-hard, and no emotion showed on her face. Enid knew to be scared when Other Mother came. She knew to run away if possible or to crouch down and let the blows come and just keep saying "sorry" until Other Mother stopped.

Enid nodded. A tear slid down her cheek. "I just wanted to be helpful. But I made her mad instead."

Her dad sighed. "I know, Half Pint. I know you didn't mean anything but good by it. She's just a little off today. I guess you had best avoid her for a while. She'll be better by dinnertime. These spells, they pass. Like yours did, a couple years back, we just need to be patient with her."

"Okay, Daddy." Enid gave her dad a brave smile, and he slipped a candy from his pocket, kissed her head and headed back to the house feeling more troubled than ever.

Enid's unexplained collapse into tears and sobbing two years back had lasted for days. Until then, everything with the little family had been perfect. The tiny infant they had found had grown into a vivacious, adorable preschooler. The walls were lined with photos of those happier moments.

Leo closed his eyes, envisioning the long hallway covered with pictures of them both holding her, their faces betraying their adoration.

The joy they had both felt after all attempts to find the girl's biological parents had failed and Enid was theirs to keep. She had been everything they ever dreamed of and more. But when that long week had hit, when

the girl stopped laughing and began
to cry, it was as if a switch had been
flipped. She was old enough to speak
by then, but she only shook her head
and wailed, tears flooding down her
cheeks. It had been terrifying at first,
and then, at least for Deena, it had
become something different,
something far worse.

"I don't know how to explain it, Leo,
but just seeing her like that, this
feeling came over me, and all I could
think was, not mine, not mine, NOT
MINE." His wife's lips had twisted, her
eyes haunted. "I didn't care about
why she was crying, only that she
suddenly didn't belong. She isn't ours,
really. And maybe she doesn't belong
here."

"Deena, listen to yourself. What do
you mean she doesn't belong? She's

ours, in the eyes of the law and in our hearts. We have loved her and hugged her and cared for her for over four years now! More than half of her life! If she doesn't belong here, where would she belong?"

Deena had said nothing, simply muttered, "Exodus 22:18."

How many times had he reached out and pulled Enid into his arms, only to say, "Your mom, she had a rough childhood?" An understatement, to be sure. Deena's childhood was one of the reasons why they had chosen to foster and adopt. Raised by her mother, a heroin addict and prostitute in Kansas City, Deena had spent the first ten years of her life saving her mother from choking on her own vomit while fending off the advances of her mother's customers. She had been at a summer camp, sponsored by one of her teachers, when a social worker arrived with the news her mother had died of an overdose. And after two years of bouncing between foster homes, Deena had eventually gone to her maternal grandparents' home and learned firsthand why her mother had ended up an addict.

Leo rubbed his chin as he walked. He'd picked up Deena hitchhiking, helped her find a job at the diner in town, and one thing had led to another. Five years of marriage, with not so much as a missed period, and Deena had been the one to suggest it. She'd been so excited, and so good with Enid, until the girl had her episode. After that, well, things had been different.

And it wasn't just Deena, Leo

reasoned, *Enid* was *different.*

Even he had to admit that. After a week of crying, refusing food, and just rocking back and forth, she had suddenly stopped one day. Not just that, but she'd brought him a bolt.

"What's this for?" he had asked her.

The little girl had shrugged. "You're gonna need it. Just keep it in your pocket."

Later that day, the combine had started to shimmy from side to side while he was in the north field. When Leo stopped to take a look at it, he could see the hitch was missing a bolt. He reached into his pocket and pulled out the bolt Enid had given to him. It was a perfect match.

Sure, it had been unsettling. But it hadn't stopped there. Enid had woken a few weeks later, crying and sobbing again. Not so different from the first time except she kept asking for Leo's dad, her Gramps. The crying jag didn't last long. It stopped abruptly when the phone rang.

His brother James on the other end, "Dad died this morning, Leo, I just got word from the hospital that he had passed."

That was the first time that Deena had invoked the bible, and especially Exodus 22:18 and the quote about not suffering a witch to live, but it wouldn't be the last. The last two years had not shown a relief, but instead an acceleration in conflict. Enid continued to evidence premonitions that were often dark and foreboding.

Her best friend, True, watched her brother die in a freak accident days after Enid woke screaming from a nightmare. The neighbor's dog, a purebred Golden Retriever, contracted rabies shortly after Enid warned its owner not to touch it. And the decline of the country, the rumors of financial collapse and the increasing utility outages and food shortages, all of them appearing just as Enid described, her childish print filling a Hello Kitty journal with dire glimpses of the future. Each time she let one slip, Deena grew more fearful, and Leo was at a loss for what to do.

That night, after Deena had performed her perfunctory duties, and it was Leo's turn to read to Enid, she had sat there in bed, sober, her piercing green eyes tormented.

"Daddy, I'm afraid." She had rested her head against his chest, errant black curls tickled his nose. Her words chilled him. What had she seen now? And what would Deena say? He'd actually seen her raise a hand to the girl last week, descending sharp and fast in an open-handed slap that sent the girl sprawling. He'd intervened, but honestly, how could he keep her safe? He was in the fields most days.

"What did you see, Half Pint?" At least she had learned to keep her mouth shut around her mother. With him it still flowed out, although he'd pay a ransom to wish it away.

She was silent and that in itself was telling. Enid told him everything, all the bumps and warts. Her mother's anger and fear had caused her to retreat in confusion and hurt, but she needed him. He could see that. He didn't shy away. It was as if the child was holding down the brake on a revving engine. She couldn't unsee these things, and with it being summer, hell, with everyone so damned spooked by her visions, she was all alone. He was the only one she had to talk to.

"I saw men," she said finally, "Soldiers, but not the good kind. They're coming, Daddy. And you..." Her voice faltered, wobbled with unshed tears, "Daddy, I can't make the things I see change. No matter what I do, they still happen."

"I know, Sweetheart." He had to wonder if such things ran in families. With her raven-black hair, pale as milk skin, and piercing green eyes, she was out of place in this sunbaked land. Who were her people? Where had she come from, anyway? And who would have been willing to abandon a child such as this? She was beautiful, sweet, and Leo's love for her grew with each day.

Sure, he reasoned, *the visions scare the hell out of me, but it isn't her fault. It can't be.*

In this, Leo and Deena took opposing positions, which was no surprise when his wife's childhood was examined. Shuttled from one foster home to another before her maternal grandparents were found and she was handed over without so much as a by your leave. Their spare the rod and spoil the child philosophy hadn't worked so well with her mother, so they doubled down on it with Deena, all while hauling her to a church that felt more like a cult the scant handful of Sundays that he had stepped inside it. Speaking in tongues, flailing about in the aisles, and handling snakes had all been part of the weekly repertoire. It had been doses of fear and hatred and then more fear and hatred on its heels - twisting teachings of the bible into warped judgments on anyone who was different in any way. Leo shook his head. How could Deena embrace that twisted world? He couldn't understand it. Although he could imagine what his dad would say.

"We all got our ways of returning to our roots, son. Good or bad, we fall back on what we know." Leo missed his dad in ways that no words could properly describe.

"Daddy, I'll try to change it this time. Okay?" And her words suddenly sunk in.

"Enid, honey, did you see something happening to me?"

The child nodded, her fist clenching his shirt. "I keep seeing it, Daddy. But it happens when it's cold out, not hot like it is today. I keep praying for it to stay summer."

"I see." A black hole opened in his stomach, and he could feel it spiraling through his body. It wasn't fear for himself, not really. Leo had always been a pragmatist. He figured when God called, you went, and that was that. Instead, the blackness was fear of what might become of Deena and Enid. Most especially Enid, without him to soothe Deena's dark moods. And then it occurred to him. What if it was more than just him? What if Deena and Enid were on borrowed time as well? Somehow, the thought of anything happening to either of them was more than he could bear.

"What about you, Enid? What about you and Mom?" Heart in throat, he dreaded hearing more, but couldn't help but want to know.

"Me and Mom will be fine, but she's going to be Other Mother. It'll get worse, lots worse, *way* worse, Daddy." Her face was solemn, pinched with fear as she stared into the distance, her eyes not on the pretty pink dresser in the corner, but far in the future. "Mom will be Other Mother until she dies."

"Can you see what happens to you, Enid? Can you see your future?" Leo couldn't help asking, his heart breaking for the child. It was a curse, of that he was certain, but not in the way that Deena saw it.

Enid nodded, her face damp with sweat, a sour smell of fear rising from her damp hair.

"I see me all growed up, Daddy. But sad too, and," she shuddered, "like Other Mother 'cause seeing all of it and not being able to change it, it makes a person bad in the head." Her tiny fingers dug into his. "Maybe I can change it, Daddy." She choked back a sob. "I don't want you to die. I *need* you."

He hugged her tight. "I love you, Half Pint. And no matter what happens, no matter where you go or how long you live, I want you to remember that. Promise me that you will."

"I promise, Daddy."

She had tucked herself against him and said nothing more while he read to her from Harry Potter and the Chamber of Secrets. Deena had objected to the books, but Leo had overridden her.

"They teach powerful lessons of friendship and good, Deena. It isn't the worship of the dark arts and witchcraft like some churches are preaching."

Many days, after he had done the bare minimum needed to keep the farm running, they sat in the field together until the sun began to creep low in the sky. The smell of frying chicken would lure them back to the cool farmhouse and out of the summer heat. Deena would make a pie or even ice cream. His wife was calm, placid even, and Leo couldn't help but hope that whatever was coming, whatever dark horse was headed their way, Enid might be wrong for once. Who knew? Perhaps she *could* manage to change the doom that approached.

That evening, the power failed again, the condenser slowly spinning down, the cool air all too quickly replaced by the hot, humid Midwestern air. The next day it wasn't on, nor the next, nor the day after that. When the natural gas piped in from town stopped working two months later, they switched back to the propane tank, a relic from before Leo had modernized and had the farm added to the gas line when the small town expanded and suburbs were laid in not too far away. The pipes had been laid on the way to a large, sprawling suburb that had been half-built before the 2008 housing collapse and never finished. It had cost a small fortune to connect, and now it appeared that they were better off with the propane for as long as it might last.

"We got at least three months longer if we use it judiciously," Leo told his wife. "I'll go into town and see what the word is."

Enid had bitten her nails down to the quick in his absence. The days had grown cool, but not cold.

Please come back, Daddy, please come back.

And when he had appeared at the tree line, she had run through the stubbled field and thrown herself into his arms. She could feel the dark horror of what was coming, slowly, inexorably marching toward them.

As the days grew colder, Deena's

mood turned dark as she watched Enid cling desperately to Leo. "That creature won't give you a minute's peace," she said one evening, hours after Enid had been sent to bed. Her tone was sharp. "She follows you closer than a lovesick cow."

"She's scared is all," he answered in the darkness, "She isn't bothering me."

"Well, it bothers me!" Deena snapped. "What's she seen? I know it's gotta be that, so what unholy vision did she have now?"

He hated talking to her when she was like this. All hard edges and sharp words, the fear of what she saw in the child, freezing the love in her heart. Leo wished he knew what to do to make it better, to change it in some way. He didn't have much time.

From the way the child clung to him, her anxiety and desperation increasing, he knew his life could be measured in days.

"Deena, stop. Just…"

"I'm not the one who needs to stop, Leo Walters! What has she seen?"

"It's nothing, Deena, nothing at all. All of this will wash away and the world will right itself again." Even as he said the lie, he knew she saw through it.

Deena sucked in a breath. "Oh no. No, no, no, no, no. You can't leave me with her, Leo. She's got the Devil in her. It's an unholy thing to see what's coming. Unholy, against the will of God." She ran out of air, the last words spoken in a rasping whisper.

"Enid isn't unholy or evil, Deena. No

matter what she sees." Leo's voice hardened. "And I'm begging you to see that. This little girl is the same little girl we found in that baby seat, spinning in the middle of that highway. The same one we nursed through the croup, through every nightmare, even the fractured tibia when she fell off the swing. Surely you can see that. She needs your love. You withhold it, and she will turn into the very thing you fear. Mark my words, she will."

Deena gasped, and he could feel her tremble in the bed next to him. "I'm scared, Leo."

He sighed and pulled his wife close. "You and me both. Promise me you will show her kindness, Deena, she's just a little girl."

And in the days that followed, Deena

did her best. A week later, with Enid sick in bed with a cold, Leo headed out to town to see if he could barter for some cough syrup and aspirin to bring down the girl's fever. At a quarter past two that afternoon, Enid awoke with a banshee wail. In the distance, mother and child could hear gunfire. Tears rolled down Enid's cheeks. Deena, her hopes crumbling to dust, shushed Enid.

"You stop carrying on. There's no need for such a racket!"

The child continued to keen, her body folded up, her entire person a sculpture of grief. She hadn't been this bad off since the week all the visions had started, some two years past. And Deena knew then, her heart crumbling to dust in her chest, that Leo was gone. There was a snap, a bowstring break in her soul as she watched Enid sob uncontrollably in the bed. Deena could feel everything good and kind wither up and dissolve to dust along with her heart.

If Enid had been looking, she would have seen the transformation come over her mother. It was more than mental or emotional, it was a *physical* transformation. One moment, it was Mom, her mother, the woman who had a place in all but her earliest memories. The next, it was Other Mother. The warm brown eyes went dark with pain and rage. Her body stiffened, hardened, her skin no longer warm and soft, her hands now bony, painfully wrapped around Enid's wrist, ice cold.

"Stop that unholy noise, you and your visions, you have brought this to pass!" A hard slap knocked the girl off of her bed and onto the wood floor. It hadn't been the first time Other Mother had hit her. It was, however, the beginning of a descent into darkness that Deena never recovered from. Enid marked it as the moment when Mom went away, never to return, and Other Mother emerged. As if the good and light had not just been locked away, but purged from her mother's body, until only darkness remained.

The days were cold, Enid's world stuck in the cycle of the seasons, held in place by duty and dread. She had seen what would come next, and in a way, Other Mother had seen it too. Especially in the last year, confined to her bed, the curtains closed in a dark, oppressive room. She couldn't say much of anything, grunts and gestures with the one hand that hadn't frozen and curled up in the wake of the powerful stroke from the year before.

Enid wondered why she stayed. Every year, as the spring thaw came sliding through, warming the frozen wasteland that had once been a thriving farm, she asked herself why she stayed. For Daddy, mostly. The memory of his kindness, his love, still strong ten years later. And partly for the woman Other Mother had once been - a kind woman who had held her and rocked her at night. Enid thought of leaving, but despite no words of love, and certainly no kindness, her dreams still showed her that Mom was there, inside of Other Mother. And especially now, in this past year, Other Mother was really nothing but a shell of the monster her mother had become. Enid could see both of them trapped inside the body that could no longer speak, or move, or care for itself.

The weak light of an early spring dawn brought a groan from Other Mother's room and Enid turned from stoking the fire in the old stove. She fixed a small smile on her face and marched into the room. "Morning Mom, how are you today?"

The contorted figure in the bed groaned, her mouth struggling to shape a sound. "Naa… nah.. nat…" She had been repeating this for days now.

"Nat?" Enid didn't know a Nat in town and certainly couldn't remember any family member or family friend by that name. She had woken this morning with a deep certainty. The woman who had dominated her life for as long as she could remember, first in the form of love and protection, then as a creature to fear, and finally as an object to care for - she was dying.

Enid could see the end coming. She had seen it a decade ago and now, finally, it was here. It was a dark cloud of certainty, approaching with deliberation and intent. Mom, or Other Mother, hell, Deena - her life was measured in moments, in hours. This Enid had seen for far longer than she cared to admit. It was what had kept her here on the farm, long after Daddy was taken from them. The dream of a life he had wanted for his small family long gone. Evaporated with invading troops, a bullet to the chest, and the fallow fields that followed. She had stayed, partly out of duty, but also because she had seen a clear, defined end to it all.

She perched herself on the edge of the bed and leaned in to wipe her mother's face with a clean cloth. Deena closed her eyes for a moment, seconds ticking by as she seemed to relax, even be soothed, by Enid's gentle touch. Despite everything, the blows, the curses, and now this complete helplessness - Enid had stayed. After all, her last fragile link to Daddy lay in the bed. Enid was no longer a child, yet some part of her needed to honor what Daddy had always seemed to stand for - peace, love, and commitment. She hadn't handled it with grace, not always, especially when Other Mother had raised her hand in anger or screamed excerpts from the bible at her, but she had done her best.

In some ways, it was more than that. It was destiny, just as her vision of the end of the world, the one filled first with plague and finally with a fireball that promised to scorch the earth like no other, was coming. She could see it so clearly.

"Nat… Natal… yuh…" The wretch in the bed groaned again and her left hand flopped and twisted on the bedsheet, a single bony finger raised shaking in the air. Enid watched her, following the finger as it rose in a spasm, shaking, pointing to the small chest in the corner of the bedroom.

"Do you need something from the chest, Mother?"

"Nat... Nat... all... yuh." The finger jabbed into the air for emphasis before collapsing back onto the bedsheet. A sheen of sweat had formed on Other Mother's face from the effort.

Enid found herself rising, moving with purpose to the chest. It was locked, the key missing, and the wood chest had strong hinges. "It's locked and I don't have the key, Mother."

Her mother said nothing, eyes closing from the effort she had expended, a tiny slick of drool sliding down her slack jaw.

And Enid suddenly felt energized. The key, it had to be in the room, it just had to be! She shoved open the curtains, dust motes dancing in the rays of the sun that shone through. Other Mother didn't flinch, her eyes were shut, her breathing shallow and erratic. Enid glanced at her and began to search the room methodically. It had to be here somewhere. And Mother had wanted her to open the chest, practically ordered her to do it. She opened drawers, rifled through Daddy's now moldering belongings, still in the drawers they had been in since the day he died. Enid pawed through underwear, then Mother's jewelry box, before finally finding the key tucked beneath a lock of hair. Hers, it seemed, a few jet-black wisps of curls with a pale pink ribbon tied around it.

The key fit into the hole with ease, and Enid turned it first to the right and then to the left, stopping when she heard the click of the lock releasing. A glance back at Mother, who lay there unmoving, barely breathing, her eyes shut. Enid opened the chest. A puff of dust and stale air, along with a faint odor of baby powder. Inside of the chest was another lock of hair tied with pink ribbon, along with a note in Deena's hand:

First haircut!

Below was her christening gown. Although they had rarely attended church, especially after her visions created a gulf between her parents and the other townsfolk, Enid knew she had been christened. Dad had mentioned it, partly in rebuttal to Mother's fears, that she was possessed by an evil spirit that sent her visions.

Something crackled then, deeper in the chest, and it took some digging to find the source. A yellowing newspaper clipping slipped into a clear plastic cover.

Mystery Baby in Car Seat Identified

The toddler was still fastened in her car seat in the middle of the Highway 49 just outside Topeka when it was discovered by a couple who hail from Atchison, Kansas last week. The couple called police after the discovery and the wife swore the car seat was still turning in a slow arc in the roadway when the couple's truck approached it.

"She was so tiny, and I thought it was a doll at first, she was still asleep!"

 The couple, who had recently completed foster care training, were able to take the child home as an emergency placement until the biological parents are located. Yesterday, Cibil Zradce was identified as the child's mother. Cibil is currently in custody and awaiting a competency hearing pending her release from The Oaks Mental and Rehabilitative Facility outside of Topeka, Kansas. The child will remain in state custody until Ms. Zradce is fully evaluated.

Enid took in a deep breath. "This is me, isn't it?" She glanced back at

Mother, who lay unmoving in the bed.
She dug further.
Two more articles appeared.

Patient Disappears from Mental Health Facility

Authorities report that a patient from a mental health facility in Los Angeles, California, with ties to the baby found on Highway 49, has somehow escaped custody.

Cibil Zradce is not considered to be dangerous, but anyone seeing her should call authorities immediately. She is described as medium height with a thin build. Black hair and green eyes.

Missouri authorities were advised that Cibil may try

to return to her child, who
is in state custody at this
time. Her mental state is
reported as unstable,
confused, and manic.

And nearly a year later...

Child Found on Highway
Adopted by Local Couple

The infant found in a car
seat in the middle of a
highway has been adopted by
the couple who found her.
The local couple has
requested privacy for their
child...

She could barely breathe. The air in
the room was stifling. The final
document was a birth certificate,
listing her name, Enid Walters, along

with the original certificate. Enid scanned it. The mother's name, Cibil Zradce, was listed and the name of the father was blank. A baby girl, weighing six pounds two ounces, 18 inches in length, named Natalia Zradce.

"I'm Natalia, aren't I, Mother? The baby in the car seat?"

The only answer was a soft rattle, the last breath of a woman who had both comforted and terrorized her for most of her seventeen years. Deena lay unmoving on the bed and her eyes, once closed, had opened into a fixed stare. She was gone.

Enid couldn't breathe, couldn't think here. She gathered up the papers, slid them back into the chest, and lifted it all up. It was heavier than she expected. She staggered out of the thick, dead air of the bedroom, down the hall, through the living room and out into the gathering sunlight on the front porch. Bright beams of light lit up the documents in her hands, and she sucked in mouthfuls of the clean morning air.

Natalia, *not* Enid.

That was her name.

Her mother, lost.

Her adopted family all dead.

"I'm Natalia." She said, the word sounding odd, different on her tongue. Had her mother sung her to sleep? Had she whispered her name in the dark and held her close?

There was so much she didn't know.

Natalia looked towards the road. A few weeks ago, a town meeting had announced that the war was over and the Reformation had begun.

Washington was gone, lost to a nuke, just like Austin, but now the provisional government of the Reformed United States of America had been formed in Chicago. Things were changing.

She turned her gaze to the barn, the fallow fields, and the farm that had been her world since she could remember. She didn't belong here. She wasn't Enid Walters. Instead, she was Natalia Zradce. It felt as if she had been reborn.

By the time the sun set in the sky, she was ready. A pack on her back carried everything she needed, and the fires had been set. By the time the townsfolk saw it, she would be long gone. The walls of the empty barn and the house blazed up in the gathering darkness, the fire gaining speed, fast, hot. Natalia Zradce walked away. Away from the farm, away from the small town of Atchison, and onto the smooth highway leading east. She walked away from the life that Enid Walters had, that Deena and Leo had, and into her own. As she did, she hummed softly, a lullaby, one filled with nonsensical words she could barely remember on her lips. Perhaps Cibil was still alive. Perhaps she wasn't. But Natalia knew one thing for sure. She knew *who* she was for the first time in her life. And that was enough.

There was darkness coming. Darkness and then fire. "Darkness and death, cleansed by fire," she whispered as she walked. "It's coming."

99 Problems

"This is the way the world ends."

"I dunno, Cal. What do we need with them, anyway?" Donnie slid lower in the bucket seat and stared at the house. "And what's for sure the old man has even got 'em?"

The plan was simple. Most of them were. Cal wasn't particularly bright, but he was sneaky and good at working out solutions to pesky problems. He excelled at finding weed when they were running low. And he could slip a six-pack out of the store right under the clerk's hawk-eyed stare when what was left over from their meager paychecks wouldn't cover it. Hell, given a chance, he could get them a hooker to share and pay her off in meth he'd made in the basement a few months back.

This, however, this was bigger than rolling some dude fresh off the farm with more homegrown than sense or stealing beer from a guy who didn't own the place. This was stepping over the precipice into dark territory.

"Shit, Donnie, don't wuss out on me now." Cal fiddled with the settings on the radio. No one was talking. The music was on an endless loop, ever since the news out of Austin. As the power outages continued, the stations were dropping off one by one, vanishing from the atmosphere as if they had never truly existed.

If you're having girl problems, I feel bad for you, son

I got 99 problems and a bitch ain't one.

"Damn, this a fucking great song." Cal turned up the volume, and the speakers gave short static bursts. Cal ignored this, slapping his hand on the steering wheel in time.

"Cal, c'mon man, let's just go back home. I don't got a good feeling about this."

Tip my hat to the sun in the west,

Feel the beat right in my chest.

Cal turned and stared at him, his eyes turning mean like they did when he didn't get his way. And everyone paid the price when Cal didn't get his way. Donnie looked at the floor, but he could feel Cal's eyes on him.

"Wake the fuck up, Donnie, the world has changed, and we gotta change with it. We need those guns and pretty soon we're gonna need food and a hell of a lot more."

   At the crossroads a second time,

   Make the devil change his mind.

"It's just a power outage, Cal, they'll fix it soon." Donnie protested, knowing even as he said it that it wasn't that simple. The power had been out for two days now, and there had been no crews on the ground, no one fixing whatever was broken.

And more than that, there were no cops, no government vehicles. Hell, not even the 24 Independence bus was running. And while some of the more tight-knit communities through the metro had come together and tried to fill the hole left after the desertion of the police, forming citizen watch groups, the rundown street that Cal and Donnie lived on was certainly not one of them.

It's a pound of flesh, but it's really a ton

99 problems and a bitch ain't one.

"Look, if you're gonna be a pussy about it, Donnie, you can just stay here. I mean, shit, I wouldn't want you to have to break a nail or pee your little panties." Cal sneered.

Donnie flushed. "I'm just saying maybe this isn't the best place to do it." He looked out of the windows. There wasn't any trash, not like on their block, and the houses were quiet and dark.

"We go up north of Independence and we'll get our asses handed to us," Cal snapped. "They got something to protect."

"What and this guy doesn't? Look at his house!" The house, its outline dim in the gloom, was large and well-built. Cal hadn't been inside it, though, only Donnie, when he was contracted to do some work there installing a tile floor in the spacious kitchen. Which was, of course, how this had all started. The man's sign, in the window of his side door no less, had been the giveaway.

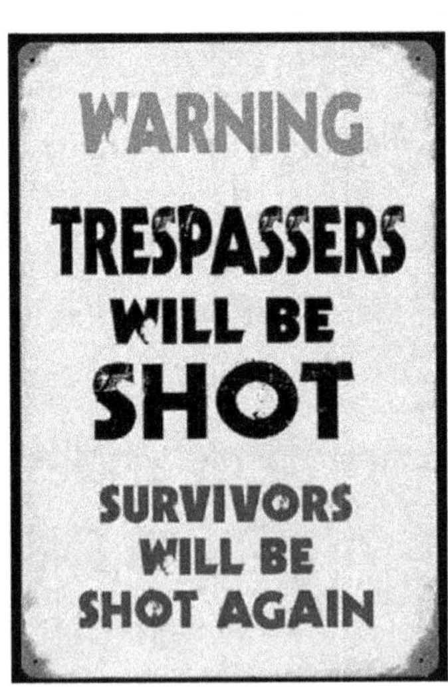

If you're having girl problems,
I feel bad for you son,
I got 99 problems and a bitch ain't one

"I'll bet he's got plenty of booze and cash besides the guns." Cal replied, ignoring Donnie's last comment. "Look, we *need* those guns. Look around you Donnie, this shit isn't getting better, and it's gonna get a lot worse. The water and gas still work, but for how long? Hell, Price Chopper was cleaned out of everything except the goddamn produce section and half the workers there were running scared. We need to defend ourselves."

"You got a gun already," Donnie pointed to the revolver sitting between them.

"Yeah, and it's got *four* bullets in it

and the gun shops were cleaned out afore the grocery store was!" Cal barked back at him, "We *need* this, Donnie, or we're gonna be deader than doornails in a few weeks' time without those guns."

99 problems,
But a bitch ain't one.

Donnie sucked in a deep breath and blew it out, "Fine. I'll do it."

"Yeah?" Cal grinned at him.

"Yeah."

Cal reached over and punched his arm. "Cool, let's do it. Just like we talked about, right?"

"Right."

Cal had come up with the plan after he had driven by the area, nice and slow, during the day. No one had been out even then. Folks were staying inside now. Not like they had been in the first few days, when the garbage trucks were still picking up the trash each week and the bus was still running. Now, with the lights off and fall quickly approaching, there were plenty of rumors, but no real, hard facts. Still, folks stayed inside, checking their smartphones that were slowly running out of juice and debating whether to run a generator which would give them a connection to the world but draw all the wrong attention in the process.

Yesterday had brought news of a nuke in Austin. Shortly after that, all but a handful of radio stations had gone silent. The tv stations were all off the air and there wasn't just a general sense of unease anymore, now it was more one of terror.

They were on their own.

Like broken glass under my feet

I could lose my mind in this heat

The sound of their footsteps crunching over gravel was far too loud. Cal hissed at Donnie, "Remember to stick to the plan." Then he disappeared into the shadows.

They had gone over it back at their cheap rental house off of St. John. Cal had said, "I'll take the way around back and set myself up around the corner of that back door. You go on up to Old Man Nichol's door and get him to come out."

That had been Cal's plan, and Donnie had gone along with it. As he approached the door, he couldn't help wondering exactly *how* he was going to get the guy to come outside where Cal could get the drop on him.

He knocked on the door.

> *Looking for the prize, but I don't want blood*
>
> *I order one drink, then I drink the flood*

One minute stretched into another and he knocked again. "Hey, Mr. Nichols, you there?"

"Who's there?" Donnie heard Nichols' voice on the other side of the door.

"Uh, it's uh me, Donnie. I worked on your kitchen floor this past spring and you said to come by if I, uh, if I ever needed more work." As the words left his mouth, he realized how stupid it all was. This guy wasn't going to let him in. Why would he?

Rather improbably, he began to hear

the locks turning, chains rattling seconds before the door opened. The older man stared at him. "Donnie? You do realize it's almost midnight, right? You okay?"

And now, staring at Nichols again, Donnie understood why Cal had been so hot to take this guy down. Especially after Nichols had given Donnie a ride home all those months ago. He hadn't really thought about it at the time, but now, staring at the man again, he could see what Cal had been hinting at.

The smile on Nichols' face was more than friendly, a lot more. So was the hand he had placed on Donnie's arm, the sensual slide down it, like a woman would do if she was looking to get some.

Donnie suddenly remembered Cal

questioning him about Nichols.

"Any signs of a woman 'round there?" He had asked. And there hadn't been. Donnie had just figured that Cal wanted to make sure there were no woman or kids to get hurt.

"He's all artsy fartsy and shit," Donnie had told Cal, "Like the carved Roman statues and naked guys and all that." And Cal had rolled his eyes, shook his head and laughed.

Well, you can come inside, but your friends can't come

99 problems and a bitch ain't one

Before Donnie could say anything to Mr. Nichols, Cal stepped forward, the weapon in motion, hammer back, the pistol pressed against Nichols' forehead.

"What the hell!" Nichols squawked in

surprise as Cal shouldered past Donnie, backing the man up until he slammed against a cabinet on the opposite end of the small enclosed porch.

"Shut your mouth," Cal said, pressing the gun hard against Nichols' forehead. He tipped his head at Donnie, "Donnie, get your ass inside and shut the door."

Donnie did as Cal instructed, hands shaking as he twisted one of the deadbolts into place. Rolling some kid for weed and a handful of cash was one thing, but this was far different. They were in this man's house. *A house is a man's castle.*

"Where are the guns, old man?"

"What guns?" Nichols gasped as Cal jabbed harder with the revolver.

"Cal, wait, just let me talk to him."

"Nah, Donnie, I got this." He sneered at the older man, "Fuckin' freak. You hot for Donnie here? Stop looking at him, you look at me. I'm the one with the gun to your head. Now you tell me, where are the guns?"

"I don't know what you…" His words were interrupted by Cal punching him hard in the gut, knocking the air out of him.

"Fine, we'll play it your way, old man. I bet that shit is upstairs, right?"

And then Cal made a mistake. He looked away. It was just a second, and that was all it took for the man to shove him hard, and then run from the room.

"Shit, he's getting away!" Cal shouted, no longer worried about making too much noise as he stumbled, struggled to regain his balance, and then pivoted and ran after Nichols.

Donnie stood there, unsure of what to do, the light from the oil lamp that Nichols had set by the door flickering. Cal turned, slowing for a short second before he disappeared from sight, "Come on Donnie, move your ass, we got to catch up to him!"

Rooms, doorways, curtains, and old furniture—it all passed with a blur—the darkness of the house far more intense than the dark of the night outside. Here there were no stars, no moon, only Donnie, Cal and Nichols, playing a nasty game of keep away. And they were running out of rooms.

It was Cal who found it first. The door ajar betrayed the light flickering within. "Holy shit, Donnie, he's got a goddamn arsenal in this room."

It was the last thing he said, past gurgling. The bullet caught him in the throat and he collapsed like a sack of potatoes on the immaculate wood floor.

Nichols stepped out of the shadows and pointed his gun at Donnie, "I liked you, kid. And I never would have hurt you. But this, you have brought this to my door. And what am I to do?"

Donnie put his hands up. "Mr. Nichols, I'm sorry. I should have never told Cal about you. It was wrong and I..."

"It's best you don't talk right now, Donnie, I'm liable to shoot where you stand and I already have this friend of yours blood fixing to stain my wood floors."

Cal gurgled and bubbled, the blood flowing freely from his throat. His gun had fallen from his grasp when he was shot, and Nichols had his foot firmly over it, ignoring Cal's efforts to claw his way toward it.

Nichols shook his head and clucked, "What to do, what to do?"

Cal had almost reached the gun and Donnie watched him with horrified fascination as Cal reached not with his right hand to grab the gun, but with his left, which held his Muela. He raked it down the back of Nichols' leg and the older man screamed, and Nichols' leg buckled, blood spraying. He fell to the floor, the gun booming in his hand as he collapsed.

> *If you're having girl problems,*
> *I feel bad for you, son*
> *I got 99 problems and a bitch*

ain't one

Donnie felt a searing pain in his chest and struggled to understand why. Nichols was on the ground, Cal's knife cleaving gouges in his flesh, gurgling sounds from both of them as Cal put the last of his energy into murdering the man whose house they had invaded.

Donnie looked down, confused, at the bloom of red, that spread slowly from a hole in his chest. His eyes glazed, his vision blurred, and he felt cold.

So cold.

Falling to the ground felt as if it were happening to someone else. More that gravity changed, morphed, and broke the laws of physics. The floor came up and greeted him in a rush. He could hear the tchotchkes clattering and breaking as they tumbled off of the side table, victims of his bulk collapsing onto the fancy spinets and arches of a Victorian era.

The floor was cold, hard, unyielding.

I got 99.

The blood pooling on his chest was filling his lungs, and he gasped, trying desperately to suck in air and finding only blood. There wasn't pain so much as what felt like a heavy rock pressing on his chest. No matter how much he tried to suck a breath in, there was simply not enough air.

99.

The darkness, which had been nibbling at the edges of his vision, now was rushing in. From far away he could the pounding and yelling. A splintering of wood from the door being broken down. Voices. The floor shook imperceptibly as others entered the large, rambling house.

99.

"What the hell happened here?"

99.

"Oh man, they got Nichols! Shit!"

99 problems.

Another voice, "Are they all dead?"

A foot nudged Donnie, and he tried to speak. He wanted to tell them he hadn't wanted to do it, that it hadn't been his idea, but the words were just bubbles drowned in blood.

But a bitch ain't one.

"This one's still kicking, but not for long."

99.

Donnie couldn't see anything now. Instead, he felt lighter than his body, his soul slipping from the flesh and bone that lay dying on the floor.

"A hidden door? Holy shit, Nichols was hiding the mother lode in guns! I can't believe it. He kept telling us that sign was just bullshit. We could have handed it to those fuckers who came barreling through last week with the AKs. Could've handed them their asses. That stingy old piece of shit!"

99 problems and a bitch ain't one.

And then Donnie was gone.

All Roads Leading to Austin

"Hope is a dance with the impossible."

Jacob

The heat of the late summer was far worse here in the Midwest. He was used to a drier heat, and the humidity in the air here just sucked the energy out of a man. His men were lagging behind, their steps slowed by exhaustion. Jacob wiped away the sweat beading on his forehead and eyed the approaching storm. It was humid, and the clouds were gray and ominous. Thunder rumbled in the distance and occasionally he could see the twist of light strobe through the thick, roiling layers. It was a bitch of a storm headed their way. It would cool them off. It already was now that the wind had picked up, pushing his damp hair away from his forehead. He needed a haircut. Hell, he needed to stop walking and fighting and watching what was left of his unit die for no damn good reason.

This town, Clinton, was a destroyed shell. Most of the buildings were either partially collapsed, burned, or mere skeletons, reaching fire-blackened brick chimneys to the sky. After weeks of fighting in June between the Western Front and the Allied South, most of the inhabitants were either dead or had fled. His orders were to clear the east side of town, confirm that the Western Front had moved on out of the area, and reconnoiter with Bravo unit before nightfall. Jacob just wanted to sit down and sleep. But sleep brought nightmares, dreams of a blond-haired boy, mushroom clouds, and radiation warnings.

His men were spread out, dog tired and stretched to their limits, thanks to the endless muggy heat and meager rations. Scouts hadn't found any food locally either. The shelves of stores had been stripped bare for nearly a year now, and it was every man, or soldier, for himself.

He had heard talk that most of the men in Tango unit had melted away in the night, disappearing like cockroaches under cover of darkness, likely heading for home or whatever was left of it. He wondered if it was time to do the same. Could JJ and Nancy still be alive? He knew how unlikely it was. But still, his heart wanted to hope against hope that they were both still out there. Divorced or not, he loved her still. No one else had come close to giving him the feeling he had when he was with her.

Nancy hadn't wanted to be a military wife. She'd wanted more. She'd wanted to finish her Master's in Art History, and who was he to hold her back? When the end had come, she had already moved to Austin and served him papers. He'd managed to come and visit and see them as often as he could on leave. But it wasn't enough for little JJ. He would cry and beg him not to leave at the end of the visit.

They had been too close to ground zero. Likely still asleep on that sunny

Saturday morning, when the nuke blew a crater into the northeast section of the city and annihilated anything within a twelve-block radius of the Arts District and the University of Texas. That's where Nancy was a student, just a year left until her degree that she had fought so hard for. He wanted to believe it had been quick, that his boy hadn't suffered, and that he hadn't died screaming like the scores of others who were farther away from the detonation site. It still gave him nightmares. The carnage that they had showed on the enormous viewscreens in the Fort Hood Commons before the blackouts took out the internet had haunted him ever since.

His scheduled leave had been that morning. He had stood there, bag in hand, planning on hitching a ride with friends after missing the train out the night before when the news hit.

"All roads leading to Austin have been closed until further notice. Authorized medical and emergency response personnel only are allowed in."

The bag had dropped from his numb hands, the ground rushing up to meet his knees, the air leaving his lungs. Hollowed out, empty. His family was *gone*.

Leave had been canceled; all troops recalled. Not all the men had returned. He knew of plenty who had family in Austin, and had likely been there at the wrong time, good men that he would never see again.

What am I doing here, anyway? How does this solve anything? We fight each other, and for what?

He knew the company line, had parroted it back to the senior officers, shouted "Yes, sir!" and told his men to keep going. But as the days had turned into weeks, and weeks into months, it had all seemed so pointless. Communications were down, and their orders, when they received orders at all, were often conflicting. The reality was, they weren't fighting an outside enemy, they were fighting themselves. And those were battles that no one could win.

Nancy

Nancy woke from the dream, a scream dying on her lips as she sat up in the pre-dawn darkness. Uncle Ray stared at her from his well-worn seat in the kitchen.

"Y'alright?"

"Bad dream." Jacob, alone in a wash of radioactive hell, bleeding, burned. The vision of it hung there, painted in her mind, the taste of ash in her mouth. She should have called him. But she hadn't, and now he was gone, lost in the blast or the radiation that followed. All it would have taken was a phone call. The father of her child, one of the best men she had ever known, *gone*.

Uncle Ray coughed. It sounded wet, thick. He always sounded worse in the morning. Eventually, given a shot of strong black coffee to loosen it up and he'd cough up a mass or two, thick yellow globs shot through with blood. On a bad day, it would be mostly blood. He should be in a hospital, but since the blackouts, and the shortages, and then the Very Bad Day, the hospital was no longer a place you went to get better.

The Very Bad Day had struck more than two months ago. And Nancy had given thanks to God every day after, for where they had been, and where they had not been, when the nuke struck Austin.

Over a million dead, probably twice that.

The fate they would have suffered, at least for her and JJ, that close to Ground Zero. It would have been quick, but still. She had seen what it had been like for those who weren't as close. Burns that wouldn't heal, hair that slipped from scabbed heads in clumps, blowing on the floors of Davis Medical Center like listless furballs, impossible to keep up with.

She did her best, though. When not changing bedpans or scrubbing the sheets clean by hand now that the power was out, she pushed a broom and tried to round up the errant hairs. It seemed to her that those strands of hairs had deserted their posts, leaving behind hollow-eyed, bald skeletons that did not seem to notice their absence. For that matter, they appeared to see nothing, eyes staring and lost, their radiation-sick bodies wasting away before Nancy's eyes.

There were dozens of them. Specters that had driven, walked, even been carried from the highways and byways leading from Austin. They had spread out, like a sickness, meandering through the country like broken homing pigeons. One foot in front of the other.

JJ mumbled in his sleep and turned over, curling up against the table leg. His hair was slick with sweat, his cheeks red from the heat. Nancy could see it was early still, the sun a weak specter sliding up into the sky, barely pushing its way through the thick cloud cover. It was hot, stifling in the small single-wide mobile home, and she sat up slowly, her back aching from the rough bed on the floor.

"I made coffee." Uncle Ray coughed again, turning away, grabbing for the handkerchief he kept in his shirt pocket. His bony frame shook, convulsed, and Nancy winced at the rattling sound that accompanied each of his breaths, in and out, in and out. He bent over, let the cough take him and gave himself to it, almost retching. He spit into the handkerchief.

"Christ."

"You watch your tongue, Raymond Withers," Aunt June said, tottering out of the bedroom at the far end of the narrow trailer. Her face was a pasty shade of gray and she said it halfheartedly, as if it took too much out of her to say more. "We give thanks to God, not use His name for curses." She looked for a moment as if she would fall, gently swayed back and forth, then slowly regained her equilibrium, and shuffled to the easy chair. It occupied the corner opposite of the table that JJ still slept restlessly underneath.

"Where's your oxygen, Auntie?"

"Out."

"What? But we got that last Tuesday! It was supposed to be full!"

"Well, it weren't. I knew it felt light when you brought it in. I took it easy on it, just like you said," she paused, caught her breath and continued, "Ain't nothin' to be done 'bout it. I'll manage."

Nancy shook her head. "I'll see if I can't get another. Maybe if they pay me less in potatoes for my work, I can ask for an extra can. You need it, Auntie."

June reached out her hand and touched her niece's arm. "Don't you... dare... that child needs food more than I need that... silly oxy... gen. You hear me?"

Hard, hot tears pricked at Nancy's eyes, "Yes, ma'am, I hear you."

June and Ray had raised her,

without complaint, after the mother she barely remembered had died of leukemia. She had been four years old when the social worker had brought her to the small one-bedroom trailer, looked it over with a jaded eye and said, "Kids are made of rubber, just let her sleep on the floor under the table. She doesn't need a room of her own." She had leaned close, speaking low, but Nancy had heard her all the same. "Better with you than with strangers and a ward of the state. You got no idea how bad it can be." And they had just nodded and taken her in.

It felt as if Uncle Ray and Aunt June had been sickly in one form or another all of her life, but not this bad, never this bad. They had moved slowly, were in their 60s by the time

Nancy entered their lives. That first fall, when it was time for kindergarten, Nancy had held June's hand and walked with her into Midlands Elementary on the southern edge of Elkins. Everyone else had young moms and dads, but Nancy's had white hair and wrinkles. It was a different way of life. Simpler, with no frills, but they had loved her and made sure she grew up healthy, with decent clothes on her back and food in her belly. Sleeping under the table hadn't been that bad, wasn't bad now, and JJ loved it. He had drawn stars on the underside of the battered Formica table and called it camping.

They had taken her in and never once complained. When Uncle Ray had called three months ago and said Auntie was in the hospital, Nancy had dropped everything, picked up JJ from his daycare and drove straight on through to Elkins, West Virginia. They had only stopped for gas, fast food meals, and what had felt like every damned rest stop along the way because JJ still couldn't hold it for long. She hadn't even thought to call Jacob until it was far too late.

They had just checked Auntie out, driven her home and settled her in her easy chair when the reports had started coming in. Chaos, screaming and crying from the folks in the park as they watched the mushroom cloud over and over and over again on the television. JJ had snuggled close, despite the muggy heat, and whispered, "It's a very bad day, Mom. It's a Very Bad Day."

The entire cell phone array was

down within minutes and it wasn't long after that the rolling blackouts started. Each one longer than the one before, until finally the power shut off completely. How many times had she tried to call Jacob over the next few weeks? Hundreds? The calls wouldn't go through, and one of the power surges that had accompanied one of the last blackouts had taken out the phone and Uncle Ray's computer, the A/C unit, and the television in one go. They were down to a radio that produced nothing but static. And no word from Jacob, none.

Nancy sighed, staring at her son on the floor. JJ asked every day, as hopeful as the day before. She hadn't told him that his dad had told her he would be visiting them in Austin, that he had bought the train tickets a

month before the nuke and swore
he'd be there. She had forgotten all of
it in the panic of getting to Auntie's
side in the hospital, scared she would
lose her. And then, staring in horror
at the images on the screen she had
been afraid to tell JJ his father was
dead, hoping beyond hope that he
would magically appear, walking
down the cracked macadam with his
duffel bag in one hand, clothed in the
familiar fatigues.

The Very Bad Day, Nancy sniffed,
JJ's name for it had stuck. And not
just with Uncle Ray and Aunt June,
but the rest of the scattershot
inhabitants of Happy Hollow Trailer
Park, which was neither happy nor in
a hollow. With the loss of power over
a month ago, many of the park's
residents had packed up their station

wagons or trucks and headed away.

"I got family out West."

"I'm a fixin' to see how Canada is right 'bout now."

"I hear the power is on in New York."

And slowly they scattered, sometimes in the morning, others in the dark of night, but most when the sun was high in the sky. JJ, who was as outgoing and gregarious a child as Nancy had ever seen, saw most of them off, waving goodbye to the frail and weak Longbottoms and their disabled daughter. Hollering "Safe travels!" to Jolene Nichols, who made the best angel food cake in the world, and the Larabies who were determined to find their youngest son.

"Not all the roads leading to Austin can be closed. He's at the University there, studying architecture, and we'll be back once we fetch him." Amber Larabie had said, her face determined, a small brave smile on her lips even as her eyes betrayed the truth of it. Their son had been in campus housing, so close to the epicenter that even his bones weren't dust. A brief millisecond and hundreds of thousands of sleeping, innocent people had vaporized.

They would never find him. And chances being what they were, they would never come back, either.

Nancy looked down at Aunt June's gray face, which held so many familiar lines and wrinkles. June smiled up at her grandniece, "Be a dear and fetch me a cup of that black tar Raymond's brewed up. That will put some power in me."

Nancy fetched her the cup, added two sugars, and noted how low the packets were in the bowl. A few more days left if she went without any, but they would run out of coffee before that. Hell, they would run out of everything by tomorrow night. She closed her eyes, her heart stranded in the dream of her ex-husband, terrified she would have to choose between eating and buying more oxygen for June, and wondering if she would be digging two graves in the next few months.

Jacob

The storm hit, fast and strong. It had been threatening it for an hour, perhaps longer, the dark clouds massing, rotating in the brisk breeze, the branches on the trees swaying.

There had been a battle here, not long ago, and most of the houses were in ruins - burned and broken. The rain was falling, thick drops, and there was little or no cover. If Jacob and his men could make it just a half mile further to the north, there was a hill with a rocky outcropping they could camp underneath. Lightning flashed, and he heard something coming from a small shed up ahead. The fence that had surrounded it, along with the house that it undoubtedly belonged to, were both splintered wooden ruins. The house had gaping holes in the roof, one wall blown completely off, and there appeared to be crude graves, complete with tilting, rough crosses.

He could no longer see his men; they were spread out too far. The same noise attracted his attention again. It was definitely coming from the shed and almost lost in the crack of thunder and the rushing of rain. What had he heard? An animal? He walked toward the shed, his finger sliding into the trigger.

He carefully swung the door to the shed open, surprised to see four faces gaping up at him in fear and shock. He stood for a moment, taking in the scene before him.

There were two young children huddled in a corner and two teenage girls frozen in fear at his feet. In the red-haired girl's arms was a tiny, pasty, limp newborn. Another flash of lightning showed he was a boy.

The baby had obviously been born mere seconds ago; his umbilical cord was still attached. They all looked at him with undisguised terror.

Corporal Jacob Daniels Sr. turned his gun to each in turn. A rifle was propped in the far corner of the shed, but no one moved. He stared at the newborn and remembered the day his son had been born. The nurse had handed JJ to him, wiped clean and wrapped in a soft blanket, and he had stood there in the Army hospital in Fort Hood, stunned at how tiny and fragile the child was.

A thousand images of his little face flickered through the Corporal's memories like a home movie. He had grown so quickly from a tiny infant to smiling toddler and finally into that precocious four-year-old who slept with a battered G.I. Joe doll that had belonged to Jacob and insisted that he was going to grow up and be just like Daddy.

The children at his feet were holding their breaths, eyes wide, terrified.

They were all children, even the older two, who couldn't be out of their teens yet. What in the hell was he doing here? As if losing JJ wasn't enough. This war, it was killing them all, ripping apart families and destroying lives. He could hear his men moving closer, calling over the radio for his status. Soon, they would be close enough to see the shed and its occupants.

Inexplicably, almost unbelievably, he lowered his gun. His body sagged slightly. He was so tired of fighting, so tired of war. All he wanted was his family back.

In a voice that was surprisingly soft, barely audible above the thunder and wind, he said, "I had a son once. It seems... so... long ago. His name was Jacob." Then, without another word, he turned away, softly shutting the door behind him and disappeared into the raging storm.

Outside, the storm raged on as he called over his radio to his men, "Move north. There's nothing here but the dead."

And the troops marched on, with Corporal Jacob Daniels, Sr. leading them. He marched through the mud, past a row of bombed-out houses. He barely noticed the crude grave markers, or the bodies lying in ditches far north of the small town. Instead, his memories were consumed with the laughter of a blond-haired little boy who had died far too young.

Nancy

"We dig one bigger grave, put 'em both in it." Harvey said, nodding to a shaded spot, "That's good soft dirt there, easier to dig into."

Nancy nodded wearily. She had found them, hand in hand, side by side on the bed that morning. The way she figured it; Aunt June had likely gone first. She had been struggling since the last canister of oxygen had run out the week before. When Uncle Ray had realized she was gone, he had gathered her up in his arms, and just let go, too. Anyone who tells you that can't happen doesn't know a married couple who have spent more than sixty years day in, day out with each other. Uncle Ray had been devoted to Aunt June. There was no sense in his living if she was gone.

The coffee was long gone, had been for weeks, but Uncle Ray would still get up every morning, shuffle into the kitchen, open the cabinet door and stare at the spot the coffee was supposed to be, as if it would magically reappear. It was as predictable as an alarm clock and Nancy would wake to the sound of the bedroom door creaking open and usually be sitting up by the time the old man made it to the kitchen. When Uncle Ray didn't wake her up that morning with his usual routine, she knew something was wrong.

A quick glance in the bedroom had confirmed it and she had slipped out of the front door of the trailer quietly, thankful that JJ slept so soundly. She had walked down to Harvey's trailer at the end of Row 3 to ask for help. Now in his late 50s, Harvey wasn't any spring chicken, but there wasn't anyone else to ask and she wasn't sure she could manage it on her own without waking JJ. He didn't need to see that. Her son was a gentle soul, even if he did keep talking about becoming a soldier like his dad. He had cried inconsolably three nights straight when his hamster died, just two weeks before they left Austin.

The trailer park was empty now. The trailers that were capable of travel had moved on, leaving gaps that felt like missing, rotten teeth. The remaining trailers sat uneven and rusting in places.

Harvey had suggested they pull the bottom sheet, wrap it around the bodies of Uncle Ray and Aunt June, and slide them on out, down the hall. Nancy had covered the open edge of the dining table with a sheet and prayed JJ would continue to sleep soundly.

It hadn't been easy, but they had done it, easing the sheet-wrapped bodies down the narrow hall and out of the trailer, down the three short steps, and to the cover of the trees.

Harvey's breath rattled in his throat. He wheezed and coughed, hacking until he shook it loose from his lungs and spat into the dirt.

"Lemme catch my breath, then I'll help you. I got me another shovel in the shed out back of my trailer."

"I got it, Harv, you rest."

Harvey harrumphed, "You ain't got nuthin' girl, you's as skinny as a rail these days." He scratched at the tufts of white hair that still sprouted in odd patterns on his mostly bald pate, "You gotta eat more to keep that energy a'going. Hate to say it like this, but, hell, leastways there'll be more t'eat now you got two less mouths to worry about."

Nancy felt a surge of anger, followed by a wash of sorrow. Harvey was plain-spoken, and she knew he didn't mean anything by it, but damn it, she wished he'd shut his trap. As if she hadn't thought of it herself, and not just today. She dug the shovel into the ground and it yielded easily, just as Harv had said.

"The previous owners had a goddamn sandbox right around here. They figured they'd have it for kids to play with. Only thing that got in it were the damned cats. There was more shit in this sandbox than there was sand. But I figured that'd make it easier to dig in, huh?" He smiled at her, his teeth yellow. One of the front ones chipped away at a sharp angle.

"Sure does," she grunted as she dug deep. The sweat was already rolling down her back and onto her forehead, the flying dirt sticking to it. Hot work, dirty work. She hadn't remembered the sandbox until he mentioned it. She'd tried to play in it a couple of times as a kid and been turned off by a rather fresh cat turd. After that, she'd stuck to the tiny yard that went with the trailer.

"Mommy?" She could hear JJ calling in the distance.

"Shit."

"Here," his rough hand closed on hers, "you go take care of your boy,

I'll keep at it." He flapped a hand at her as she cast a look at the bodies, the hole, and then back at the trailer in the distance. "Go on with you, I can handle this."

"I'll be back soon." She jogged away, trying to formulate the words to say to him.

Jacob

He woke up on the hard ground, the sounds of fish splashing in a nearby lake. It wasn't quite dawn, and by now they would have noticed he was missing. It was time to move, put some miles between him and his unit, and, more importantly, the superiors who would do their best to find him and make an example of him.

He wouldn't build a fire and heat up one of the MREs. He'd just down a protein bar, some water, and get going. Later he could chance a fire, but not yet, maybe not even tonight.

It'll have to depend on how far I get.

Jacob felt a cold knot of dread form in his stomach at the thought of them hunting him as a deserter. The Army was all he had known. They were more family to him than the laundry list of foster homes he had stayed in.

That's what drew Nancy and me together - a wish for family - both of us missing out growing up, even if she did have her aunt and uncle.

Jacob paused mid-swallow.

That's it. If she and JJ are alive, they'll be in West Virginia. I need to head there, not to Texas.

No one would think of looking for him in West Virginia, or on any roads heading north or east. They would expect him to go to Texas, which made sense. But Nancy's family was in West Virginia.

She loves Uncle Ray and Aunt June. If she made it out, that's exactly *where she will be.*

He dug out the protein bar, swallowed another gulp of water, and filled the canteen with lake water, using the carbon filter. The filter wouldn't really help make it taste good, but he'd avoid getting parasites and would stay hydrated. After all, he had a hell of hike in front of him.

Jacob hefted the pack onto his back. He had maybe twenty meals, twenty-five if he stretched it. That could get him pretty far along before he needed to look for more. And he had his gun, so he could hunt in a pinch. He pointed himself towards the east and began walking, slapping at the mosquitoes that were beginning to gather in the cool, shaded areas.

He tried to calculate it. West Virginia was over eight hundred miles away. If he maintained an average of 3.0 miles per hour, and walked at least six hours each day, it would take at least forty-five days to reach his destination.

I could have stolen a Hummer and been there in a couple of days of driving.

He shook his head and kept walking. Hell, if he'd stolen a vehicle, they would have tracked him down and locked his ass up in the brig. That is, if he was lucky and didn't get shot on sight for desertion. At least this way, he had a chance they'd just give up. He wasn't the first to desert, and he certainly wouldn't be the last.

Nancy

The trailer park was quiet. The fall morning air was crisp, just a hint of what was to come in another month, perhaps two. The garden was full of fall crops - kale and spinach, along with a bumper crop of carrots. Nancy had helped Harvey cannibalize several of the older trailers for their windows, and they had built several cold frames that would allow them to continue to produce through the winter. The park was far away from main roads, and she was thankful they were isolated.

Elkins had been hit hard. First by the Allied South duking it out with the Central Unionists, then some damned neo-Nazi group had come in a series of deadly raids, scooping up drugs from the pharmacy inside of Davis Medical Center and kidnapped a Somali widow and her two children. Anyone who stood in their way was shot with terrifying efficiency. Fearing another raid, Nancy and Harvey had downed a large tree across the cracked and winding mountain road that led to Happy Hollow Trailer Park and dug out the battered sign that advertised its presence.

Two families, both from Elkins, had picked their way down the road, over the fallen tree, and brought a large dog kennel full of chickens with them. Later, a pregnant goat, loose in the woods, had been rounded up and given birth to a kid. With luck, they would find another and have some breeding stock that could add meat to their diet. With extra hands on board, the garden had tripled in size, the earth surprisingly rich as it yielded forth bountiful harvests over the long summer. With hard work and no small amount of luck, Nancy was reasonably sure they would make it through the winter.

Nancy had climbed the radio tower twice before and she climbed it a third time, braving the winds that tore at her and stared out at the mountains, curving roads, and ruins of Elkins in the distance. Here and there, she could see campfires that rose up and blended with the fog that often crept over the mountains and married the treetops to the sky. Their corner of the world was quiet for now.

"Jacob, if you are out there, you need to come back to me." Her words were snatched away by the wind and her eyes hurt as much as her heart did. "I'm sorry I didn't try harder, but I know now how much I need you. Not just JJ, but me too. Come back to us."

She clung to the tower, half-sitting, half-standing, her legs and arms firmly wrapped around the rungs. The cold was creeping into her fingers through her gloves, though, and it was time to go back down. Nancy took one more look at the road that led to the trailer park, a speck of movement catching her eye. A deer, perhaps? They had bagged one over a month ago, and nothing since.

What I wouldn't do for some venison.

The tree cover was too dense. She thought she saw something, but what it was, she couldn't be sure.

Jacob

The thin mountain air held a chill. It had since he approached the edge of the Monongahela National Forest two days ago, skirting his way around a settled area, and heading towards Elkins.

Day 62 - Damn, but it's taken a lot to get here.

His boots, designed for war, for marching, along with his fatigues, were still in decent shape, although his clothes were stiff from dirt and he wondered if any amount of cleaning could be able to get the stench two months of living out of them. Everything hung loose on him. He had seen his reflection in a glass window, one of the few intact ones in the town of Elkins, and been shocked at how gaunt he was. He had walked through the town, unnerved by the silence. Several times, he was sure he had seen a curtain twitch as he moved past some of the more intact buildings, but no one had ventured forth. This had become routine as he walked the highways and streets. His uniform marked him as a soldier, but no telling which faction, and most of the countryside had seemed to have had their fill of soldiers. They didn't venture out, but he hedged his bets by not approaching, either. He had walked too damn far to get shot now.

The last week had been the hardest. The miles had been eaten up quickly the first two or three weeks of his journey, especially once he had made it to Interstate 70, which was, barring bridge collapses and warring factions, still a nearly straight shot to the beautiful mountains and the outer edges of the Monongahela National Forest.

He had been born there in Elkins, and lived the first eighteen years of his life in one shitty foster home after another. The only bright memory was of Nancy and a couple of other high school friends. Nate had made it out and had been in California last he heard. His foster brother Joe had ended up serving time for burglary in Tygart Valley Regional, and Perry had been studying to be a mortician like his dad. And, of course, Jacob had ended up marrying Nancy. It had been a no-brainer to get hitched when she realized she was pregnant. He had loved her, still did.

If I had been better at those little

things, the little gestures, maybe we would still be together.

Instead, he'd focused on his role in the Army, moving them from town to town until she had had enough.

"I'm always having to leave my friends behind, Jacob. I can't go to college. JJ won't make friendships that will last more than a few months, and it's just too damn *hard* to live like this."

He had brushed her concerns off, ignored them, until the papers were served and she had taken JJ and moved to Austin. He didn't blame her, not one bit. He'd been the one to take her for granted, to not listen, and here they were.

He was getting close. If they were here, and he wanted to believe they were, how would she feel about him showing up. Would she welcome him back into her life again? Or would he just be an unwelcome reminder of the past?

He stumbled, tripped on an uneven portion of pavement, and nearly fell. He was tired, bone tired each and every day. Not enough food, lips dry and cracked, dehydrated since losing the water filter last week crossing a ravine to avoid troop movements.

His feet guided him to the lonely, tree-lined road that led to the trailer park. Just a few miles now. He looked up and saw a small flash of sunlight, some lookout up in a tower, and slipped to one side of the road where the trees covered him. What was he walking into? He had stopped at a farm a few days back, helped the old man with the harvest in exchange for food and gotten an earful about a group of extremists in the area, making trouble.

"You see anyone moving in a pack bigger than two and do what I do, *hide*," the old man had said, waggling a bony, spotted finger in his direction. "Those damn neo-Nazis been rounding up women and kidnapping any of them *ethnics* that they can find. I hear they use 'em as slaves. Goddamn *slaves*!" He had spat on the ground then, shook his head, "As if we didn't learn nuthin' the first time 'round."

He had offered Jacob a permanent place to stay, shaking his head when the younger man refused. "The offer stands. It's dangerous out there, son, so find what you gotta find, and come back if you can. You and yours would be welcome."

Jacob saw the tree straddling the road in the distance. The sign he had seen a thousand times, battered yet legible, was missing. He moved off of the road, stepping quietly now. The world, even one he knew like the back of his hand, had changed. Who knew what was waiting for him up ahead? He slid the rifle off of his back and double-checked it. There was a round in the chamber. The safety was off, and he crouched slightly, bending his knees and choosing his steps carefully, taking his time.

He swung around, moving higher up the north incline, moving carefully as he circled around to a side of the trailer park. They wouldn't be expecting him to come in on, on the opposite side from where the road led in. The sounds of children playing, laughing, were the first signs that someone still remained. As the trees thinned, he could see an extensive garden located in the sunny, central patch next to what had been the trailer park office. Many of the trailers were missing, but the ones that remained were a mix of obviously occupied as well as others with gaping holes where the windows had been. A hundred yards from the garden was a rough corral that held a handful of goats. Chickens strutted about, loose, pecking at the grass and winding their way through the cold frames on the ground.

A burst of laughter and several children came into view. Jacob blinked, barely able to believe his eyes. A tow-headed boy was being chased by two smaller children, a boy and a girl, all of them screaming and laughing as they tore around the garden, chickens scattering in their path. Jacob stepped out from the last cover of trees and the boy looked up, stopping in his tracks so suddenly that the other two slammed into him, collapsing on the ground in surprise.

The little boy looked up at him and grinned and hurled himself into Jacob's arms.

"Daddy!"

Jacob hugged his son to his chest and sucked in a breath, "Hey JJ."

After all these months of not knowing. Hoping against hope. He had found him. He opened his eyes and saw Nancy running towards them.

"Jacob? Oh my God, JACOB!" The

strength of her embrace took his breath away and his fears dissolved as her lips found his.

His son was alive.

Nancy, his first kiss, his first love, was here, in his arms.

And after far too long away. After miles of endless road and plenty of hungry days, Jacob knew one thing.

He was finally, and incontrovertibly, *home*.

Run While You Can

"When you can't save others, at least try to save yourself."

Arriving at Clinton had been a letdown. Serena had seen it in Brad's face. When it came to the town, there wasn't much to be done. Brad had stopped dead at a burned hulk of timbers and said nothing. His face held a mixture of fury and anguish, his lips worked silently, and his fingers whitened as they gripped the pack on his back. After several moments of silence, he had turned away. Which really said everything. His family was gone. So was his home.

Max and Annie hadn't said a thing,

not even a whine of complaint. They followed as he turned on his heel and marched them towards the east, to the outskirts of town. There they had found the same scene; the only difference was the wide space between the farmhouses. The corpses of horses, and of other animals of an uncertain breed lay rotting on the ground, spread out randomly across the wide drive. The farmhouse they stopped at was in ruins, nothing but the blackened bricks of a chimney stood among the collapsed, burned timbers. Nearby, a barn was in the same shape, but several smaller buildings appeared relatively intact and they ended up bedding down for the night.

It wasn't their final destination. A half-collapsed building in the forest marked the end of their journey the following day. A tree had fallen against the house years ago. Its branches poking through what were now open holes along the back edge. The house hadn't been occupied in years, and the remains of the front of the property were desecrated with graffiti and empty bottles of beer and whiskey. And it seemed that someone had collected the cigarette butts, arranging them in what were now moldering pyramids, black with mold.

"It's remote," Brad had said, "off the beaten path." He shrugged at Serena in what might have been an apologetic way, but he'd been so quiet since seeing the remains of his family's home that she wasn't sure he was even capable of that. His expression had settled into a blank darkness, and he pulled away from her that night, instead staying up to provide watch, despite the proclaimed safety of the location.

The first night, they slept in the filth and mess. By the next morning, however, Serena was determined to make a go of it. She didn't have long, after all. The baby would be here soon. Any day, by her estimate. So as the dull rays of the sun peeked intermittently through the low cloud cover and the chill of the morning hung around them, she roused Max and Annie and set them to work. Some of the bottles could be rinsed in the nearby creek and made use of. Others could serve as the base for an outdoor cooking pit once the clay soil warmed enough to be dug up and shaped into an oven. By the third day there, they had settled into a routine of sorts. There were plenty of destroyed buildings to pick through. There were only so many clothes or blankets people could take when running for their lives, and from the looks of it, the troops that had blown through the small town had killed anyone foolish enough to stay. Serena thought about what Jess had said as they parted ways. "Don't go to Clinton. There's nothing left there but bones and ash."

Jess had been right. There was no one left in Clinton. If there was, they hid themselves well. Most of the homes in their area hadn't even had a good pick-through. Serena had certainly seen her share of empty homes in the past few months as she and Brad had slowly made their way, mostly on foot, from the time they had escaped the Western Front in Mississippi. By now she could tell when one had been picked over versus one that had not. Most of the places they scavenged were untouched, and Serena couldn't help but feel afraid. Untouched did not mean safe, not at all, and she listened carefully for sounds of footsteps, anything really, that would betray the presence of others. No matter how quiet it was, she couldn't shake the feeling that they were being watched. The night that they had spent with Jess and the kids was the last snow of the season. It had melted away within days and the air had warmed quickly. The warmer temps and the discovery of a cache of seeds in a dented old box near the ruins of another farm had curtailed any additional scavenging and instead become a race to get the ground ready for the spinach, kale, and lettuce seeds. The storm clouds gathering in the west promised them a wet reward and Brad had pointed out that any seeds they could get in the ground now meant not starving in a few months when their supplies ran out.

It was there, in the middle of the fourth row, that Serena had stared down at her legs, confused at the sudden rush of warmth and wetness. She stared at her legs, rooted to the spot, and felt panic wash over her.

Why didn't I insist we go with Jess? There was a hospital there, Research Belton. I can't give birth here!

Brad, consumed with the work, had moved ahead of her down the row

with his shovel, Annie followed behind
with a hoe, breaking the dirt up
further. Serena felt Max tug at her
hand. "Sweena? I plant more?" His
hands were covered in dirt. He had
followed behind as she carefully
dropped seeds at intervals and gently
pushed the dirt over them. Brad
turned back then, took in the wet
pants and dropped his shovel,
pushing past Annie to close the
distance between them.

"Is it the baby? Is it time? It isn't
those hick contractions again, is it?"

"Braxton Hicks, and no." The
contractions were coming, fast, hard.
She stood there, lip trembling, tears
running down her face, "It's different
this time, way different." Her stomach
twisted, and she felt the baby slide
down even further, pressing hard

against her pelvic bone.

Brad was at her side then, holding her steady. "Okay, it's gonna be okay, babe. We planned for this, remember?"

In a moment of wild optimism three days ago, she had told him that women had been giving birth for thousands of years, and all they needed was some hot water, towels, and something to cut the umbilical cord.

Prepared? Oh God, I want a hospital. I want doctors. I want a fucking epidural! Why did I let him talk me into coming to Clinton?

Slowly, they moved back to the house, and she gritted her teeth as the next contraction knifed its way through her.

That evening, the storm was fully

engaged over the pitiful remains of a ghost town once known as Clinton. Lightning flashed and rain dripped through the roof of a dilapidated house, forming a puddle.

Serena screamed at the top of her lungs for anything that could stop the pain. Another push and scream and the head and shoulders appeared. Brad let go of her hand and reached down to cradle the tiny head, holding the baby as it slid out and coughed. A sharp, thin wail issued from its mouth.

He looked past the umbilical cord. "It's a girl. Baby, we got ourselves a little girl!" He smiled, yet Serena could see he was disappointed. He'd talked endlessly about having a son and the evening before he had brought home a stack of baby clothes, all in blue. Serena fell back against the blankets, exhausted and exhilarated at the same time. She'd done it all without a hospital or doctors or even an epidural. She wished her mom was here. Mom hadn't thought much of her, always chiding her for being a delicate flower - she would have been in awe of her girl managing such a feat.

Brad gently wiped the baby down, cut the cord, and then wrapped the tiny infant in a clean blanket, and handed her to Serena, who looked both excited and exhausted. The lightning lit up the room, and the baby squawked in fear at the loud thunderclap. Serena took in the baby's features, her shock of jet-black hair, and met Brad's steady gaze. He knew the baby wasn't his, didn't he? For just a moment, the same look

Brad had on his face when he saw the remains of his family home resurfaced as he stared at the tiny infant swaddled in a soft blanket. But he said nothing, shook his head quietly. Was it sadness? Anger? Hurt? She wasn't sure. She felt a lump of fear and guilt form in her throat. She hadn't ever come out and said the baby was his, but as the months had passed and they had become a family of sorts, he'd just sort of stepped up. He'd been excited, especially after they found Max huddled alone and starving as they made their way out of Mississippi.

"I always wanted kids," he had said, his gaze landing on Annie and Max as they walked down the road hand-in-hand behind them. "I guess I never imagined it quite like this, though."

She had relaxed a little, hoped for something good to come out of it, and started thinking of Brad as the baby's father. Now she had to wonder, had she been wrong? Would he reject the baby, hell, maybe reject her as well?

He smiled then, reached out, and stroked the baby's cheek. "She's beautiful. What should we name our baby?

Relief washed over her. "My mother's name was Rebecca. We'll call her Becka for short."

"Becka it is."

It stormed for two days and the wet and the cold returned. Not as bad as it had been in winter, but certainly far from comfortable. They huddled inside and Brad and Annie handled the meals while Serena breastfed

Becka in a pile of bedding and pillows scavenged from the wreckage of a partially burned home nearby. The smell of smoke riddled most of bedding, sometimes overwhelmingly so, but Serena soon learned to ignore it.

When the storms passed, the warmth of spring returned in earnest. The seeds sprouted and were soon joined by new rows of carrots, parsnips and potatoes. Serena nursed Becka, and Brad took care to see that she ate plenty of food. Occasionally, when he didn't realize she was watching him, she could see his true feelings on the subject. Especially when the standard blue of her newborn eyes began to pale and become the all too familiar ice-blue. They were quick flashes of anger, possibly resentment, but Serena could see that he was trying hard to push the negative away and focus on the good.

"Which do you think trumps the other, nature or nurture?" He asked once, in an offhand way.

The kids were outside playing in the warm summer evening, the sun low in the sky. Annie still wasn't talking, but occasionally Max would do something exceptionally cute, in a way only a three-year-old can do, and Annie would giggle softly. At the moment, he was covered in dirt and so was she, as they dug into the soft earth underneath a nearby tree. It was the day that Becka's eyes had changed, lightened to the ice-blue she remembered so well.

She said nothing for a moment.

Becka was already fast asleep. She was a good baby, and by the end of two months was sleeping well through the night. Serena thought of the monster who had raped her and wondered, just for a moment, if he was still alive. She hoped not. Men like that, rapists, murderers, they didn't deserve to live. But how Becka had been made, how Jess's son Jacob had been made, that was nature. What happened next was completely within their power.

"Nurture," she answered, looking up at him. "It's the one thing we can control."

In the gloom, Brad's face was difficult to read, but she saw him nod slowly. "Yeah, that's what I think too."

Serena saw an opportunity then and took it. "I knew this boy in middle school. He was quiet, shy even, but really sweet when you got to know him. We studied together after school. Totally platonic, just great friends. He had to move, though. Out of the area, East coast. His mom wanted to return to the family there. We kept in contact for years. He finally told me about his dad after the man died in our junior year. He had been a long-haul truck driver. That is until they sent him away for multiple rapes and murders when Joe was twelve. Joe was the gentlest person I ever knew. Once, we were walking home from school and we saw a little squirrel get hit by a car. Killed instantly. He insisted we bury it." She paused, "If a kid can have a dad like that and turn out okay, then I have to believe its nurture."

It was a small lie, the story. She hadn't known Joe, not personally. Sure, she'd waved hello to him in the hallways and shared several classes, but he was on the outer edge of her friend's circle. Instead, her best friend Shelly had known him, even kissed him once behind the bleachers on a dare. The rest of it had been true, so really was it a bad thing to lie about?

Nonetheless, it had the desired effect. After that quiet summer evening, she hadn't caught him looking at Becka with anger or resentment. Which was a relief, to be sure.

By the end of summer, they had managed to accrue six hens, three of whom managed to survive a rash of raccoon attacks that stopped abruptly when Brad brought back a large roll of chicken wire and reinforced the tiny doghouse turned chicken coop.

Brad spent most of the daylight hours ripping the damaged back wall off of the house, patching sections of the roof, and framing in a new section. It wasn't pretty. He wouldn't be winning any architectural awards, but it would keep out the elements. And that was important, come winter. They didn't have much in the way of meat, which was a problem. However, the garden had produced more vegetables than they had expected, thanks to the warm temps and regular rain showers. It was a delicate balance. Too much rain and plants suffered, not enough rain, and their growth was stunted, but the growing season had been kind. Even better, Brad and Annie had discovered hundreds of empty dust-covered canning jars in a church basement a mile to the west.

Whatever they could can, and probably even some of the things they shouldn't, had been quickly put up in the old jars with their zinc covers. Serena hoped desperately that they weren't setting themselves up for a nasty case of botulism, but Brad was insistent.

"Hell, my mom canned everything, even potatoes, chicken, you name it, if it could fit in a jar, she canned it and we ate it."

Serena had her doubts, but Brad was so self-assured, so certain, that eventually she just went with it.

They hit gold in early October after a particularly violent storm toppled a length of fencing. One adolescent bull wandered away from a small herd that had evaded all of Brad's efforts to catch them now that he was out of bullets. His mistake was fatal. He crossed a section of the downed fence and ended up tangled in the barbed wire. Wet, wounded, and wrapped up like a present, he roared his distress, which woke them in the pre-dawn hours.

Serena watched as Brad killed the young bull quickly and efficiently. He definitely knew what he was doing in this department, and he grinned like a schoolboy as he began the butchering process.

"Steaks for dinner, Babe!"

She was thankful for the abruptly cool temperatures. The flies were few and far between and the mosquitoes had already died off, were hibernating, or whatever mosquitoes do when the temps drop into the 30s and 40s. Serena didn't know or much care, as long as they weren't buzzing her ears at night and raising welts on the kids' arms.

Most of the meat had to be smoked in order to preserve it for more than a few days or weeks, and Brad set into doing that. There was already a smoking shed on the property, luckily. Brad had pointed it out when they first arrived. Meat had been in such short supply that he hadn't gotten a chance to smoke any of the fish he caught. There was no need to smoke what they desperately needed in their bellies at the moment. But the bull was a different matter. It wasn't possible to eat the meat before it went bad, even in the colder temps.

"I know where I can find some mesquite wood, up there at the Ace Hardware," he said as he hacked away at the meat, his knife cutting off strips of steak. They had been eating beef for the better part of a week and the newness had worn off, Serena was happy to add it to a soup filled with spinach and root vegetables, but she was well and over the thick steaks they had eaten day in and day out. "I saw it near them chimney things when I was over there scavenging."

"Chiminea," she corrected, laughing. Becka cooed from her spot on the blankets at the far end of the room and gummed at a piece of dried meat in her hand. She had cut two teeth in the past week and been an angry, fussy mess until Brad had handed her the meat. She had chewed on it constantly, the two lower incisors working their way through the gums, a mess of drool and meat juice on her chin.

"What?"

"It's not a chimney, it's a Chiminea."

"Whatever. Anyway, that's where I saw it." He flapped a hand at her, "I'm just wondering if going there is such a good idea."

"Why?" Serena asked, frowning.

"Well, I know there's got to be others around here. Seen evidence of 'em. Stuff moved. Just wish I had bullets for that rifle I brought home last week." He had found it lying underneath a body, not far from where it appeared, at least from the bodies and spent ammunition, as if the Western Front had engaged a different faction, likely the Allied

South.

Serena's hands felt clammy and she could feel her heartbeat increase. "Others? As in... soldiers?"

Brad slid his hand around her and pulled her close. "It's just folks who live around here, Babe, nothing to worry about. I'm just being cautious is all."

Serena still had nightmares. At first, they were so bad that she had punched and kicked Brad a couple of times, her sleep-addled brain convinced she was back in the camp, back in Tent Five. After months on the road, and the birth of Becka, they had slowed down. Instead of having them nearly every night, it had dwindled down to once a week, then once a month, but it made no difference. Unless the others that

Brad had seen evidence of were a woman or a child, they weren't safe, she was sure of it.

When Brad announced he was heading to scavenge later that day, after washing the blood and gore from his hands, she had asked if he was going by Ace. She hadn't even realized she was biting her lip until the taste of copper flooded her mouth.

"Don't worry, Babe, I'm not gonna go anywhere near there," he had told her, his eyes avoiding hers, "I'll be back in an hour, two at tops." He'd kissed her forehead, turned and walked away, heading into the forest to the northeast. He had devised several routes this way, varying his paths, in order to avoid creating a visible path back to their small family.

Serena watched him disappear into a thick copse of trees, his brown hair and camo jacket quickly disappearing into the last of the greenery. Soon, the leaves would be gone from the trees and they would have to face a cold winter.

Serena found herself wondering yet again if she had made the right choice. Jess had seemed so certain that her home, a large town of over 20,000 people, would still be there. Clinton hadn't even had half of that number, and from the looks of it, those who hadn't fled had died either in the fighting or when the Western Front had done its best to torch the town. Those that were left seemed to have no interest in showing their faces. Between being pregnant and then caring for a newborn, she didn't have an opportunity to get out, but Brad had. He provided her regular updates that were curated, no doubt, to avoid alarming her. Two months ago, he had come back scraped up, a black eye, and blood on his ripped shirt. She knew he had been lying when he said that he had fallen, but she hadn't said anything. He'd stayed close to home for weeks after that.

By the time the sun slipped behind the trees and darkness set in, Serena knew something terrible had happened. Either he had run into someone armed and dangerous, or he was afraid to return and bring whoever was around back to their small family. She stamped out the fire in the smoke shed and buried the haunches of meat after wrapping it in a sheet. She would have preferred to sink it in the creek, but that was too far of a hike to risk, even in the dark. Becka had already fallen asleep, as had Max, but Annie was wide awake and Serena could see the girl watching her every move, eyes wide, lip trembling. She still didn't speak, not a word, but Serena could tell the girl definitely had something to say.

That Brad hadn't returned was a bad sign. They were exposed, unsafe, here. Serena cast about in her mind for any potential solutions, her thoughts interrupted by terrifying questions.

Was he dead?

Did whoever had killed him know where she and the kids were?

Were they coming for them?

Sleep was elusive and fragmented that night. And the next. And the one after that.

"Where is Brad dad?" Max asked. The little boy was relentless, asking over and over until Annie would reach over and put a finger against his lips and shake her head in warning. He wouldn't listen. Becka, only six months old, had been fretful and fussy. It wasn't a new tooth, Serena had checked. No, it was Brad's absence, and the rising fear in all of them. Becka could sense it the same as the rest of them.

Brad would have returned if he could and by now Serena was sure he was dead. Nothing else explained it, nothing else made sense.

Despite the chill in the air, Serena's hands were clammy with sweat. As the sun set each night, she found herself shaking uncontrollably, her leg muscles tight, ready to run. Day in and day out, the fear did not abate, and she was a shaky, sleep-deprived mess by the time a week had slipped by.

Annie tugged at Serena's sleeve. Becka had been fussing and unwilling to take a nap, but the baby had finally collapsed in her mother's arms, drunk on milk and stripped of the energy that had caused her to fuss for nearly two hours straight. Serena glanced down at Annie and raised her eyebrows in the gloom.

"What?" she whispered, then winced as Becka moved restlessly against her chest.

Annie pointed towards the back of the house and tugged again, clearly indicating she wanted Serena to go with her. Serena nodded, turned back to the baby long enough to settle her gently in the bed and pull another blanket over her before she followed the girl into the gloomy interior.

Without any intact replacement glass available, Brad had simply boarded over the broken windows. This made the back half of the house dark and somewhat treacherous to walk through, thanks to some rotting flooring. The kids slept upstairs and seemed to manage just fine while Serena, Brad and the baby had occupied the front room near the front door. It meant less privacy, but it was warmer near the fireplace. Max had been complaining about the cold and Serena had known it was just a matter of time before they would all be crammed into the same room. Winter was here, and with it the bitter cold.

Along the back wall of the house next to the stairs going up, Brad had patched the wall where a large hole had been knocked out by the tree. His repair job hadn't been pretty, but it had done the trick. Water wasn't getting in, despite some strong storms during the spring and late summer. Annie walked over to one part of the back wall and knelt down, pulling and shoving at a small piece of wood that had been tacked in place. With some effort, she wrenched it up and to the left and then pointed out the newly made hole.

"A way out?" Serena asked, "In case people come for us?"

Annie nodded.

"That's good thinking, Annie. Thank you."

She fought to keep the tremor out of her voice as her stomach dipped, thinking again of Brad, wondering what had happened to him.

He's dead. And really, what else do you need to know other than that?

She winced at the thought of it, leaned over, and hugged the girl gently. "We'll be okay, Annie, don't you worry." She sat there for a moment, wishing she could do something to help the girl feel safe.

"I think maybe it's time we headed for Belton. Maybe we can find Jess and her family. What do you think?"

Annie's head nodded and the girl, normally so reticent, reached her hands around Serena and hugged her back with a strong grip. It took Serena by surprise.

"Okay. Make sure and get a bag

together, keep it by this back wall and we will just see if we can't plot a course for Belton before it's too cold."

Hell, it's already too cold. But what else can I do? Chance staying here all winter without him?

Serena reviewed her options.

I can try staying here and likely starve halfway through the winter. I could try to find whoever is still out there and do whatever it takes to stay alive. Or I can take the kids and head for Belton, maybe even Kansas City.

She knew the chances of them all surviving the winter were slim to none, with the first two options. With a tiny baby and a preschooler, the entire burden of survival would rest on her and Annie's shoulders, and Annie was barely more than a child herself. The chances that whoever was out there would take her and the kids hit her anxiety triggers like nobody's business.

Whoever was out there likely killed Brad. The only way they would want to use me or Annie would be nothing better than a return to Tent Five. And Annie already tried to kill herself once before I got her out of there. As for Max and my baby, who knows what they would do? All I know is that I can't risk it.

Serena tried to remember how far away Belton was. Some fifty, no, close to sixty miles away. Her brain nearly stuttered to a stop as she tried to imagine how they would get there, the four of them, all alone, on foot. How fast could a child walk in a day, anyway?

A brisk walking pace is three miles

an hour, so figure half of that through mud, off-road. And maybe six hours a day of walking per day, tops, between Becka and Max. That was, what, a week of walking every day? They would need to carry food too, and how will I take care of Becka's diapers?

Brad hadn't had any luck finding diapers, so they had made do with strips of cloth and safety pins. There were only so many cloths, though, she'd run out just a few days in and have no way to clean and dry more. The image of a baby crying loudly as they made their way through unknown territory was enough to send her shaking uncontrollably.

Shit, shit, shit. No matter what she did, no matter how she chose, she couldn't see this ending well. And as the night closed in around them, Becka hugged to her chest, with Max and Annie now spooned against each side of her. Serena was more afraid than she had been in a long time.

Serena silently cursed Brad for carving up the tent to use for several projects, including a cover for the front door, which had been hanging on by one hinge and hadn't even been good for anything more than kindling. Without the tent, they were going to be cold, damn cold, as well as exposed at night as they walked all that way. Not to mention the fact that she would have to be carrying Becka and likely Annie would have to help Max. In the end, just two days later, there ended up being no choice at all.

They came late in the day, the sun had long vanished behind thick, heavy gray clouds and the temperature had plummeted. They had just finished eating dinner, a large jar of green beans and onions, along with a side of the beef she had kept in the house. It had begun to turn, but not enough that she was willing to waste it. Becka had slipped off into dreamland and Max as well, curled around the baby, a thumb in his mouth. It was Annie who heard it first. An errant step onto the now frozen ground, and a branch snapped. Her eyes rounded, her head snapping to Annie, who had been carefully adding another blanket to the heap. She froze in the gloom, stiff, alert, and stared back at Serena.

Serena said nothing, just pointed to the back of the house and reached for Becka. There was no time to do anything more than slip her sleeping daughter into a backpack, zip it up as far as the surrounding blankets would allow, and try to move without sound to the back of the house where the escape hatch was. Annie passed her, a very sleepy Max in Annie's grasp. They could hear voices now, several, and despite the cold, Serena felt a rivulet of sweat trickle down her back as she waited for Annie and then Max to slip through the hole before handing out Becka in the backpack. The sounds they made were small, but in the night, they sounded so loud. Luckily, whoever was out there had been drawn to the remains of the bull, which they had slowly continued to strip off all meat over the past few days since Brad had disappeared.

"You were right, Buddy, damned if that young bull didn't end up getting snatched," an older voice commented. He sounded grizzled, old.

"I knew that guy wasn't alone, either." A younger voice said from inside of the house, "There are more. Got the remains of a vegetable garden over near the smoke shed. Blankets are still warm and I smell food."

Serena prayed to whatever gods were still there that Becka would stay asleep. She eased the straps over her shoulders, keeping the pack against her front, and tugged at Annie's arm, pointing in the direction of the trees. They needed cover, and to be out of sight, but there was at least one hundred yards to run across open field, something they needed to do as quietly and as quickly as possible, before the men thought to look behind the house. Max, despite his age, seemed to understand enough to keep quiet. He took Annie's hand, and they all began to run.

"We got movement!" The old man shouted, "Buddy, get over here! There's movement in the back field!"

Time didn't stop, so much as blur. Serena heard rifle shots and increased her speed, legs flying across the stubbled, uneven ground. Max and Annie fell slightly behind and Serena didn't falter, couldn't bring herself to slow down in the slightest. In truth, she felt nothing but horror and panic - the rest of the world washed away in white noise. Her only focus was the dark shelter of the trees. They were close, so close, and the fire in her lungs barely registered as she willed her feet to go faster. Becka was making small squawks of distress as the backpack strapped against Serena's chest heaved and thumped with every footfall.

She felt, rather than heard, the gunshots. One came close as she entered the woods, hitting the tree next to her head. The bark exploded into shrapnel and she dove to the right, into a thicker part of the woods, as an agonizing streak of what felt like an electric shock tore down her left shoulder and arm. Serena didn't allow herself to think of it, or to stop. She just kept running. The men back at the farmhouse continued to shoot. The bullets, such small and seemingly inconsequential things, parted the surrounding air.

Behind her, she heard the children doing their best, but losing ground, falling behind more with each moment that passed. Then there was a strangled scream, a thud of a body hitting the ground, and then nothing more but her own feet grinding through the forest, a stampede through the fallen leaves, rustling, sliding.

Her arm hurt. A deep ache that finally turned to a throbbing stab of agony. She slowed, the darkness fully encapsulating her now, her breaths hoarse, ragged. She couldn't continue like this.

Serena slammed into a tree with her right shoulder and wheeled about, unable to go on. She had run so far, and for so long, that she could no longer see Annie or Max or anything but the thickness of the trees all around her, even in their leafless state. The sky above was dark, as was the forest that surrounded her. She couldn't even hear the men now.

I didn't even try to save them. Oh God, I just let them fall behind and be shot!

Serena felt the guilt surge through her. As she regained her breath, Becka stirred, the sudden lack of movement waking her where the panicked run had not. She whimpered, twisting in the tightness of the backpack and blanket, her tiny feet kicking. Becka quieted quickly when Serena pushed up her shirt and pressed her breast into the baby's mouth.

"Shh," she whispered, and Becka's body relaxed against her, slowly nursing before falling back into a deep sleep. While she sat there, her body pressed against the hard, cold ground, Serena listened, trying to ignore the heartbeat that still roared in her ears. Had they stopped? Or were they still following her? It was dark now. So dark that Serena could barely see beyond the small clearing she was in. Worse, it was beginning to snow.

If I can get to the highway, walk it at night, I could make better time. And now that it is just me, I can walk faster, maybe twice as fast.

She felt another surge of guilt at that last thought.

As she slipped Becka off of her breast and struggled to place her back inside the backpack, her left arm burned in agony. She realized then that the wetness on the blankets was blood and her right hand crept up to feel the wound on her arm. It burned like fire when she touched it, and she hissed at the pain of it.

Is the bullet still there?

She couldn't tell, but the blood was still coming. She dug into the pack and found one of Becka's spare diaper strips and wrapped it around her arm. That would do until daylight, when she could see it better. Now she just had to figure out where the highway was and get moving. It wouldn't do to stay here; the blood trail would make it all too easy to find her come tomorrow morning. There was no point in going back. She knew she couldn't help the kids, even if they had survived. She suddenly remembered a story she had read in high school, from a former soldier in Vietnam who had been the lone survivor of his regiment.

"When you can't save others, at least try to save yourself." At the time, reading those words, she had been horrified. But now she understood it better. There was no way she could have saved them. Hell, she would be lucky if she could save Becka and herself. Still, the tears tracked down her cheeks, freezing in the cold of the night. She began to walk, her feet slipping on the leaf-covered forest floor, heading west toward the highway. Becka's warmth was heavy and still against her chest. She was thankful that the baby had not been woken, and that she would likely sleep most of the night through while Serena walked. And walk she would until she could move no further. Her life, and Becka's, depended on it.

Serena put one foot in front of the other. The mile markers would have told her how far she had come, and how close she was, but she was no longer in any shape to read them. She struggled to keep her focus on putting one foot in front of the other.

Her left arm was swollen, hot to the touch, and her feet felt like two lead weights soldered crudely on. She had walked and walked, stopping only to rest, if she could, for a few hours at a time. The snow had continued to fall. This was unusual for the area. Typically, the storms blew through, dumping a couple of inches before moving on, never lasting for more than a day. This snow, however, had turned to sleet and then back to a powdery fine snow that felt hard and painful. The infection in her arm had begun almost immediately, and it had turned Serena's thoughts to mush, especially once the dull headache had set in.

She walked, chewed on a piece of bark from a willow tree, remembering that it could help with pain, and winced at the terrible bitter taste before spitting it out. Pieces of the bark stuck to her tongue.

Her mouth was dry, her lips cracked, and after three days of walking, she had moved beyond hunger and into something else. Becka cried against her chest, but Serena couldn't help. It had started with a clogged milk duct on the left and then the fever and infection had set in and all Becka did was cry when she tried to nurse.

Serena ignored her child. It did no

good to stop. Every time she did, it was the same. Her breasts were on fire as well now and there was no sustenance, no respite for the hunger her baby felt. Becka would suck at the breast, flail and beat at Serena's chest with her tiny fists, and then wail in frustration. She hadn't eaten in over a day. The only thing Serena could do was somehow make it to Belton, and hopefully find Jess or anyone who might help.

Jess will help, I know she will.

She remembered what Jess had said to her, in those quiet moments when the children were playing and Brad was off gathering wood for the fire. Serena had been overcome with fear, afraid of how she would feel about Becka when she was born. She had leaned close to Jess, so the others couldn't hear and whispered, "I pray every day that this baby is Brad's. But I know it isn't. It's that bastard's, I know it is." She had looked up, gazed hard into Jess's eyes, "Do you think I'll be able to love it? Even if it is from *him*?"

Jess's reply had been simple and direct, "Yes."

Serena had liked the girl. Why had she listened to Brad? If she had put her foot down, insisted on taking the kids and going with Jess, she wouldn't be here right now. Max and Annie would still be alive. Her mind occupied with these thoughts; Serena barely noticed the sign by the side of the road. It had been cut down and covered up, only the metal supports jutted out of the ground. As she concentrated on her putting one foot in front of the other, her eyes were caught by the sharp stubs barely peeking out of the snow. She stopped, tottering in place for a moment before she left the road and she pushed the branches away from it.

Five miles. Just five more miles to go.

Night was coming. And with it, darkness that was impossible to navigate through. Her foot slipped, then the other, and Serena fell. It wasn't the first time. Her knees ached from the impacts of multiple falls. She got up, slow, and continued to walk down the empty road.

One mile.

Another mile.

When Serena lost her way in the dark, she slipped hard on the slick macadam, tumbled down the small embankment, and landed, unconscious in the ditch. She heard nothing. Not the wails of her child, who had somehow been shielded from harm by Serena's body as she rolled down the hill, and certainly not by the two young men who realized with shock that she was still alive. It wasn't until they moved her, jolting her injured arm, that she woke with a scream of pain on her lips.

"It's all right, we got you. We're gonna get you to a doctor, ma'am, just hang in there." The one who said it was young, maybe late teens. He and the other man each had rifles slung over their shoulders. They exchanged glances, one crouching beside her, the other letting out a low whistle as they pried away the blood-encrusted bandage.

"She's in bad shape, Jake. We best get her back to town and have Ridley take a look at her."

Serena struggled to speak. It impossible. The world was bright and white, but she felt so heavy, so tired. "What... town?"

"Belton," was the younger one's quick response. "Where you from?"

"Clin... ton. Tell her."

"Tell who?"

"Jess Aaron..." her words slurred and Becka, all cried out, gave a pitiful whine in the backpack still strapped to her chest.

"Jess Aaronson?" The one standing above her asked. "You know Jess?"

Serena managed a small nod before her eyes slid closed. She had done it. She'd managed to get Becka to Belton and these men would help her find Jess. Becka would be safe. She smiled then, a thread of gratitude and relief intertwined. As she felt herself lifted, Serena relaxed for the first time in more than a week. She was safe now.

Loved and Lost

"In war, there are no winners."

Wes held the receiver so tight that the plastic creaked in his iron grip. "What do you mean, you've got nothing?"

"I'm sorry, Mr. Perkins, sometimes these things take time." The private eye's voice crackled and faded; his cell phone connection as poor as ever. "I tracked them to Memphis, but then the trail went cold. She might be here, working for cash, staying under the radar, or she might have headed for a big city, like New York."

Wes gritted his teeth, his jaw tight and aching as if he had chewed on an entire half pound bag of House of Jerky in one go. His free hand

clenched as hard as the one holding
the receiver and he could feel his
short, stubby fingernails digging deep
into the flesh of his palm.

"It's up to you," the private eye said
as if he didn't have a care in the
world, "but I'll need another two
thousand if you want me to keep
working the case."

How he wanted to reach through the
phone line and rip the smug little
bastard's throat out. He had damn
near zeroed out his savings as it was.
And now with his boss cutting his
hours down to thirty hours a week
"until the financial crisis blew over" he
had even less coming in. Where the
hell could he going to find another
two thousand dollars?

"Keep looking," he ground it out, his
knuckles showing white on his left

hand. He opened his fist and counted the four crescent moon shapes his fingernails had left in his skin.

The line crackled and the private eye sighed. "Mr. Perkins, I'll need that deposit by tomorrow evening."

"Stay in Memphis. Find them. You'll get your goddamn money." He slammed the receiver down and punched the wall. The drywall, which was already sporting a sizable dent from the last time he had hit it, crumbled, leaving a gaping hole. A splinter of wood from the edge of the stud dug a gouge into his hand. "Fucking shit!"

He stumbled away from the phone, his mind spinning on how he was going to generate two thousand dollars by the end of the day tomorrow. He tripped over a Power

Puff doll and slammed his hip into Laura's beloved rolltop desk. It rocked back and forth and a figurine of a dolphin that Cody had given her last year for Mother's Day fell and smashed on the floor, breaking into several pieces.

Wes limped into the small, dark hallway cursing, and fumbled for the light switch. Nothing happened when he flipped the switch on, which wasn't surprising. The rolling blackouts had become more frequent in recent weeks, and it seemed like the power was off more than it was on these days. The sharp edge of the medicine cabinet raked his hand, and he fumbled in the dark for a box of band-aids only to find the damned box was empty.

"Fucking kids," he muttered and

tossed the box, now smeared with blood, toward one of the children's rooms. Sarah had probably used the last of them on her baby dolls or herself. The smallest of wounds, imaginary or real, were instantly solved by his daughter raiding the medicine cabinet for a band-aid.

He wiped his bloody hand on his pants and walked back into the living room, grabbed a bottle of whiskey from the corner table where he had put a serious dent in it the evening before, and settled into his easy chair to drink some more. The fridge was empty, and he had finished off the last of the canned soup and crackers on Sunday.

Fuck it, whiskey for dinner sounds just fine to me.

He didn't bother with a glass, just

tossed the cap in the general direction of the overflowing trash can and tipped the bottle up to his lips, feeling the liquid burn as it slid down his throat.

In some ways, having Laura and the kids gone was pretty damn nice. No nervous looks from Laura or the kids, no scuttling about like they had something to hide or were somehow scared of him sitting there. No complaints about how there wasn't enough money to buy food because he'd gone and bought an economy size of the Jim Beam, or her pursing her lips in disapproval like his mom used to do to his dad.

It has to be a thing they all learn at their mother's knee, that tight-lipped look that gave the appearance of a stick being shoved firmly up their asses while simultaneously saying without words what a disappointment a man is to them. All the women I've ever known had that look mastered. Like it's a fucking art or something.

He took another hard swallow. The alcohol burned less this time and he could feel the slow heat spreading from his stomach to his limbs, loosening the angry set of his shoulders.

Four weeks now and not a goddamn word. No phone call, the bank account hadn't been touched, and that damned useless private eye had lost them in Memphis. They had stayed in a rundown roach motel for two days, cash only transaction. Wes knew that much. But the private eye had fucked it all up, spooked Laura before he could get off his shift at the plant and head for the address. He was left holding his balls, the television in the corner still warm and set to Channel 39, the Disney Channel.

He'd only hit Laura that one time. Hell, he'd apologized, brought her flowers, everything. But it hadn't mattered. He'd seen the wary look in her eyes and she'd tiptoed around for two days before taking the kids and disappearing, poof, with no one willing to look him in the eye up at the police station or help him fill out a missing person's report.

"Ain't a missing person if they leave of their own volition," the deputy had said. "Go home, Perkins, maybe she'll come round. Things are really tough right now. She'll have a hard time finding work. Hell, she'll be back with the kids before you know it."

But she hadn't been back. And the house wasn't the same without the kids squabbling over who got to watch what, or Laura in the kitchen whipping up something amazing.

Did I tell that private dick to check the diners and cafes? She could've gotten a job as a cook easy as pie. She was that good.

He frowned, downed another jolt of liquid medication, and jumped to his feet at the loud backfire that sounded outside on the street. Standing there, Wes swayed a little, unsure of why he was standing there or why his heart was pounding so damned hard, his pulse jumping in his neck, the hairs on his arm pricking up.

Just old Dowsey's car backfiring. Nothing to worry about.

He sat back down. It had been like that ever since he came home from Afghanistan. A loud noise, a car crash or siren. Hell, he was a fucking mess when the 4th of July came around.

His hand ached, and the blood was drying, except around the wound, which continued to leak. He looked down at his dingy white shirt. It was covered with red smudges of blood. That would have set Cody off big-time. Laura had been worried he had autism or Asperger's or some kind of fucked up syndrome of some kind. When the kid saw blood, he freaked the fuck out.

That's what comes of having a woman raise your son while you're off killing sand niggers and defending America.

His lip curled in disdain at the

memory of Cody losing his shit in Wal-Mart when Sarah fell down and got a bloody nose. She was crying, but Cody, two years older and lacking the balls a boy his age should have, had started screaming bloody murder over the blood on his sister's dress. Wes had taken him into the men's bathroom and backhanded him, shocking the boy into silence.

And how Laura had given me The Look then. As if it was my fault the boy had no balls and screamed like a girl over blood.

Wes hit the bottle again, then again, until suddenly, the last drops were dribbling out on his tongue and everything felt warm and fuzzy. A nice big blur that intensified as he tried and failed, to stand up. He tried again, and the room tilted as he wobbled towards the dark hallway. The last light of the day was pouring in through the living room windows cloaking the room in red and he heard the hum of the electric start up, the fridge motor turning on, as if after hours of being off, and a checkered past two weeks of infrequent electrical spikes that there would be anything inside worth preserving any longer.

He wove his way into the bathroom, belching as he peed into the toilet. The light in the bathroom was dim, probably because all but one of the three lightbulbs had burned out. He turned and tried digging in the closet for a box of bulbs. He was sure it was in there somewhere. And just as quickly as the lights had come on, they flickered once, twice, and were down again.

Wes backed up, but not far enough. In the pitch black, and in his drunken state, he stood up too soon and cracked his head on the shelf above. He didn't see stars so much as streaks of hot white light burning across his retinas, his head exploding with pain.

"Fuck!" He fell back, the ground tilting and moving under him, and passed out on the floor of the bathroom, too drunk to try to find his way back to the living room or the empty bed.

Dawn came stealing in from the east, lighting up the hallway in a weak orange light. But the dawn wasn't what had woken him. The impatient honk of the truck outside had. Wes groaned and clutched his head as Maynard pounded on the front door and rang the doorbell.

"Perkins!" He could hear his friend's muffled yell, "We're gonna be late!"

Wes struggled to his feet, removing the Hot Wheels car that had slid up his pant leg and lodged painfully against his ankle. It clattered and slipped away, banging into the far wall. He winced. The back of his head had a lump where he had slammed it into the shelf, but that was the least of his ailments. His tongue felt thick and coated, swollen, yet also dry and parched, and his injured hand ached, the wound having finally stopped bleeding. The weak sunlight filtering in was enough for him to see his reflection and he instantly wished he hadn't. He looked like hell. He looked worse than that.

Eyes sunken, dark smudges under

them like he'd been in a fight, and his lips cracked. He stood there, shaky, a sour taste in his mouth, and his teeth were coated with gunk.

How long's it been since I brushed my teeth? Or took a damn shower?

Maynard pounded again and then thought to try the door. It was unlocked, of course. In a town the size of Tiptonville, everyone knew everyone. You needn't bother locking your doors.

Maynard turned the handle and walked in, saw Wes shuffling out of the bathroom and shook his head in disgust. "Christ, Perkins, you ever give that whiskey bottle a break? We're gonna be late to work and you look like the walking dead. What the hell? Did you forget we got the early shift the rest of this week?"

Wes flapped his hand and shuffled to the bedroom. "Gimme five minutes, I gotta change my clothes."

It took seven minutes, and Maynard revved the engine of his truck as Wes slid into the passenger seat. "I can't afford to be late man, you're gonna have to find someone else to take you if you do this again to me."

Wes mumbled under his breath and his friend looked at him, his lips set in a thin line before he squealed the tires and pulled out of the gravel drive with an impatient jerk. The plant was just to the north of town, and there was no traffic to speak of. The men were silent. Maynard fiddling with the dial on the radio the entire way, flipping incessantly from channel to channel. They made it with one minute to spare, sliding into one of the last parking spaces left in the small lot.

"Best avoid Boss Man, you reek of whiskey," Maynard said in a low voice as they approached the building.

His warning, however, was in vain. Boss Man, also known as Ethan Hurlbut, the owner of Hurlbut Manufacturing, was waiting at the door. Maynard nodded at the man, "Mornin' Boss," and sidled past. Wes wasn't as lucky.

"Perkins, if I could have a word." The older man's face was grim, and Wes felt his guts twist.

Maynard threw him a sidelong glance that spoke of pity mixed with unease and scuttled out of sight around the corner. Wes could hear the punch of the clock seconds later and the far door open, releasing the loud hum of machinery, before clicking shut behind his friend. He knew he would not be walking onto the floor today, and possibly any other day.

He licked his lips, which felt dry, stretched, as if the whiskey had sucked every ounce of water out of him. Hell, his skin felt so dry that his eyeballs ached in their sockets. He hadn't felt this bad coming off a drunk since Afghanistan and the IED that had blown up his patrol vehicle, sending him to the hospital with a concussion, lacerations, and a week's stay in the infirmary. And he had been the lucky one.

"Don't bother, I got a feeling about where this is heading," he rasped, glaring at Ethan Hurlbut.

Boss Man had spent time in the

Marines, been drafted into a stint in Vietnam, and then re-upped for one more tour. When he had come back, he had taken over Hurlbut Manufacturing from his dad after the old man suffered a massive heart attack and died in the dingy cafeteria directly under a hand painted sign that read, "Here at Hurlbut we don't haul ass, we hurl butt!"

And Ethan ran a tight ship. A lesser man, a man who hadn't served his country like Wes had, wouldn't have lasted a month coming to work hung over. But Boss Man had watched Wes, even given him an advance two weeks ago so he could hire the private dick, and even let him take off that one day to find Laura and the kids in Memphis.

"Wes, I've been where you're at,"

Hurlbut began.

"Save it for someone else, boss. I don't need an intervention."

"No, you need to stop killing yourself. Which is what you're doing. And I can't have you operating machinery when you're still sauced from the night before. No can do."

Wes waved a hand, weaving slightly as he walked away, heading for the road. "Right, got it." He didn't look back, but he could feel Boss Man's eyes on him.

The walk back to town took most of an hour. It gave him time to think about how fucked he was.

No wife or kids. No job. No fucking money.

He sobered up as he walked, the May sun warming his bones, the brightness of it painful at first. He stopped when he got to Main Street and instead of heading home, he walked into the Sinclair gas station and dug into his pockets for the wrinkled dollar bills he had dug out of Cody's piggy bank that morning before getting in the truck with Maynard.

Leslie Cobain and her husband Phil owned the gas station. They alternated shifts, and it was Leslie's turn to man the station. She looked up with a smile that faltered at the sight of Wes.

"Hey there, Wes, you look like you have been through the wringer." She clucked her tongue, "I heard about Laura and the kids. You had any luck on that yet?"

Wes knew it was all over town.

Hell, can't take a dump without the

entire fucking town hearing about it.

He shook his head, his mouth dry as a bone.

"Well, grab a cup of Joe and sit for a bit."

He didn't want to head back home to an empty house. He had no job to go to, and Wes couldn't remember the last time he'd just sat and talked to anyone. He grabbed a cup of coffee, added a couple of pieces of ice to cool it off enough to drink, and pulled up a stool next to the counter. He had dated Leslie for a few months in high school. It hadn't been serious, a casual friendship that got a little hot and heavy and then, once the anticipation was done and over, had dwindled back to casual again.

Phil wasn't the jealous type. A year ahead of Wes and Leslie, he had been friendly, and Wes and Laura had been invited to several get-togethers over the years. Hell, Phil had drunk him under the table a few years back now.

"So how are you, Wes?"

"Shit, you got eyes. I feel like hot shit bagged in a layer of lava." Leslie wasn't blind, and he knew he looked like hell.

She laughed and stood up, walked to a cooler and grabbed three large Smart Water bottles and two orange Gatorade, then set them down on the counter in front of him. "On the house. You'll feel better if you can flush some of that whiskey out of your system."

"Hell, whiskey's a food group, Les, didn't you know?"

Her eyes were kind, full of empathy, "Drinking it like its water isn't going to bring Laura and the kids back."

He cracked open one of the Gatorade bottles and downed half of it in one go. He could feel his body sucking it in, felt the cells expand, and his skin felt a little less tight.

"Well, now that I'm fired, I got nothing to buy any more with anyhow." His headache, although still a whopper, began to ease off. His stomach growled, loud and long, and Leslie looked amused as she tossed him a bag of jerky.

"You'll be in good company soon enough. Ethan doesn't have the funds to keep anyone on after the 18th, anyway. All this financial mess, the power issues, and more..." she shook her head, "It's gonna get worse before it gets better."

Wes took a piece of jerky and began

to gnaw on it. The taste of the teriyaki-flavored meat filled his mouth and soothed his angry stomach. "Whatcha heard?"

"Mostly it's been through Phil when he's up at the clinic getting his dialysis treatments. They are saying things are going to get a whole hell of a lot worse soon."

Wes shrugged, "Economy goes up, it comes down, it goes back up again. Big fucking cycle. What's to worry about?" Before Leslie could answer, the question struck him. "Hey wait, what's going on with Phil that he needs dialysis?"

Leslie's face twisted in pain, her lips quivered a little as she tried to smile, to put a brave face on her fears. "His kidneys are failing and his liver is starting to fail. What with all that's going on in the world, the list of donors has dropped off. Especially here in flyover country. The doc says it's likely they won't find a donor liver in time, so he's got maybe three, six months if we're lucky."

"Jesus, Les, I'm sorry." He reached out and took the woman's hand, his mind reeling at the thought of Phil, full of life, father of four, dying. Hell, they weren't even middle age. "This shit isn't supposed to happen in our 30s, damn it."

She shrugged helplessly, "It was the drinking. He drank like a fish for years. Nobody really saw it. He started in high school and just never really stopped. I don't know why I didn't say something, do something, especially after seeing my dad and mom kill themselves slowly. Instead, I was living with it, covering for him, *enabling* him instead of drawing a line in the sand. I covered for him here, at home, and it just got bad, really bad. And one day he went in for a checkup. He hadn't been feeling well, been vomiting blood, peeing blood, the works. And they told him he was going to die if he didn't change his ways."

"Overnight, he changed. He checked himself into English Mountain, that rehab center up in the Eastern hills, and he got himself clean and sober. It was amazing and wonderful. I got my husband back; the kids got their daddy back. And things were good, better than good, until late last year." There were tears in her eyes. "And now, well, now I get to watch him die, just when things were turning around."

Wes squeezed her hand, unsure what to say, when suddenly Leslie grabbed his hand and held onto it with a strength that took him by surprise. "You only get this one life, Wes. This one, here and now. You can waste it or you can make the best of it."

Before he could reply, there were voices, shouting, a flurry of activity from down the street near the Trade Mart.

"What the hell is happening now?" Leslie asked, her eyebrows furrowed as she stared out of the glass. A handful of men and women, more than the usual group that held court in front of the Trade Mart and smoked cigarettes and gossiped, were gathering.

One of the women shook her head and Wes and Leslie could both hear her shouting, "No, no, NO! The news reports are wrong. They have to be!"

Wes stared at Leslie, "We better go see what's going on."

Wes untied the body of the deer from the pole. He had gas in the truck, but instead of driving he had walked the ten miles, choosing to enjoy the stars and camp for a day or two before taking the buck, field dressing it, and returning to town.

He'd spent the past two months clean and sober, even though the DTs had hit him hard soon after the news of the limited nukes in Austin and D.C. had come out. That day, standing there in front of the Trade Mart, listening to the scant, and often contradictory, news coming over the radio, reality had struck him like a freight train.

Thanks to his PTSD and heavy drinking, he had lost Laura, Cody and Sarah. Most likely forever. There was no way of finding them, no clues as to their whereabouts. Thanks to The Collapse, the United States was in shambles, the government gone, and rumors of civil war were spreading. The country he had known, the one he had gone to a foreign land filled with sand and violence to defend, was no more.

There in the gravel driveway, he glanced up and saw Leslie sitting on his front stoop. She looked as if she had aged ten years in the last two months. But then again, losing your husband and your only way of making a living thanks to The Collapse will do that to you. No tankers to bring gas, as of a month ago, no gas to sell, and Leslie had finally just walked away from the gas station. The shelves were empty by then, nothing to sell, certainly nothing to steal, and she had sat by Phil's side until he drew his last breath.

Wes had been bringing her hunks of meat since May. He knew that others were helping in whatever way they could, as well.

"Hey there, Les. I got a nice-sized back haunch for you."

He eased the carcass down off of the sling. A combination of metal poles, wheels, and a heavy-duty tarp had made hauling the deer back to town relatively easy. As it was, he was feeling more fit than he had since his high school days. He spent most of his time hunting, alone in the woods outside of town, and the isolation had helped. Having meat helped. He traded it for other things, like produce from the Perdue's farm, or the heavy home-style bread that Sadie brought every Tuesday and Friday to the Trade Mart to barter for her family's other needs.

Leslie smiled, a small one that faded fast. She looked tired. No big surprise there. She had four little ones to look after and her husband hadn't been gone three weeks now.

"Hanging in there, Wes." She looked at the deer carcass. "No head?"

"Already dropped it off at the Perdue's on my way in. Old man says he's gonna make head cheese with it and the tongue."

Leslie nodded. "I wasn't coming by

for meat, although it's kind of you to offer, but I wanted you to come to the Fourth of July picnic folks are planning for tomorrow."

Wes snorted, "Fourth of July? Hell, there ain't no Fourth of July anymore."

"Don't be silly, of course there is." She waved a hand in the direction of Main Street. "Hell, I know how you feel. I'm not really up to a picnic myself, but it will be good for the kids. They haven't been out much since the funeral."

"Yeah, well, I ain't going."

"Wes, stop it. You cleaned yourself up, everyone can see that, and some of the menfolk they've been asking about your military experience. We could use a militia in case those rumors turn into something more.

You've got training, experience."

"Yeah," Wes snorted, "I got real good at getting shot at."

"Don't be a pain in the ass, Wes Perkins. Come to the picnic and bring some ribs. You need to be part of the community; this town could use your expertise." She stood then, and she moved slow, slower than she should at her age. "I'll expect to see you there."

The next day had dawned and with it, storm clouds on the horizon. Wes looked out the window and thought of what Leslie had said. She'd been right about his drinking, and she was probably right now. He hated the 4th of July. At least he had these past five years or so, back from Afghanistan where a damn car backfiring had him on his feet looking for an attack.

The rumors that were swirling of the supremacist militias and the malcontent'd remnants of soldiers left unpaid and leaderless in the economic collapse, all of it added up to bad news. Wes cinched his belt a notch tighter. He'd lost two waist sizes since Laura had left, taking her mad cooking skills with her. He ate meat, usually jerky, and wasn't drinking, so the extra pounds he had put on since he'd been overseas had melted off.

Hell, maybe I can fit into a size large shirt again.

He dug into the back of the closet and found a stack of old shirts Laura had put away when he'd drank enough to make them too tight. His mouth quirked up at the third one down from the top, an outrageous red and yellow Hawaiian shirt, garish in design. It had been a Father's Day present shortly after he'd returned from overseas. Back when things were still good, or relatively so, a time when Laura had still loved him. He slipped it on, buttoned it up and felt his mouth turning up in a happy grin. The first one in months.

It fit. It actually fit well.

Fuck it. I'll go. It'll shock the shit out of most of those gossipy old busybodies to see me show my face.

He stared at his reflection in the mirror and his smile slipped as he thought of Laura and the kids. Chances were, he might never see them again. He had hoped, when things got bad, that they would come back. He dreamed of it, waking up in the middle of the night sure he had heard Sarah's voice, or Cody's husky whisper, the one where they think they are being quiet but instead are shout-whispering. But there had been nothing. No sign of them, not even a postcard or letter before the mail service had shut down completely. They were gone, and he was here in this empty house, reminded of them at every turn. Reminded of how he had failed to be the husband and father they deserved.

Hours later, as he stood on the edges of the crowd, the rack of ribs he had brought slowly browning on the large grill that had been set up in the middle of the street; he found himself questioning why he had come. Most of the women wouldn't meet his glance, and the men were all gathered in a group, with Ethan Hurlbut at the center, talking about starting a town militia. Leslie had come over, smiled and squeezed his arm, gave him a small hug before having to run off and deal with her youngest, four-year-old Eva who had fallen down and had a nasty scrape. The girl was wailing, a mess of tears and snot over a tiny little patch of blood on her knee.

He stood there, alone. His shirt felt like a damned neon sign that proclaimed, "Look at me! My wife left me and took my kids thanks to me being a drunken asshole!"

Another hunt in the woods sounds really good right about now.

"Hi."

Wes blinked. The woman standing in front of him could not be talking to him. He looked around, first to the left and then the right, before he turned back to her. Her lips twitched in what could only be amusement.

"Me?"

She said nothing, but a smile grew on her face. She handed him a slice of cake tilting on a cheap paper plate. "Leslie said that lemon cake is your favorite. I'm Angie, by the way."

She tipped her head back towards the group of women where Leslie was holding her youngest. Leslie looked up, winked at him and smiled before returning to petting Eva's hair and wiping the last of the little girl's tears away.

Dessert before dinner. Why the hell not?

"Uh, thanks." Wes took the cake from her and managed a weak smile in return. "I'm Wes." He took a bite of the cake. It was delicious. How long had it been since he had eaten lemon cake? At least six months, probably longer. It wasn't as moist as Laura's, but still.

The light shifted, dimmed, the clouds that had been in the distance had finally moved in and the day took on an unprecedented coolness as the storm began to move in, thunder beginning to rumble.

"Uh oh," Angie looked up, grinning, "it looks like we are about to get some real weather."

The way she said it, her odd accent, and the fact that her face wasn't familiar, reeled Wes in. He stepped closer. "Where are you from? Not from around here, I'm guessing."

"No," she said, shaking her head. She cocked it sideways and grinned like a fool at the darkening sky.

"California. I was visiting friends, and well, things went to hell and I figured why not stay here for a while."

She turned away and studied the clouds, her eyes examining them as they roiled and moved, the wind picking up her hair, blowing it. Behind them, folks were scrambling to pull the tables inside of the Trade Mart. Even the grill was being moved to under the overhang of the building as fat drops of rain began to fall.

"You act like you've never seen rain before." He shoveled half of the cake into his mouth, watching her with obvious delight.

She turned back. "There's plenty of rain, but without the thunder and lightning. Just a downpour, no light show." Her grin stretched impossibly wide, her teeth were uneven, but bright white. "Do you think we might get a tornado?" She said it with a hopeful look, eyes wide with excitement. She jumped as a streak of lightning lit up the horizon and thunder boomed.

"I think we are more likely to get hit by lightning if we stay here." He swallowed the last of the cake, licking his fingers. "C'mon, let's get under cover."

Without thinking, he took her hand and led her away. Not towards the Trade Mart, but towards home. It was instinctual. He had been ready to run when faced with the crowd already, and somehow, having just met her, he didn't want to say goodbye. She didn't question it, didn't look nervous, just laughed as the rain began to fall, heavy and their feet were soon splashing through puddles as they ran through the side streets.

The heavens let loose as they made it to his door. The rain hammering the roof, filling the gutters and gushing over in two places, the water overwhelming the gutters, and spilling down in a solid line where Cody had dented the spot of guttering over the eaves with a football the year before. The kid might be a pansy over the sight of blood, but he was strong.

"Wow, that changed from sunny to downpour in nothing flat!" Angie laughed, pulling at her soaked t-shirt and wiping at the drips that ran in rivulets from her hairline. She looked around the living room and Wes felt a wave of embarrassment crash through him.

What had he been thinking when he

brought her here? The bottles of Jim Beam were all gone, but he hadn't cleaned, not once, since Laura and the kids left. Dirty laundry lay scattered on the floor, a pile of dirty dishes covered the coffee table, and he was suddenly acutely aware that he hadn't cracked a window to let fresh air in. It smelled almost feral, as if he had brought her to a wolf's den, not a home. He grabbed a tall candle, a floral scented one Laura had liked so much, and lit it with a match. He shook the box. He was down to the last handful of them. Hopefully he could pick up a box at the Trade Mart next time he had some meat and skins to trade.

"I, uh..." Wes was surprised to find he felt nervous, worried this stranger would want to leave as quickly as she had arrived. "I didn't really think about how messy it was in here. I, uh..."

"You weren't expecting a strange woman to come home with you?" Her face was guileless, and she cocked her head to one side, assessing him with her warm brown eyes.

"Yeah, I guess so. I mean," he paused, suddenly out of his depth, "I mean, is that what we are doing here?"

She threw her head back and laughed. It rang out, so bright and melodic, that he was shocked by it. "You tell me, Wes, you led the way. I just followed along!"

He felt attraction then, a strong pull of it. It wasn't just the fact that a real, live woman was standing in his living room. That she could have taken home top spot in a wet t-shirt contest or that he hadn't had any for longer than he could remember. There was something about her. She was confident, yet not brash. She smiled at him and he felt like he could lose himself in that smile. It reminded him of how Laura had looked in the early days - when the first blush of their love had been simple and overwhelming and pure. Before Afghanistan, before Cody, and responsibilities and bills had replaced those hedonistic moments of making love on his narrow futon in a sun-drenched apartment with neighbors bickering on the other side of the wall. Before the explosions and the whiskey, he drank to keep his nerves from feeling like white-hot pokers in his brain.

He smiled back at her, felt the unfamiliar stretch as the corners of his mouth lifted up. She nodded then, "That's better. You looked so solemn before. A smile looks good on you."

It slipped then, and he looked away. "I'm not so good with people these days."

She stepped closer, reached up, and touched his cheek. "Really? Maybe you just haven't been with the right people." She leaned in, her breath smelling of lemon cake, and kissed him lightly on the lips. He returned the favor by putting his arms around her, pulling her close, and losing himself in a deep, passionate kiss.

He slept late that next morning for the first time in forever, opening his eyes to hear Angie moving about in the living room, humming away. She had stayed the whole night, and the sun was pouring in the bedroom window, promising a hot, muggy morning after the odd weather of the day before.

He stretched, listening. What was she doing? He sat up, grabbed his jeans, and slipped them on. Her back was to him and she gave a small yip of surprise when he spoke, jumping as she turned, toys filling her hands. He looked around the living room, saw it neat and clean, the dishes washed, the tables cleared.

"You're awake." she looked down at the toys in her hands. "I'm an early riser and, well," she shrugged, "I like to clean. I hope you don't mind."

He didn't and realized his face probably told her something different. The scent of meat cooking got his stomach rumbling, though, and it let out a large, low growl.

Angie laughed, another one of her carefree, musical laughs that had him grinning in return. He scuffed his bare foot on the floor, "I guess I worked up an appetite last night."

Her eyes widened, eyebrows arching, her grin infectious, "Same here, I'm positively *starving!*"

It felt strange to see her in Laura's spot at the table. But as she talked about the life she had left in California, "It was so expensive to live there!" and her life here in Tennessee, "Did you know that cows actually do that?" he found that she fit in some odd, refreshing way.

After breakfast, they sat on the front porch and she waved at Dowsey as he walked past, his decrepit Buick neatly put away in the garage. The old man was pushing ninety. He had lived on his own since his wife of sixty-five years had passed the year before, and he still didn't even need glasses. He nodded at the two of them and kept on walking.

"Tell me about your family," Angie asked, matter of fact, right to the point.

Wes stared at her. "I imagine you've heard the stories."

She shrugged, "I'd rather hear it from you."

Yep, and this is when she's gonna high tail it out of here.

"Laura, my wife, she took Cody and Sarah and left about four months ago now. I hired a private eye to try to find them and he got close. By the time I got to the motel in Memphis, they were gone and there's been no word since." He paused. "Is that about what you heard?"

Angie nodded, then asked, "Would you consider yourself a good husband and father?"

She's direct. A woman after my own heart.

He drew in a breath and let it out, sighed, "No, I wouldn't. I tried to be. I really did. But I fucked up. I drank too much, yelled at the kids, and lost my temper with Laura. She didn't deserve it, not one bit of it." He looked away, down the road, wondered where they were, whether they were okay, if they were safe. He wondered if he would ever know the truth.

"She did what she had to - to be safe, to be a good parent to the kids. She did it because I wasn't changing, and the situation was getting worse, not better. I was mad as hell, ready to drag her back by her hair if I found her. I lost my job, lost most of my friends, and I've sat alone in this house and wished I had another chance to make it right."

He stared into the distance, afraid to look at the woman by his side. She sighed too and slipped her hand into his. It was small, delicate.

"Thank you, Wes. For your honesty."

He snorted and shook his head. "And now is when you're gonna run for the hills, right?"

She laughed and bumped her shoulder against his. "Nah, I think I'll stay awhile if you don't mind."

Relief flooded through him. He'd been lonely and there was something about Angie that captivated him. His voice was gruff, "I don't mind."

"Good."

They sat there in silence and listened to the town wake up around them.

"I fixed you the last of the tea." Wes set the steaming mug down on the dining room table and turned back to his packs. The first cold snap and a hunting trip were long overdue. He added his fletching knife, which he had sharpened the evening before.

Angie's hair, normally neatly coiffed in a bun, was in disarray and she was still in a nightshirt, a thick woven blanket around her shoulders, her knees drawn up to her chest, heels balanced on the worn wood of the chair, a faraway look in her eyes.

Wes looked back at her. She hadn't touched the tea. "You okay?" He pulled up a chair, sat down next to her. Something was wrong.

She looked up, uncharacteristically somber. He attempted a smile. "I suppose you could keep your nightshirt on while hunting, and just flash the deer. The shock of it might keep them from bolting."

A corner of her mouth twitched, but it was fleeting, and he could see an anxious look in her eyes. "I think I had better stay here. I'm not feeling so well."

"It was that damned Anderson kid, wasn't it?" She had been helping out with running the small school in town, reading to the younger children while others taught the older students. Bella Anderson, a normally feisty four-year-old, had been rosy-cheeked with fever, glassy eyes and a runny nose when he stopped by with lunch for Angie the day before. "I swear they've got some cold or flu on a constant running basis. With seven kids in the house, it's practically a rotating array of disease."

"It's not little Bella," Angie picked up the tea, sniffed it, and then set it down again and pushed it towards him. "I can't enjoy it, my stomach's all crazy right now, you go ahead."

Their fingers connected and Wes felt a ball of wonder beginning to rotate in his stomach. Laura had been the same way with both Cody and Sarah.

"Oh shit." He breathed it out, shock mixing with anticipation, even joy. Her eyes met his, worry and even fear so clear in her soft brown eyes. "You're pregnant, aren't you?"

"Do you want me to go?" Her voice

was childlike in that moment, and he could see she was waiting for him to give her a sign, anything that would indicate decisively how he was feeling.

"Do I want you to go?" Why would she think that? And then he thought of Laura and Cody and Sarah. They had spoken of them, many times, and in all of those times, she had never once asked what would happen if they did come back. For that matter, he hadn't wanted to think of it either. And now the question was there, in front of them. This existence, this thing that they had together. What was it?

His mouth opened. And then it closed. He couldn't explain it. He couldn't put it into words, the emotions he was feeling. That if he told her how he felt about her, it meant closing the door on the life he had with his wife and children. What if they came back? This child, this baby growing inside of her, it changed everything.

"I can't... I can't talk about this right now." The words sounded harsh, distant, and they fell out of his mouth before he could stop them, before he could explain how complicated this all was. The love he felt for her, so different from the love he had felt for Laura. Different, because they were different people. He pulled back, hating himself as he saw his retreat in her eyes.

He reached out then, took her hand, stared at how the fingers were bare of jewelry, no ring that said she was his, and his own still wearing his wedding ring. It was simply part of his hand, it had never occurred to him to take it off, not even after Angie had moved in four months ago.

Four months, they had done nearly everything together. She had hunted with him, sleeping on the hard ground, cussing out the mosquitoes that swarmed near Reelfoot Lake, and learned to trap right alongside him.

"Stay here. I need to think. I need to..." His brain was spinning, "I just need some time, okay?"

He could see the beginnings of tears in her eyes, "Okay." It hadn't been the response she had obviously been hoping for, more of one she had feared.

Her fears manifested. Will I ever stop hurting the people that I love?

He squeezed her hand. "I'll be back

tomorrow, next day at the latest."

He grabbed his packs and left then, escaping to the woods where there were no people, no noise, nothing but the woods and him and the creatures he was hunting. All of his cares, all the things that pulled him back to civilization, they fell away and he could think.

Wes walked; each step chosen carefully. No high hide this time. A bullet in the chamber, locked and loaded, and he picked up fresh tracks near the stream's edge, heading away into a deeper brush.

A baby. He remembered Sarah's birth so clearly. Cody's, he had missed, thousands of miles away in the desert city of Kandahar when he got the news that his son had been born a month early, two weeks before his scheduled leave. Laura had been young, just seventeen, and he had gotten leave to come home and see his new wife and son. Red and small and squalling, that had been his impression of him.

And if he were honest, that was pretty much how he had always found Cody, at least the squalling part of it. Sarah, despite her love for baby dolls, was tougher. She had been a happy baby, seemed impervious to pain, and had climbed trees better than her brother. He hadn't been there for them. Neither of them.

And he would be there, every step of the way, every moment for this one. Not fucked up, or desperate for the alcohol to blunt the noise, the memories.

The tracks intersected with another

creature's prints, and Wes could see he was on a main thoroughfare for the animal life here. A superhighway to the watering hole. Ahead he saw the path open up, and there at the edge of the lake, a doe and her two fawns had stopped to drink. He lowered his rifle. He wouldn't take a doe, not one that had babies to care for. Across the way, a hundred feet away where the land held on, fighting the lake for dominance, he saw a majestic stag. No doubt the sire of the two fawns that drank water silently, mere yards away from him.

He lifted his rifle once again. It was a long shot, but he could see just where to put the round. There was no wind, nothing to interfere with a quick death. It would take a good twenty minutes to walk through the brush and around the edge of the lake to retrieve the kill, but it was a good one and Wes smiled, eager to return to Angie, to say the words she needed to hear. The stag's ear twitched, but it didn't move.

He closed an eye, sighted down the barrel, and focused on the place where the round would hit. Center mass, slightly to the right of the breastbone, a tad elevated to account for distance. His finger tightened gently on the trigger. And in the split second before he fired, the sound of gunfire erupted from the distance. The stag wheeled around, sprinted away with a mighty crash and was out of sight in less than a second, random crashes in the brush betraying his existence as the creature fled for its life.

Wes stopped, looking in vain to see if he could see anything. It was a lot of gunfire, and it was coming from town. He dropped the two packs he had brought with him. They didn't have anything he couldn't retrieve later, and certainly nothing that he needed. What he did need to do was get home as quickly as possible.

He ran, settling into a steady lope. A ground-eating pace he had learned in the service, one made easier by not having the sixty-pound pack of camping supplies and tools on his back. The '65 Enfield was strapped to his back and at this rate he would be back in town in less than an hour.

Too long, gotta get there faster.

He lengthened his stride, felt his boots dig into the brush, crackling with frost, following a game trail rather than seeking the road.

There had been rumors of troop movements, in at least two directions, one from the west, and others to the north. Tiptonville was small, remote even. The initial tension and attentiveness to the world around them had faded as the months stretched on and the small town was forgotten by the world at large. An oasis of calm, it went unnoticed for so long that many had come to believe they would be able to ride out The Collapse with little more than inconvenience. They had taken their peace for granted, assuming it would continue. And now, from the sound of the gunfire, the town was paying for that mistake dearly.

He was winded, his heart pounding in his chest, but he continued to push his body forward, yards disappearing beneath his feet, his entire focus on returning to Angie. Would she stay inside? Or would she step out of the door, run towards danger?

In the past three months, Angie had proved herself to be strong, capable, tough. He had shown her how to fire a gun. She had lain on the hard ground beside him, handled gutting and cleaning the kills, and even taken a buck of her own over a month ago. A clean shot to the chest, with the creature dead before it hit the ground.

Stay inside. Hide. Stay inside. Hide.

The silent plea repeated itself over and over. If only his wishes were enough to keep her safe.

He faltered, his ankle a hot pulse of pain as it twisted on a rocky section of the trail. He ignored it, followed the tree line, and burst out between two backyards a block over from his house. The fence between the two yards had been on the decline for a decade, but it was helped along by a particularly strong spring storm. The neighbors, an older couple on one side, and the other house long empty, had not bothered to fix it. A quick road trip to Home Depot was no longer an option.

He slipped through the gaps, avoiding the fallen panels and crossed the road. The gunfire was concentrated in the north part of town, to his right.

Perhaps they hadn't even come through this area.

His hopes were dashed when he saw the first body. Dowsey lay crumpled on the ground on his stomach, one gnarled, aged hand lying limp at his side, the other tucked under him. He wasn't moving and there was a wide circle of red in the middle of his back. Wes didn't stop. He passed another and another.

His heart hammered in his chest as he turned the corner, and he saw her then, her dishwater blond hair splayed out, half on, half off the front stoop. His Ruger, the one he had given her to practice with, lay on the ground next to her limp right hand. And blood, so much blood.

If he had any breath to spare, he would have screamed then. But each molecule of oxygen served to move him forward to bring him to her side. He slid to a stop, his lungs desperate for more air than he could give, his heart shattering as he brought her up to him and held her against his chest.

Minutes passed. Time enough for his heart to slow, for his breathing to return to some semblance of normality. He sat there and held her. When he could speak again, he told her how much he loved her, that he was sorry he hadn't said it that morning, that he was a fool. He told her all the words he knew she had wanted to hear, all the words that had occurred to him on the long walk out. He spoke of his dreams, the dreams made real by the news that he had another chance, another moment, a life to spend with her and their child in this house. That he didn't want her to go anywhere but instead be here with him. He held her, rocked her, and described what it was like to see Sarah born. To know that a piece of himself had become a person, something whole and separate from him, and that, no matter what, they would make it work.

And when he was done. When there were no more words and her blood had drenched his shirt, his jeans, he laid her gently on the ground, carefully closed her eyes, and went to find the men responsible.

Hours later, in the darkness, in the burning flames of the buildings the invading troops had set on fire, Wes exacted his revenge on the last two soldiers left.

He had been far too late to catch the men responsible. Those who had commanded the troops were long gone, on to another town, and better conquests. The town militia was in tatters. Their head, his former boss and ex-Marine Ethan Hurlbut lay dead, partially crushed by the fallen water tower, his body riddled with bullets. Of all of them, Ethan's voice had been the loudest, warning of the possibility of this happening. He had been their leader, but most of the men in the militia had never seen combat. They were gun owners, hunters even, but not soldiers.

The two soldiers, wounded, left behind when their Jeep headed down the wrong side street, separated from the Western Front, if the violent, murderous remainder of the army could even be called that now - the two soldiers were taking a long time in dying. Both of them shot in the legs, they couldn't walk or run or even crawl. Hell, they couldn't escape from the Jeep which was now on the side of the road into town, pushed there after Wes had assumed leadership of what few remained of the militia.

It was Wes that called for the gasoline can. And as he set fire to the Jeep, he ignored the screams of the men inside as they begged for their lives. He had stood there, long after the crowd had dispersed, long after they had scuttled away, back to the ruins of their homes and their lives, and he had waited for the men inside to be burned clean of their sins. He had waited until only their skeletons remained.

He walked away, into the dark.

"Wes?" Leslie, her arm in a sling, put a hand on his arm.

A new day had dawned. He hadn't

slept. He'd cleaned Angie up as best he could, but there was no water pressure left in the lines now that the water tower was down. He'd wrapped her body in a sheet, loaded her onto the tarp they had used to bring back the deer carcasses and begun the long walk out to Reelfoot Lake.

He hadn't noticed Leslie following behind.

He had dug the hole there in the first campsite he had taken her to. It was on a hill, surrounded by willow trees and carpeted in wildflowers. He had just been settling Angie's body into the grave when Leslie spoke.

"I'm so sorry." Her voice was flat, her eyes bloodshot.

"She loved this place. Said it was magical." His hands shook, and he stared at the shovel, realizing he hadn't washed the blood off of them yet. *Her* blood.

"It's beautiful." Leslie said, her voice choking. "She is, well, she was..."

"I know. She told me." He took the shovel and prepared to begin digging.

"Those soldiers," Leslie's voice was a whisper, "the ones in the Jeep."

"I thought it would make me feel better." He said, his eyes taking in her burns, the dried blood on Leslie's clothing, her hands. "Seeing them burn after what they did to Angie. What they did to this town."

"And did it?"

"No."

"In war," Leslie said slowly, "there are no winners."

"No, there aren't."

And with nothing left to say, Wes dug the shovel deep into the soft earth.

This Fractured Nation

"The world is not what it was. Our nation is in ruins."

I noticed the dog first. She watched me, at attention, her body close to a small girl with red hair who sat near a young woman with golden blond curls snaking down her back. A few feet away, a blanket was covered with a small mound of tiny pups, all of them sleeping deeply.

The dog gave a short bark, then wagged her tail at me. The young woman looked up, surprise on her face. I wondered if it was surprise at the dog's reaction, or was it that I was a stranger? Perhaps few people came this way, I wasn't sure.

This had to be her, though, the girl I had been looking for. She was younger than I expected. She looked to be in her late teens, perhaps early 20s.

I thought for a moment that, given the right set of circumstances, this girl could be my daughter's age, if Anna had lived. And for a moment, the pain slammed into me, barely dulled by twenty years, still as gut-wrenching as ever. When menopause had come on last year, early at the tender age of forty-six, it had been a relief. I didn't need the monthly reminders that my ovaries and uterus had conspired against me, that they were not capable of bringing viable life into the world. It was a relief, really.

I forced the memory away, met

Jess's gaze, the corners of my mouth turning up in a friendly smile, and I raised my hand in greeting. "Hello there! You must be Jessica Aaronson." I reached down and scratched the dog's ears as she nosed my leg, "And this must be Quincy."

Quincy licked my hand, then settled down near Jess's feet again, her tail a steady thump against the ground. Her latest litter of puppies squirmed on a blanket nearby, beginning to wake up, their bodies of mass of tiny noses and twitching tails.

I wondered what Jess must think of me. Now in my late 40s, I had slim, long legs, and I was taller than most women, far taller than my mother had been. My hair was long, straight, and dark, and I kept it braided in one thick rope down the middle of my back. The hair at my temples had begun to show gray last year, as did one long streak that ran the length of my long hair. Despite the cool fall day, I was wearing shorts and a sleeveless tank top with a rucksack resting on my shoulders. When Mother was younger, they had often pointed to me and called me her mini-me. They said it even as I grew taller than Mother, eventually towering over her by nearly six inches. So much for a mini-anything. But that had been years ago.

Jess stared, "Uh, hello." She sounded hesitant, but polite. Not afraid, but not overly friendly.

"I'm Penelope," I said, sticking my hand out. The girl fumbled with the lamb's ear and then quickly stood up to shake my outstretched hand. "I see you are collecting lamb's ear seeds." I said, "Do you work with other herbs?"

Jess nodded, but did not elaborate.

I smiled, curious about the girl's knowledge. Perhaps she was the one I needed to ask after an apprenticeship, not the young girl that the town doc had mentioned. "Do you know anything about the properties of lamb's ear, Jess?"

"Only that it's making me feel nauseas. I don't like the weird smell." The young woman grinned ruefully back.

I laughed, "Stop for a while and I'll take over. I've gotten used to it." I sat down on the stoop, took the bucket from Jess, and began plucking at the dry flower heads. "The leaves can be picked early, before it flowers and can be dried and used in tea. You could also eat it in salads, or steamed, but most people object to the furry aspect of it. The best use of lamb's ear is for small wound care—it is absorbent and soft, and plentiful. But that isn't why I came here." I finished with one stalk and started on another. Suddenly I wasn't sure what to say, or how to say it. Here was the girl I had been looking for, for nearly five years, I was sure of it. But how do you jump into that? Instead, I found myself saying instead, "I've come to speak with you and David about Tina and a possible apprenticeship."

Jess looked at me, frowning slightly, "Tina's only ten years old."

My hands didn't stop moving as I turned toward Jess and gave her a long, appraising look. I had spent time in the heart of the town, talking to Sarah Turner. She had described Jess as the "go to" person for information on the town and its residents. After a few days of trade and work, I knew enough of the girl's history to know that she and her house full of kids had struggled through some pretty tough times in the past six or seven years. Sarah had been forthcoming with details about Jess, telling me that Jess was busy writing down the lives and accounts of most of the residents of Belton and compiling a history of the area.

"She goes from house to house, usually during the winter when there's not so much to do," Sarah had said, "She writes down whatever memories they have—of this war, of their families, of the time before—whatever someone wants to talk about, really."

The woman had shrugged. "I wasn't born here, but she even wanted my story."

I had been as circumspect as possible. I had been searching a long time for the author of the letter I had found in the cave. I was sure that this Jess Aaronson was the one that had seen Mom through her final days, and buried her in the cairn outside her beloved cave.

If you are reading this, then you undoubtedly know Madge. My name is Jess Aaronson. I'm sixteen years old.

The letter was crumpled and tattered now, worn from reading and re-reading it over and over.

"Well, I've heard from Dr. Ridley that she knows a lot about herbs and healing." I smiled and turned back to the lamb's ear. "I've also come for a different reason. I've been looking for *you* for a long time now, nearly five years. You see, you knew someone very important to me."

I let Jess digest this in a long moment of silence. When I looked over at Jess, the expression on the girl's face had turned from one of curiosity to one of fear. Sarah had hinted that the girl had been through terrible experiences before she returned to Belton nearly seven years ago.

I stopped and said, "I'm sorry; I didn't tell you my full name. It's Penelope Falling Water Aster... Dr. Madeleine Falling Water—you may have known her as Madge—she was my mother."

The girl said nothing for a moment, her mouth falling open in shock.

"I, she, oh my God. Grandmother Madge. She…" the girl couldn't manage to put the words together. And I watched as the tears welled up in her eyes.

I watched her for a moment. I had read the letter so many times, but I had still had my doubts. Had this girl and the other children truly loved my mother? Had Mother been at peace, surrounded by someone, anyone, who may have cared for her? Had they said the prayers that my mother's spirit required in order to find peace in the hereafter? Watching the younger woman now, seeing her reaction, it seemed that the letter had spoken true.

Before I tell you how your friend or mother died, I want to tell you how she lived. How she gave us sanctuary and saved our lives, by leading us here, to this cave...

The four of us, my newborn son Jacob, David, and Tina, both orphans from Clinton, and I have been here since September.

I reached out and hugged Jess as my own tears began to slide down my nose. We were still hugging and crying when a young man in his late teens walked up a few minutes later, followed by a girl who looked very much like him. They both stood and stared at the two of us sobbing, frowning.

I am sure I do not need to tell you how special Madge was—or how much she came to mean to us. I lost my best friend in the world just days before she found us. I couldn't think; I was scared and lost.

"What's going on? Who is she?" The girl asked the young man. He just shrugged and kept staring at us. The young girl's question, however, was enough to reduce the crying and elicit some basic explanation of who I was.

Two hours later, the sun had slipped low on the horizon and dusk was gathering. My husband, Kip had joined them and they had just finished nibbling the last kernels of corn off of the cob.

I kept stealing glances at little Erin, the little girl with red curls. At nearly four years of age, she appeared to be in a growth spurt, her pants coming to rest high on her ankles, her top stretched tight, and her sleeves ended long before her wrists began. She was slender and pixie-like, her freckled skin slightly sunburnt, and her hair a mass of bright red curls. She maintained a steadfast silence, never speaking, except for the occasional giggle when David, the young man who had come upon them crying, tickled her.

As dinner wrapped up, there was a quiet silence that descended upon the group. I looked at the bunch of them and marveled at their resilience. Jess was tall and graceful. Her skin was tanned a golden brown from working in the sun, and her hair fell in long curls down the middle of her back. David was in his mid-to-late teens, and his arms and chest were muscled and lean. They had served some stew with turkey and wild greens in it and Jess had pointed to David, noting that he was the one who had landed them the turkey using his bow. It was the same bow that Grandmother Madge had taught him to use.

The end was peaceful. We were with her, holding her hands, and my baby Jacob nestled beside her. She loved to hold him, and he adored her. We all did.

The sun had slipped down beyond the horizon, pink and red streaks colored the clouds, the crickets had begun to sing, and the evening had a chill. They had spent hours describing their time with Grandmother Madge in the cave. Kip and I had pelted them with question after question, Kip especially seemed shocked that they had all spent a winter there. As dinner had wound down, Jess had put a pot of chicory coffee on to boil, and handed out mugs full of it. I tasted it and was pleasantly surprised at the sweet taste. I raised my eyebrows, and Jess grinned.

"I sweeten it with sugar beets. We grow them over there, two houses down." Jess said, pointing to the east.

They had expanded their gardens to several yards, those they identified as having good soil, and others that had intact, tall fences. Especially when it came to foods that deer liked, the high fences had been effective in keeping out the local deer population that was exploding in spite of regular hunting.

"Grandmother Madge said you were in Europe, or was it Africa?" Jess asked, dying to hear about the outside world. "How did you get here?"

My face grew grim, as did Kip's. We glanced at each other for a moment and I held out my mug to Kip for a refill. He was nearest the coffeepot.

"That has been an adventure, let me tell you. Have any of you heard much of what is going on in the outside world, outside of the former United States?" I asked Jess and David. David frowned and said nothing.

Jess answered, "We heard that The Collapse spread past our borders. That it was kind of like a domino effect. First the economic collapse and then multiple civil wars and uprisings in places like Greece, the Middle East, even China after the U.S. dollar collapsed. There were a lot of problems with the Euro before the Collapse. But afterwards," she shrugged, "we lost power and internet and my parents stopped talking about what was happening out there."

She stared into the gathering darkness. "Maybe it was too big, too frightening even for them. And then afterwards, after I returned with David and Tina and Jacob, well, we haven't exactly welcomed outsiders in Belton until more recently. The world has changed, I'm sure, but we only know what is nearby. There have been plenty of false starts into reasserting government on a broader level, but nothing that's stuck." She gestured toward the town center, "We have a militia, a mayor..."

"For whatever they are worth," murmured David in disgust.

Jess shot him a glance, "... and a basic town government in place. Every so often someone gets their britches in a knot and wants something more, and starts talking about money and taxes and the federal government. That doesn't last long."

I nodded. "When the United States collapsed, much of the world was already on the brink of complete chaos. The riots in Greece were just the beginning of what became an uprising, civil war, and eventually a full war through Europe."

"Even Switzerland couldn't sit this one out. And Africa had already been a hotbed, right along with the Middle East; so much infighting, along with the scourge of HIV and so many young people growing up without any parents, without any direction in their lives."

I took a sip of the dark, heavily sweetened chicory and continued, "We were traveling with an independently funded humanitarian aid mission in Uganda. The Lord's Resistance Army controlled much of the north at the time. The word got out that every American had better get out now, or else." I grimaced, "As if it were that easy."

Kip, who had said little until this point, took up the story. "It took us nearly two years just to get out of Africa. Everything that could break down did—communications, monetary systems, and the American embassies, or any embassies friendly to United States interests were either closed, burned to the ground, or abandoned. The fact that we were Americans was suddenly a very bad thing. Luckily, we had friends, those who had been helped by our organization, by us. We stayed with a string of them until it became dangerous for them to keep us there. We eventually found our way to the Mediterranean and tried to enter Europe via Italy, and later Spain." He shook his head.

I continued, "It seemed that all of Europe was either involved in uprisings, civil war, or fighting each other. More than anything, though, we, well, *any* Americans were turned away. We ended up with several others from our aid group on a freighter, bound for Port-au-Prince. It was the closest thing we had to the U.S., although anyone we spoke to told us there had been nukes set off in the south and there were plenty of pointed fingers."

I took another sip of the chicory, now cooled in the mug, and continued, "In the end, we don't know how it started, or who pushed what buttons, but there were nuclear detonations recorded in Austin, D.C., and Los Angeles. It looks as if the Star Wars defense program took out most of the satellites in space at right around the same time—effectively ending world-wide communications."

I stared at the bottom of my cup; my vision clouded by the events that came next.

Kip waited for me to speak and then he continued the story, "We knew the chances of finding Madge were unlikely. There had been such chaos in the cities. We wondered if she ever even made it out. Not to mention that she had told Penelope of her illness and that she didn't have long. Penelope had been scheduling a trip back to the States when everything went to hell. We just didn't hold out much hope. We stayed in Haiti for nearly eighteen months trying to stay alive and figure out where to go next."

I sat there for a moment, my eyes and mind miles away, lost in memories of Haiti. I didn't want to tell them of the disease, the murders, or how many times we had fought for just enough food to survive. I didn't want to talk about the children she saw lying dead in the streets.

I shook it off with some effort. "Florida was impossible—there were nearly a dozen naval bases there that banded together once communications with D.C. ceased. They patrol the waters and allow no one in. It's a fire first, ask questions later situation. We couldn't get close enough to tell them we were American, not that it would have mattered. They had locked it down to Florida residents, anyway. Texas was a fallout zone, as was much of the Caribbean and the southern states." I pursed her lips, "Not that they told Florida citizens that. They actively denied it even after the first reports of radiation sickness. Once the Western Front started moving east into the Plains states, other factions of former military, along with extremists, rose up to define their own areas of control."

Kip chimed in, "The Allied South struggled to consolidate Louisiana, Arkansas, Mississippi, Alabama, Georgia, and parts of South Carolina. Mexico had surged into Arizona, New

Mexico, and the most southern section of California and there was chaos there—lines drawn between the white, Hispanic, and Native American populations. The drug cartels made a move for power. The east coast had three different contingents—the Northern Allies who were struggling to define the borders of half a dozen small states, the Unionists that controlled some parts of the southeast, and the Patriots who were hopelessly divided through infighting in Kentucky, Ohio, and Indiana."

Jacob and Becka, who likely understood little of the states being discussed, having been born after the Collapse, were silent. Erin had curled up in David's arms and was sucking her thumb, listening intently.

I continued, "We finally found entry

just west of Biloxi, Mississippi. There had been a radiation fallout scare, and much of the area was deserted. We headed up Highway 49. After that it was a zigzag route. We entered Tennessee, tried to go through the northwest section, but there was a chain of small towns, all with militias, and we were turned back at Tiptonville." I took another sip. "The Western Front had torn through that region and everyone was on edge. If you weren't a resident, they turned you away, no questions, no argument." I smiled wryly. "After all, they were the ones with the guns. You can't argue much with the business end of a gun."

Kip spoke up, "We spent a winter in Arkansas. There were migrant groups moving through the areas, many of them working crops, building or reinforcing town borders, living like gypsies as they searched for a place to stay. We moved in and out of these groups—diseases we hadn't seen in decades in the Western world ran rampant. Cholera, bouts of dysentery, and a host of other illnesses could be found in any group we joined. But the alternative was to go it alone, without some of the protection a group could provide. Sometimes it was worth it, other times it wasn't."

I picked it up from there, "And eventually we moved through parts of Oklahoma, Kansas, and then finally Missouri. Once we hit Missouri, I was determined to find my mother. I had thought about it a lot, wondering what she would do, where she would go if she knew she only had a short time to live. I doubted that she would have stayed in her home there in Kansas City, and we were close to the archaeology site she had been working on for the last few years. I had been given the opportunity to visit the site the first year they had begun work, so I was familiar with where to find it. I figured if she wasn't there, I would try finding her in KC. I wasn't holding out much hope either way."

I paused, drained the last of the chicory from my cup, and said, "I noticed the cairn immediately. When we arrived at the cave, I was convinced that the full team had to have been there, since there was evidence of more than just Mom. It took me a while to go deeper into the cave. I was wondering where everyone went, even though it was obvious it had been a while. I had completely forgotten about the long passage. Finding your letter, even as it raised more questions, gave me some measure of peace."

My eyes brimmed with tears. "She wasn't alone when she passed. That means so much to me to know that she had someone with her as she passed into the world of spirits." I wiped at a tear that had escaped and began trickling down my cheek. "And eventually we came here, looking for you, Jess."

Jess's cheeks were also wet with tears. "Those months we spent with Madge were beautiful ones. She gave us so much—love, acceptance, and peace—even now, I remember it like it was yesterday. My faith in humans and life in general had been sorely tested and Madge reminded me of all I had left to live for, all that I could be for Jacob, for myself and my family."

Grandmother, that is what she asked us to call her, took us in, and taught us how to survive here, in this cave through the winter. It is now March, late March, and no snow has fallen in several weeks. The temperatures are rising and it is time for me to try to finish my journey home.

"I have her journal. The personal one that she kept," Jess said suddenly. "I can get it for you."

I held up a hand. "Tomorrow. Can I come again tomorrow?" The sun had set, and the darkness had closed in. "We are staying in town. That they let us in at all was a surprise. We tried months ago and were turned back.

But apparently the militia is allowing traders and migrant workers in these days, and we had goods to trade, so we will be here for another day or perhaps two."

Jess nodded, "Yes, yes, of course. Come by tomorrow."

As we walked away from Jess and her family, I could feel their eyes on our backs, watching us. Kip slipped his fingers into mine. "Have you asked after Tina? She's pretty young, younger than I thought."

"The town doc vouched for her. Says she's smart as a whip. Young as she is, it's kids like her who will help us climb out of this hole we are in, and return to a better future."

I don't know you, and you don't know me. But I'm writing this letter and then hiding the box where only

The next day, David seemed better. They had worked on the house, repairing a section of the roof, and then weeding several of the beds of potatoes and lettuce. Jess had made up her mind to tell Penelope they weren't interested, that Tina was far too young. What possible apprenticeship could apply to a young child? As she watched Penelope approach, her long-legged stride fluid on the broken pavement of the street, Jess could see that Sarah Turner had joined her and that Penelope's husband, Kip, was not with them.

Sarah was a kind woman. She had always treated Jess as an equal—and during those first months and years, she had championed the younger woman's cause, and that of their motley group of children more than once. Sarah was quite protective, in fact, which made Jess wonder about the older woman's past, and that of her children, who were nearly the same age as Jess. Sarah had always been rather close-mouthed about where she had come from, or where Cody and Laura's father were.

What would Sarah have to contribute to all of this? Jess wasn't sure what to think. A quick glance at David's face signaled trouble. Tina was *his* sister, and he had a right to his opinion, but for the first time, Jess wondered what Tina wanted. Stay or go, wasn't it up to her? After all, Tina was nearly the age that David had been when they all first met in Clinton. He had been old enough to make a decision then, a decision that taken him away from everything familiar, everything that reminded him of home. Shouldn't Tina have the right to make that same decision? Even at the age of ten years?

Jess was conflicted, and she knew it showed in her face. Sarah took it in, smiled at her, and gave her a warm hug. "Good morning Jess!" Since her daughter Laura had married Todd Stevens, the laugh lines on her face had deepened. The births of Laura and Todd's two boys had brought happiness, along with something Jess could only describe as longing to

Sarah's face. Jess wondered if Sarah was thinking of the husband she had left behind. Jess had listened to so many stories, so many unfinished, unknown fates of loved ones. It was perhaps the most haunting part of her job as historian—the unknown fates of so many. Sarah's story was one of dozens.

It was hours before dinner and they had had lunch just two hours earlier, but Sarah produced a loaf of her sourdough bread, a favorite of David's. That was combined with a bag of fruits that Kip had sent along, payment for some picking work they had both done earlier in the day. Jess and David, along with Tina, Sarah, and Penelope, sat down for a bite to eat and some conversation. It was stilted at first, mainly due to David, who felt cornered and resentful. Jess laid her hand on his knee, reminding him silently that she was his ally. He stared at her hand as she made small talk with Penelope and Sarah, concentrated on the long, tapered fingers. They were rough with callouses, but still delicate. He looked at them and tried to calm his fears—of losing his sister, knowing how much she wanted to go.

Tina had come to him that morning, the sun barely peeking over the horizon, and quietly folded herself on the floor of his room, quietly so she didn't wake Jacob. Her room was right next door, shared with Becka and Erin, when one or the other wasn't curled in bed next to Jess. "I want to go with her," was all that she had said when he opened one bleary eye and focused on her. They had engaged in a silent contest of wills, him glaring, her just staring back, until he had finally turned away and pulled the covers over his head and tried to ignore her. When he had turned back over a few moments later, she was gone.

The small talk had progressed while he was woolgathering. Penelope was describing her mother's house in Kansas City. "It's over 130 years old and solid brick. Surprisingly, it's rather intact considering the dire situation that most residents were in before and during the collapse. Most of her books are still there," Penelope smiled at Jess. "She wrote about all kinds of recent history, as well as anthropology. She had quite an obsession with Jesse James and also had notes on Pendergast, a corrupt political boss in the early 20th century." She turned toward David, who just shrugged and shook his head. He had never heard of Jesse James or Pendergast.

"In any case, the house was gone through, but not much was taken and it was empty when we visited it last week. We are planning to stay there and work with a medical group that is forming." She looked at Tina and smiled at her, then back to David where her smile faltered a brief second. "If it would be all right, Tina could come with us to Kansas City, and stay in the house. There is plenty of room and there are other students who she would be learning side-by-side with. You could come too, David, to see for yourself, if you liked."

A long silence ensued. All eyes were on David, until Tina spoke up. "I want to go to Kansas City with you, Penelope. I want to learn how to be a doctor. It's all I've ever wanted to do."

David closed his eyes for a moment, remembering her tiny hand in his, her matted hair in those weeks and months that had followed the deaths of their parents. The feel of her tiny body nestled against his. He remembered farther back, the first time he had seen her in the hospital, a tiny red face, impossibly small, mewling cries that sounded like a tiny, sad kitten. They had never fought; with nearly eight years between them, he had always been the oldest, the one she looked up to. And when they had been alone, lost in the rubble of a dead and broken town, she had depended on him for everything.

It was only here, in Belton, that she had come into her own, as young as she was, defining her future, writing it on the wall with nothing short of an indelible marker. Her abilities, her intuitive understanding and curiosity about the healing arts had given her this opportunity. And who was he to say no? How could he? David thought of her being absent, not someone he saw every day, not in the garden or walking into town with freshly picked herbs for Dr. Ridley, and something deep in his chest twisted and pulled. She was all that he had of their former life. The only evidence he could show of the parents that he had lost. The words to say all that seemed to elude him.

In the end, he simply stared at Jess's hand, still on his knee, and said, "If Tina wants to go, then, I guess that's what she should do."

But if you find this, know that she died surrounded by people who loved her. She was at peace, and I miss her dreadfully.

Yours, Jess

Take the Shot

"How far would you go?"

Jonathan

Farley's underground bunker was a well-kept secret, one that the mayor took pains to keep. No one needed to know the extent of his wealth or his resources. During the past two winters, especially. He had said nothing, not a word about it to anyone, since the Western Front had overrun the town, looting, snatching people up to join their ranks, and burning half of the damn town to the ground in the process. After that, food had been scarce, and he had even considered, if only in passing, limiting his intake of the food stores he had collected in order so as not to bring attention to his door.

He had thought of it, sure, but continued to avail himself of the fine foods, the rare liquor, while others in town starved. The fact was, he didn't give a damn what the other people in this town had to go through. It was their fault, for being the mindless sheep that they were, and this was the natural order of things.

The only exclusion to this was his son, and sometimes Jonathan Farley wondered if he had made a mistake allowing James to know as much as he did. The boy was hotheaded, impetuous, and worse, loose-lipped, with a few drinks in him.

Farley shook his head and swished the glass of port in his hand gently. It was chilled, thanks to the reusable ice cubes he had plucked from their bin in the freezer. Here in his hideout, his secret lair at the end of a fifty-foot-long tunnel dug fifteen feet deep in the earth, the only access to a rusty hatch hidden behind the hay bales in the barn, he could relax. Not even James bothered him here. Well, not usually. Really only at Farley's behest. Tonight, or in the morning, he would be coming by to report on how the transaction had gone.

James had never shown a preference for port, or any of the near priceless bottles of wine Farley had trucked in here, one case at a time. And he hadn't told his son about the rest of the liquor, the higher-end stuff that he didn't feel he needed to share. He had made sure to throw everyone off the scent by installing a significant number of items that he could use as a trade. The rest, everything stored here in his hidey-hole, well, that was for his personal use.

In the depths of the earth, it took some juice to keep the coolers full of meat, seafood, and more running. But not nearly as much as it would have on the surface, where it could exceed a hundred degrees in the summer. The humidity often brought it to a heat index of 103 degrees, and despite the chilly temperatures now in play, Farley could still remember how the sweat caused his clothing to cling to his body. He shivered at the thought in the cool of the wine room. It was late November, and the winter had long since descended, capturing the Midwestern states in its icy grip.

There was one oversized chair of tufted leather and a high back in the middle of a room surrounded by wine racks, the outer circle of which held the freezers full of foods against the outer stone walls. This deep underground, with nothing but stone surrounding him, and it was a constant fifty-five degrees. The only thing that varied was the humidity level.

The port was sweet and heavy on his tongue. Since the Collapse, Jonathan Farley had placed his fingers in even more pies than he had already had them in as the bank president and town alderman. The town was lucky to have him, though he was sure that the sheeple wouldn't see it that way. His wheeling and dealing had helped ensure that no one else invaded, and that was important, because the town of

Belton, a mere 26,000 souls before the Collapse and invasion of Western Front troops, was now down to a fraction of its size. And it wasn't as if the land surrounding them was empty or devoid of life. Before the Collapse, there had been more than two million people in the Greater Kansas City area. Two million, and while many had fled, or died in the fighting or of starvation and disease, there were plenty left. It was enough to warrant more than just a town militia to defend their borders. It meant deals, brokered arrangements, and shady compromises.

Belton had always been a rather white town, but before the Collapse, you could still see diversity, however limited. It was that small amount of color difference that had been the first to fall. When the chief of police James Wingo had sensed a change in the wind, one that would eventually carry the Western Front to their door, he had sat Farley down and had some strong suggestions for how the future of their vulnerable town could be secured with a few changes. Those few changes had included dozens of well-placed evictions. That several of the evicted had the temerity to suggest that Belton, Missouri, had become a sundown town was met with ridicule, even if it was accurate. Shutting down that talk had led to what seemed inevitable, a slippery slope into what some might even call human trafficking. He preferred to think of it as improving their community with a side benefit of getting some folks a future they were far better fitted for. Farley sniffed and took a large gulp of port, then nibbled on a rich brownie that Sarah Turner had baked with the last of the chocolate. At least, it was the last chocolate that *she* had. He had at least thirty pounds of it in a box down the hall. His thoughts briefly strayed to exactly how he was going to "find" some more chocolate, and better yet, not have it shared with the others in town. Sarah wasn't a native to Belton, but his control over her and what she was able to do at her small cafe on Main Street had slipped slightly as the years wore on. He grimaced and swallowed more port. She was rather popular now, no doubt thanks to her mad baking skills. Those who hadn't learned how to go back to basics and bake their own bread often brought their rations to her and she managed to make the magic happen. The fact that she didn't ask anything in payment for the work also worked in her favor. It was hard to argue with people's stomachs and it had led to her and her two children being welcomed into the fold by most.

The trade in people, more specifically those less fortunate or those who were not raised as well as they should have been, had been an unfortunate, yet necessary, course of action. His town, as Farley liked to consider it, needed the best. People who would work hard and follow his directives. Those who couldn't, or who asked too many annoying questions, well, they needed to move on, disappear even, so long as they stopped interfering with Farley running the town in the manner in which it needed to be run.

People disappeared all the time these days, after all. Wingo had already taken the lead on handling the drug production and trade in the area, something that kept those undesirables left who still had some use, quiet and compliant, but he had tasked Farley with making sure that a steady trickle of people - unwanted or non-compliant - were provided to the surrounding areas in exchange for protection from invasion. What they did with the unwanted. Well, that wasn't his business, was it? The Collapse had changed everything but human nature. There would always be the haves and the have nots, and Farley was determined to fall into the latter category.

As the bombs had fallen, and the world at large had descended into chaos, losing the electrical grid and communications array had sent their once-proud nation back to the Dark Ages. And here, in what Farley thought of as the unlikeliest of places, they had found some kind of balance in what could only be described as a form of city-state. The remnants of the political structure had shifted and morphed into a mix of "get whatever you can and hold on to it" and a territorial shifting of priorities, one that re-created the warring city-states of ancient times.

What most of the citizens of Belton didn't know or understand was that the currency had changed. They no longer operated in fiat currency, instead it was trade. And while food crops, even cattle, were highly prized, the trade he personally specialized in was not trade that most people accepted. In the new, post-Collapse world, food, drugs, and human beings were the new currency, and Farley and Wingo, working together, controlled them all.

James was heading up the collection of a woman who would provide a tidy solution to an imminent problem. An addict with loose lips, and one time worker for Wingo, she had become a problem that needed solving. He had told his son to check in with him once the deed was done.

Farley gathered the last rich crumbs of brownie goodness from his plate and drained the last drops of port from his glass. He didn't let morality interfere with his life. That was something Evelyn would have done. His late wife had been the religious one, the moral one. At least, she had been until the cancer began to eat away at her brain. It had turned her into a hate spewing, paranoid creature. Their son, James, had been in young, ten maybe, when the delusions had really set in. Farley had put her in an institution immediately. That kind of behavior, created by illness or not, simply had no place in his orderly existence. It had been a short stay. The cancer, while relentless, had been mercifully quick. Just six months from diagnosis to death, and Farley had found himself raising the boy all on his own. For a child he hadn't particularly wanted, it had been an onerous burden. Figure in the Collapse a handful of years later, and it was almost too much to bear.

He'd increased the enormous life insurance payout in a number of financial wheeling and dealing, which had quickly tripled the amount he had been paid. He had then engaged an out-of-state contractor to dig the tunnels and lay in the solar when the rumors of a financial collapse began to circulate. While most of the nation was focused on elections, or Black Lives Matter, the latest epidemic, or rising food costs - Jonathan Farley was stocking foods, supplies, weapons, and any other creature comforts he could think of. Let the world burn. He was ready for it.

The Western Front blowing through had both helped and hindered his position. He'd been lucky that he had the sniffles that day and not gone into work. He had been an alderman with dreams of more power, but with several seasoned candidates in his way. Almost to a man, they had died during the invasion. The one who had been left, the lone female alderman with plenty of clout and her fingers in every pie, had been spared, only to lose her husband and grown son in the attack. Marjorie Brown hadn't lasted long. The first round of a bad flu had taken her that first year and the path to the mayorship had been cleared for him. In that sense, he certainly had the Western Front to thank. But the damage they had done had been substantial. By the time the fires had been put out and the dead and missing accounted for, Belton had less than one-tenth of their population left.

From a town of more than twenty thousand people to one that hovered in the range of around eighteen hundred.

Farley shook his head at the thought. His father, had he still been alive, would likely have been sorely disappointed in him. The old man had aspired to far more, and he had dabbled in politics as well while making his fortune in several investment firms that were nothing better than Ponzi schemes. But power was power. If the town had still had its population intact, it would have been far more difficult to control. Farley knew this for a fact. He wasn't a pie in the sky dreamer, and he understood people rather well. He knew himself better than most, and he could see that others respected him only for the power he wielded, not for his sparkling personality. He was good at making money, better at keeping it, and he made sure to keep his supporters well-plied with the occasional rare gift.

Farley was as happy as could be expected in these trying times. And if he positioned himself right, he would continue to profit, and grow, come what may. That was the goal, at least. And the challenge of profit, through cold, hard cash or the wealth of choice when others had little of either - that was one he embraced.

He poured more of the port and picked up a remote, aiming it at the enormous speakers on one wall. A moment later, Vivaldi blossomed forth. Farley smiled and settled back to wait for his son.

A warm glow was beginning to spread through Farley's limbs when a chirp of alarm sounded. "Front hatch… open," chimed his security alarm. It was disabled. He'd been expecting his son, but not for a few more hours. He was handling a transfer tonight. The girl was a particularly troublesome one. And Farley had certainly been happy to assist Wingo when she didn't make good on payment for services rendered. The girl had made certain promises in return for a hefty amount of meth, and she hadn't kept up her end of the bargain.

As far as Farley was concerned, the ones who couldn't afford their addictions tended to be the worst of the riffraff, causing troubles in other areas - theft, disruptive behavior, and more. The fact that she had been one of the former alderman's kids made it all the sweeter. He would be all too happy to hand her over to the gentleman's club that had been restarted some forty miles outside of Kansas City on I70. His connection there had made sure to take care of his son James' needs as well, but Farley had little time or inclination for such cheap things. In truth, he had hoped for a little more with Sarah Turner, even though he could see she had no interest.

Better that I live a simple life, monastic in nature, he mused as he slipped the last crumbs into his mouth and followed it with the last mouthful of port. He stood up and turned to greet his son as he emerged from the long tunnel.

James looked worse for wear, and that was being kind. His nose, chin, and the front of his shirt were a bloody mess. His eyes were wild with panic. Jonathan felt a rush of fear flow through him.

"What happened?" he barked at James.

"We have a situation, sir." His boy looked afraid, but at least he kept up decorum. Long ago, likely long before the boy's mother's cancer had eaten her brain, Farley had insisted the boy call him sir, just as his own father had done. It was the small, yet meaningful traditions like that which kept them above the simpler folk.

Farley set his glass down and wiped his mouth with a cloth napkin. He kept his composure, but he hated the sight of blood, and James' face was covered in it.

"Go on."

"The crazy bitch got the drop on me. Damn near broke my nose and hit me on the head with something. By the time I came to, she was gone."

Farley stared at his son incredulously. "Why are you here? Get Wingo, and a couple of men you can trust and go after her!"

"I just thought..."

"No, no, you didn't think. If you had been thinking, we wouldn't be having this discussion, would we? Get Wingo, get Payton and Trey and get her back. Now! Before she flaps her mouth to anyone in town."

The chances that anyone would believe Cici Baker, daughter of drug addicts and an obvious addict herself, were small, but if they got wind that James Farley, the son of the mayor, was involved, then things could get sticky. Farley shook his head.

Stupid boy. Should have known better than to expect him to do this job right.

He dusted a few crumbs off of his shirt and barked at his son, "Go on! Round her up and I'll get Wingo to pitch in. She isn't going far. Stupid girl has alienated anyone willing to help her long time back."

And if she got out, if she talked to anyone, it could mean real trouble for all of them. Until the girl had shown what a real mess she was, they had used her for production and distribution. It had been a while, a year or more, since she had shown herself to be unreliable.

Why didn't I push for her to be removed back then? Hell, I could've had Wingo give her too big a dose and just had her OD. Too late for that now, though.

He felt anxiety ratchet up his pulse. Best they caught her quick. There was talk on the wind of a Reformation, and there hadn't been any fighting for quite a while. The time for these murky transactions was coming to a close and that little skank Cici had been involved in far too many of them. She wasn't particularly smart, but now that she knew James was involved, it didn't take much for anyone of any basic intelligence to look farther past the boy to the real source. And Farley couldn't have that. Uh, uh. In a few years, the world would reset itself, climb out of the darkness and society would go back to what it had been before the dollar had collapsed and the bombs had fallen. Life was cyclic like that. The bad times didn't last, but neither did the good. Existence between birth and death was far messier than most would care to recognize.

"Find her, and I'll meet you at the rendezvous north of town." Farley barked at his son.

James, who had been gingerly wiping at the caked blood from his face, nodded, his shoulders hunched, and disappeared down the tunnel without another word.

Jeremiah

Jeremiah Flanagan woke from a doze, the ground hard and cold beneath him. Dani, her tiny body spooned against the inside of his, slept hard, a bundle of warmth tucked in tight. He did his best not to wake her. She was exhausted, dark rings under her eyes from lack of food and the endless walking. She hadn't said much, not since they had left New Mexico behind some four weeks ago.

He slid one leg out of the thick extra-large sleeping bag and then the other. Easing out of it, wincing at the cold air which sucked his energy away. His stomach grumbled, and he knew they would need to find a town soon. One that might take them in, if only for a day or two. One that would have work for him to do, so they could re-stock on supplies before hitting the road again.

He'd been a fool to try to do this now, in winter, but really, what choice did they have?

Dani shifted as a gust of cold air invaded the sleeping bag in his absence. She didn't wake, however, and Jeremiah slipped on his gloves before he tried to stoke the campfire back to life. He winced at how stiff they felt, the cold affecting him in a way that he had never experienced until now. New Mexico got cold, sure, but this, this was bone-aching cold. It slipped in and surrounded you, enough to make you wonder if you could ever be warm again. And it would only get worse, especially when he thought of where they were heading. Canada in winter. He shook his head.

What kind of fool heads north, on foot, with a preschooler, in winter?

It hadn't been cold when he left, not

at all. The weather had been warm, short sleeve weather, as Shannon had called it, and consumed with grief and loneliness in the wake of her passing, it had seemed like the right thing to do. His mother's older brother, his uncle Jaime, had settled outside of Winnipeg not long before the Collapse. His last emails, before the power had failed, and the nuke hit Austin causing a string of chaotic events, had been to invite Jeremiah and Shannon there to his farm, an extensive parcel that was self-sufficient and safe. But Shannon hadn't wanted to leave. New Mexico had been home to the de Silva clan for generations, and she had never so much as stepped foot outside of the state in her entire life.

Neither had Dani, for that matter.

Shannon had given birth to their daughter nearly five years after the Collapse, surrounded by her mother and sister and a cousin who had been a doula since before Shannon was born.

Jeremiah poked at the fire, pushing aside the layer of white to reveal the glowing red embers beneath. He added a piece of old, weathered fencing, all that he was able to gather the evening before, and tossed a handful of dead grass on top. The glow intensified, smoke curling, a crackle and spit, before the flame jumped to life, heat emanating from it which felt good on his chilled face but also pulled the already dry skin tighter until it felt as if he were wearing a tight mask. He added another piece of fencing and watched the flames lick up the worm-riddled wood.

Dani stirred then, stretching at his feet, her eyes fluttered open for a moment before she burrowed deeper, out of sight, in the folds of the sleeping bag. Her red hair was a mass of tangles. He'd forgotten a brush, and it had descended in a matted mess of snarls and the occasional twig or mashed leaf.

I suck at this, Shannon. God knows I do.

He watched the flames grow, hypnotized and lost in thought. Those last moments with Shannon, watching the fever take her in its clutches and not let go.

"It's dysentery. I'm sure of it. The Lakewood's down the way had it and it presented just like this," Shannon's mom had said at the end of August, shutting the enormous tome she regularly consulted in times of illness. The Lakewood family had all died within days of each other as they ran high fevers and vomited and shit themselves. It had been sudden and fatal. But the antibiotics were gone, long gone, and although there had been rumors of the Reformation, it certainly hadn't made it to their little hamlet of Hatch, New Mexico.

Jeremiah closed his eyes, turned, and let the heat of the flames warm his back. Rosalia de Silva had survived the dysentery that gripped her and her daughters. It had left her a weakened wreck, however, especially after Shannon and Sonora had both died. He stared at Dani's small shape, now completely hidden within the sleeping bag. Her torso rose and fell rhythmically. Rosalia had been a formidable woman when Shannon had brought him home to meet her, and it was only her own bout with the disease, and the loss of her daughters, that had robbed her of the strength to fight his departure.

The heat pulsed into his back, the fire crackling merrily now, spitting sparks, the ancient wood engulfed in flames. His stomach grumbled, and he reluctantly left the warmth of the fire to dig through the backpack for the last cans of food they had.

Dani roused from the sleeping bag, her tiny fists rubbing at her eyes.

"Hey sugar plum."

She mumbled, "Hi Da," and pulled the sleeping bag close to her, a tiny shiver racking her body.

"We've got corned beef hash and

peaches for breakfast."

Jeremiah watched as her lower lip began to tremble. She said nothing, but tears filled her green eyes.

"It's all we have, kiddo. At least until we get to the next town." He reached out and plucked a crumpled leaf out of her rat's nest of tangles, paused and remembered how his wife had been with her. He leaned down, cupped her tiny chin in his hand and kissed her forehead just as he had seen Shannon do a thousand times.

"Did you sleep okay?" He asked, reaching for the cans of food. Nights were the worst for her. There hadn't been one night without tears, not one.

Dani nodded, but said nothing more. He felt his chest tighten. His baby girl missed her mom. Hell, he missed

Shannon so badly it felt as if his heart had shriveled up and died with her. But for Dani, who had been Shannon's shadow since the day she could walk, the loss of her mother had been the most traumatizing event of her life, seconded only by leaving the only home she had ever known.

You goddamn fool. You should have stayed in New Mexico.

Was it a fool's errand, this quest to find Uncle Jaime's farm?

Most likely you'll both die out here. At best, you don't, and you actually find this damn farm only to learn he's moved on or died or the place has burned to the ground.

At first, they had ridden a sweet 3-wheeled bicycle he had bought shortly before everything went to hell. But after a couple of close calls on I-35, the third time of which had seen them running for cover as troops moved through, Jeremiah had more than enough. Which faction of troops they were, he had no idea, and he wasn't willing to find out. He had ditched the bike, and they had hidden within the forest, moving deeper as he watched several of the soldiers stop at the bike and then look toward the line of forest. He hadn't wanted to know whether they would take what little the father daughter duo had, or simply shoot them. Later, as dusk stole over the land, he had snuck back close enough to see that the bike was gone, no doubt taken by the soldiers. That was okay. Two of the three tires had already begun to leak. And without a spare, he was on borrowed time with it, anyway.

They had stuck to smaller roads and occasionally cut through forests or wide grassland. It was better to avoid the towns when possible, and the terrain had been slow-going, but they hadn't managed to get as far on foot as he had hoped. His back, neck and arms ached from carrying her on his shoulders and Dani's shoes were sporting cracks in the soles, and the thin canvas wasn't enough to keep her feet warm as she stumbled along the ground beside him.

Something had to give. They still had at least 800 miles to go and winter was here. Jeremiah struggled to remember how in the hell he had thought it would take a month, maybe two at most, to travel over sixteen hundred miles with a three-year-old. The math had seemed simpler somehow when he was imagining them riding the bike, Dani perched on the custom seat he had built in the back, the wind blowing in her hair. On foot, however, reality had set in. Still, he could have turned back. He had been closer to Hatch, easier to return, admit defeat.

It was his Irish blood. That's what Shannon would have told him, laughing as she threaded her long delicate fingers through his red hair or spread aloe vera over his ever-present sunburn. Shannon, with her dark brown curls, olive skin and hazel eyes. God, he missed her. The dysentery had taken her so fast, faster than any of them could have been ready for. In his darkest moments, he had hated her for leaving him, for leaving Dani who hadn't smiled once, not once in the eight weeks and five days since they had lost her. Shannon had been the glue that kept them together. The one who had stood up to her mother and insisted that Jeremiah was her choice and her love, defiant in the face of maternal disapproval. Without Shannon, he had no chance of withstanding the hurricane that was Rosalia deSilva.

Jeremiah slipped off a glove and hooked the pull tabs on both cans of food with his fingers. Gently easing them back one at a time. He couldn't afford an injury or cut. Not now, not on the road. A week earlier, he had stepped wrong. One minute he had been fine, the next he had been on his knees. It had hurt for days and slowed them down. The ground was uneven here, whether it was forest or open prairie, and occasionally, after examining their surroundings well in both directions, he would slip onto a gravel road, grateful for a more even-footed stretch to walk on. Still, it wasn't a good idea. He'd seen what some of the troops that barreled through the main roads had done. Whatever side they were on, it wasn't that of anyone unfortunate enough to run into them. There had been one hair-raising encounter at least two weeks past, with three men dressed in fatigues, all armed. Jeremiah had been lost in thought, and Dani had been draped over his shoulders, a slick of drool escaping from her mouth, dozing as he walked. He'd been so busy picking his way through the forest he had walked into their encampment before he had even realized they were there. The dark muzzle of a shotgun in his face had nearly caused his bowels to loosen, but it had been the larger of the three men, sitting on a fallen tree next to their campfire, and the lascivious look that he had fixed on Dani that had turned Jeremiah's blood ice cold. It had all happened so quick. But the man holding the shotgun had waved Jeremiah away when he learned he wasn't a local.

As he had put tracks between them, picking up his pace to a jog shortly after their camp disappeared in the trees behind him, he had wondered if they really were soldiers.

There had been plenty of talk, rumor really, of what was happening in the country. After the reports of nukes, a wave of silence had hit. It had left them to wonder, fear, what was really happening. Rumors had flown thick, especially from anyone who dared to travel. Several factions of soldiers were fighting for control of what remained of the United States.

Although really, what is left, after all? Jeremiah had wondered more than once. *D.C. is a nuclear wasteland, so is Austin.*

Nevertheless, the various factions found something to fight about. Considering how dirty the three soldiers had been, Jeremiah couldn't help wondering two things - was there anything worth fighting over and were the men deserters of whatever faction they had originally sworn allegiance to?

Dani's small hand on his arm brought him back to present. She handed him the can of corned beef hash. There was more than half left.

"Sugar plum, you gotta eat your share. Here, take one more bite." His daughter made a face, but opened her mouth obediently to the spoon he held out to her. He looked at the can of peaches, untouched, in his hand, and speared several slices with his fork. "And I need to take my own advice, don't I now?" He shoved the sweet, dripping mess into his mouth, wiped the drop of juice that escaped down his chin, and handed the can to his daughter.

They would need to find food soon. Dani was looking peaked, tiring earlier and stumbling along the way as they walked, and he wasn't faring much better. Walking took a lot of calories out of them, more than they were taking in, and that was for sure. Especially now that the weather was colder. Perhaps he could find a way to pay their way to overwinter in the next town.

"Da? Carry me?" His heart wrenched at her request. He was tired, exhausted even after a night's sleep, and he forced a smile on his face.

"Sure Sweetheart, just for a little way, though, okay?" He could manage a short distance, maybe the first mile or two, even. She sat and watched him as he broke down their camp, rolling their sleeping bag up and zipping everything away neatly before he lifted her onto his shoulders. She felt lighter as he lifted her, but as soon as she was settled on his shoulders, he regretted having agreed to carry her. Her little butt was bony and dug into his shoulder blades. She had lost weight over the long journey, of that he was certain, but so had he, and it was hard enough carrying all of their equipment. He teetered off balance for a mere moment, and she clutched at his hair in fear.

"Easy there, Sugar Plum. I need that hair to keep my head warm," Jeremiah said, wincing as she clawed for safe purchase.

The sooner they got to the small town of Belton, the better. He grimaced, hoping that Dani's elfin face turned their hardened hearts into puddles of kindness. If it didn't, they had a day, maybe three at the outset, before either of them would simply stop being able to travel at all.

It was simply bad luck what

happened next. If Jeremiah had known whose field he was stepping into, if the sign that read Keep Out hadn't been felled by a recent storm, and if a particular, highly private trade between two parties who prized their anonymity above all else had not been happening at that very moment - Jeremiah and Dani's lives would likely have been very different.

Dani had seen the sign. Her head, a good foot above Jeremiah's, had given her that extra range needed. It was on its side, wrenched from its hole and turned away by the tree that had felled the section of fencing they were now walking through. She recognized the letters, at least some of them. Her mother had been teaching her letters earlier in the spring, tracing the shape of them in the dirt outside of their house. Dani could see a K, which was a letter she loved.

"K is for Kitten," Dani could still hear her Mommy's voice in her head, see the stick in her mind as it scratched through the dust, making shapes.

Dani had been trying to find out where mama cat had hidden her new kittens for days and days. Likely under the front porch, which was off limits due to fears of snakes or scorpions. She had wanted a kitten more than anything. And the K, well, it looked perfect, a shape that promised happiness. Just a moment to glance at the sign, though, before Da moved on into the small clearing surrounded by trees. The K had been followed by two Es and a P.

"Da? What's K and E and E and P?"

she asked.

Jeremiah lurched to one side beneath her as he stepped over the uneven terrain.

"K... E... E... P, Sugar Plum?" He lurched again, swearing under his breath, "That spells keep."

Dani nodded and said nothing more. She hadn't read the bottom half of the sign. There hadn't been time, after all. The small clearing was not empty. There was a series of low-slung buildings in various stages of disrepair. No wood smoke, though, so likely they were abandoned. It was too cold out for there to not be wood smoke and both of them started with surprise at the sound of voices coming from the boarded-up house to the left.

It was two men at least, and their

voices sounded angry. A second later, and a woman's voice. The words were not clear, but the woman sounded scared.

Jeremiah stopped in his tracks and gently slid Dani off of his shoulders, bringing his face down close to hers, a finger to his lips.

Dani

"Da?" Dani began to speak, and Jeremiah shushed her. The look on his face was clear. He was afraid. Before Mama had died, he had only looked like that once, when Tuna, Grammy's dog, had gotten bit by a rattlesnake by the back shed where Dani liked to play. Tuna's leg had swollen up, impossibly big, and he had died. Da had grabbed her arm and told her not to go anywhere near the back shed. The next time he had looked like that, Mama had died. And the time after that, it had been when the soldiers took their bike.

Dad didn't get scared very often, but if he was afraid right now, so should she be. Dani clamped her mouth shut, eyes widening, and took his hand, sticking close to his left hip.

The voices were louder now, clear, despite there being boards over the windows and the others being inside while they crept by. There was a small creek in the distance, along with another thatch of trees. Da pointed to them, making sure she understood. That's where they needed to go. That's what would get them away from this place, and the angry voices.

"You can't treat me like this! I kept my mouth shut, never said nothing to no one!" That was a woman talking.

"She knows too much, Farley. We can't trade her to the whorehouse, she'll open her goddamn mouth and now, thanks to Jimmy screwing this up, she knows you are in it too." The voice was low, closer, and Dani realized with a start that the two men were standing *outside* of the ramshackle house, in clear view. They hadn't noticed Dani and Da, but they would at any moment. The taller one, the one who had been speaking, left the shorter, fat man standing there and walked inside.

"Oh, shit!" shouted another younger man's voice inside, and an aborted scream from the woman as a shot rang out. A loud thump followed.

Dani had tried to be silent. But even she knew something bad had happened. A sharp gasp from her, and the fat man's eyes shifted, suddenly seeing the father and daughter there, and he jumped a little in surprise.

Da said nothing. Nothing at all. As he grabbed Dani's hand in a brutal grip and began to run through the tall, dead prairie grass. Dani could feel her feet flying, the grass whipping against her, feet not even touching the hard, cold ground. If she could have looked behind her, she would have seen the fat man turn back to the house, wave at his partner to come back out, and the man give chase. Instead, she simply held onto Da's coat as they flew, everything a blur of browns and yellows and golds mixed with snow and eventually ice-cold water as they entered the stream

and then the trees and did not stop.
It felt like an eternity. Eventually,
Dani could hear Da's breaths coming
in rasps, huge heaving gasps of air as
he continued to run. The trees that
had closed around them had twisted
and turned with the stream, lining it,
providing cover, but also a challenge
of twists and turns. They rose and
lowered on each side of the stream,
the terrain far from even. The man
shouted at them to stop, but Da didn't
listen. He kept running, and with him,
Dani simply held on. She felt like she
was flying. It might have even been
enjoyable in any other circumstances,
but this, this was all too fast and
scary.

"Someday, Sugar Plum, I'm gonna
take you on a roller coaster." Da had
told her. "They're all closed right now,

but soon, soon the world will turn right again and I'll take you on a roller coaster and you'll scream and be scared and love it all at the same time."

Da had traveled all over the world. He'd been born in a place really far away called Ireland. "Across the pond," he'd said, but a bigger one than they had near the farm. A super-big one that was deeper than anything she had ever seen. Da had told her about coming to the United States, traveling all over, and that his car had broken down in a tiny town in New Mexico and, "I fell in love with your Mama, Sugar Plum, and suddenly traveling the world didn't seem half as important as staying right here and being with her."

Da's red hair and bright green eyes

were an oddity there in their small hometown. But his voice, it was his voice that always drew the stares. Dani loved it more than anything.

As he ran, slower now, his breaths coming ragged and harsh, the trees thinned out onto a large open patch. Nearby was the continuing line of forest and trees. It had diverged from the stream, charting its own path.

In the far distance, she could see the tops of what looked like houses. A town, possibly. It was then that the shot rang out and Da jerked and fell into the stream. They had come so far. Dani couldn't even see the ramshackle house or even the men that had been chasing her, but Da lay in the water and Dani, flung in a sprawling heap at the side of the stream, stared at Da, waiting for him to get up. Her backpack had ripped as they fell and it cushioned her fall, only a small tear in the knee of her jeans and a pinprick of pain to show for such a heavy, abrupt fall.

Looking at him, he didn't seem hurt. There was a tiny rip or hole in the back of his jacket, but nothing else. She pulled on his arm and he moaned. That was when she saw the water moving away, sluggishly, and colored a dark crimson red.

Dani couldn't make words come out of her mouth. A whine of fear escaped, similar to the one that had caught the fat man's attention back at the clearing, but nothing else.

Da shifted, groaned, and blinked. His mouth was bloody. Dani could see it now that he lifted his head, barely moving, just lying there in the icy water. His lips moved, and she knelt down in the stream, ignoring the ice-cold water, trying to hear what he was saying. It wasn't louder than a whisper.

Closer. Closer.

"Run, Dani. Run away." The words were Da's, but they were so quiet, so low, it felt like a nightmare where nothing sounds or works right. Dani shook with fear, her teeth chattering with her feet and knees soaked in the ice-cold shallow water. Da raised his head again and choked, blood speckling the smooth rock in the stream next to his head. "GO!"

And somehow, she had. She picked herself up, focused on the nearby forest, and ran. As she did, she could hear men's voices. Mainly they shouted at each other, but once or

twice they shouted at her to stop. She
didn't listen. Da had told her to run
and run she would. As she entered
the trees, a second shot rang out.
Dani didn't stop, however, she just
kept on running until she tripped, her
small body catapulting over a half-
buried tree branch and then sliding to
a stop in a culvert filled with brush
and leaves.

It hurt. Vegetation scraped her face
and hands, and she winced as she
tried to tuck the injured hands into
her pockets. The culvert that she had
landed in was rather deep on the side
she had fallen in on. To one side was
an enormous dead tree protruding on
the edge of rocks and a dark crevice
of dirt and leaves provided a nest of
sorts. She crept into it, pulling the
leaves up and around her like Da had

taught her the other day.

"Sugar Plum, if you ever get too cold out here and for some reason you are all on your own, just make a little hole and pull the leaves and dry vegetation up all around you. It'll help warm you."

She could hear his voice in her head, warm and rich. A tear slipped down her cheek, then another, and another. It mingled with the dirt, fat drips falling muddy onto her hands. The men were coming. She could hear them now.

"A little kid, by the looks of it. She can't have gone far." The older man's voice rang out, dangerously close, and Dani tried to hold her breath. She flattened against the earth and rocks, her body disappearing from view, the leaves thick and comforting, a great thick blanket of them. She tried to hold still though, for fear that the very things keeping her safe and helping to warm her would be the same things that gave her away. She listened as the man's footsteps came closer.

A younger man's voice, his breathing labored, spoke up, "She's just a little kid. What's she gonna do, really, Chief?"

"She could point. Tell someone we shot her daddy." The older man, Chief, responded.

Another body came in, his breath rattling as he wheezed to a stop. "Christ, Wingo, why the hell did you do that? You shot that man. There's no covering that shit up. Cici, back at the farm, *that* was justified, but I could have talked to the guy, sent him and the kid on their way or something."

Dani couldn't be sure, but she thought it might be the fat man that had been back at the ramshackle house that was talking, well, wheezing. Three men. The older one that had been outside with the fat man and was called Chief or Wingo, and the young man, who had been inside the house.

She wanted to make herself smaller, but she was afraid the leaves would make noise and give her away. They were close, so close.

"Any sign of her?" Was all that the older man said in response, ignoring the other two.

"Not that I've seen."

"How old d'ya think she is?" Wingo asked.

"I couldn't tell you," the fat man

responded, still wheezing, "Small, maybe two or three years old?"

"Old enough to talk then."

In the trees above, a soft pattering began and, as Dani watched, ice particles began to fall, landing with ever-increasing rapidity on the fallen leaves all around them.

"The storm's rolling in," Wingo said, his voice further away, back the way they all had come, "A kid that small'll be dead by morning from exposure. End of problem." Dani could hear him walking away, twigs snapping and the leaves crunching as he left. "I'll take care of the mess back at the house."

"What about the guy in the creek?" the younger man called after him, still standing close to Dani's hiding spot.

"Fuck him. He's no local. Folks won't give a damn about someone who got shot after he was creeping around fixing to rob them." Wingo's words hung in the air, and then there was silence.

"Damn, but this all went to shit." The younger man whistled slowly.

"You think?" The fat man spoke, his breathing mostly back to normal now, and he sounded angry. "You made a mess out of it. I should have never agreed to this human trafficking bullshit, not with you making a hot mess of it from the get go. And shooting that man, hell, Wingo's damn near lost his mind."

A branch snapped above Dani's head. "He's right about the kid, though. She's likely to die of exposure out here, so I'm thinking we might as well be on our way. I've had enough nasty business in the past hour to last a lifetime."

Dani could hear him slowly walking away, his departure noisy, his feet heavy on the forest floor.

"You coming? We need to get that nose of yours looked at."

"Yes, sir." The crunch of leaves signaled his departure as well.

Dani listened as the men left. Part of her was sure that they would be waiting, like the bogeyman from a nightmare, just out of range of hearing, waiting to grab her and hurt her like the Chief Wingo man had wanted them to do. She took a chance, adjusted herself deeper into the drift of leaves, and closed her eyes. Just as quickly, she opened them, looking at the empty woods. Around her, the storm began to pelt the forest with sleet. She would have to leave soon, likely go back to the stream where Da was.

Da. I need Da.

The leaves were warm, however, warmer than she had felt in a long time. Dani's eyes slid shut, and she sunk into a fragmented, restless doze.

When Dani's eyes opened, the small amount of weak sunlight that had greeted her that morning on the road with Da was gone, replaced with gray. Sleet now fell solidly, a relatively loud, continuous sound. For a moment, Dani didn't remember where she was. The momentary confusion that had her back in New Mexico, staring at the alien forest around her. And then it all surfaced at once, the argument in the ramshackle house, the gunshot, their panicked run and Da falling in the streambed.

Her mouth formed his name, but her lips failed to speak it aloud. The leaves that covered her exploded out as she scrambled out of her hiding place, intent on getting back to the stream, back to Da. Her feet scrabbled up the embankment, up out of the culvert, slipping and sliding on the newly wet and slippery leaves.

It was cold, ice cold now, but she didn't notice. All of her focus was on returning to Da, to the streambed, to the only source of safety and comfort she had left since Mama had died and Auntie Tia too. She slipped and fell twice before emerging from the cover of the trees. As she ran out into the open, she could see his form, dark and alone, still sprawled in the streambed. Some part of her gabbled in fear at the thought of the men that had chased her and Da, could they still be here? But she kept focus on reaching Da. That was all that mattered.

Her chest was heaving, her breaths sharp and ragged in the bitter cold, as she slid to a stop next to him.

She had seen Mama, right after, before they had sealed her in the box and lowered her in the ground. Da, he looked like that, only covered in blood and his eyes open, not closed like Mama's had been. Still she couldn't help but cling to him.

She thought of a rhyme Mama would say at night, while they sat on the porch and looked up at the dark, night sky and the panorama of stars.

Mama had smiled and whispered, "Star Light, Star Bright, first star I see tonight. I wish I may, I wish I might, have this wish I wish tonight."

But there were no stars out. It was still day, although it was dark and gray and the sleet kept falling, a steady patter as it covered the browns and golds of the dead vegetation. And there were no wishes that could bring back the dead.

How long she stayed there, Dani could not have known. Long enough that she felt cold all the way into her middle, and her fingers and toes were stiff, cold and aching. Tears she hadn't realized she had shed, coated her cheeks, mingling with the pellets of ice. Dani was alone. Worse, she had no one left to run to. Her stomach rumbled, but she had no way of accessing the last of their food, Da's backpack was wedged underneath his body and there was no moving it, nor accessing the zipper. And even as her stomach rumbled, Dani felt too scared to do much about it.

In the end, she had kissed Da on his cheek and stumbled away. Not back to the forest, but slowly, in the growing gloom, towards the buildings she saw in the far distance. Her feet and legs automatically moving, one step, then another. Away from Da, toward the unknown. By the time she reached the first of the homes, her coat was coated with ice. Her limbs felt stiff, unwieldy, and she kept falling.

The first house was a burned-out ruin. So was the second, and the third, and after the fourth one she lost count. It seemed that most were burned, but others were simply dark, empty things. Their doors gone, their contents removed, whoever had lived and loved and laughed inside of them long gone. She wandered up and down the streets, past burned hulks of cars, and skirted the edges of roads.

The house wasn't big, or even much different from the others she had seen walking in, but Dani was drawn to it. It had signs of occupancy. The large yard in front had been cultivated. Not now, of course, but Dani could see the remnants of orderly rows that had once held plants. The rest of the houses on the block were either in ruins or obviously empty, but this house, someone lived here. The smoke curled from the chimney and one of the windows allowed for a small glow from the fireplace within.

By now, the darkness of night was complete and Dani was afraid. What if the bad men were here? What if they wanted to hurt her? She was tired, though. So tired. And the front stoop she found herself standing in was well-protected from the wind. The snow, piled high just a few feet away, actually seemed to insulate the entryway and Dani slid down in place against the front door, seeking warmth, but also trying to marshal her reserves. Every part of her ached with exhaustion, grief, and her eyelids felt like heavy doors that would not stay open. Outside in the open, the wind howled its own grief, and she cried with it, the tears leaking down her cheeks in the darkness.

Somehow, despite the cold and the

hunger and her grief, Dani slid into a restless sleep.

The day dawned bright and light. The storm had moved on, the clouds pushed away in the wind the night before, and the sky was clear and blue.

A boy had appeared at the door. The inside door, that is, whereas Dani was against the outside door, huddled in tight. He had talked to her, but Dani had been so tired, so cold and scared by then, that she had no words for him. No words at all to encompass this yawning chasm of loss. It had hit her then, that Da was gone, and Mama was gone and everyone she knew and loved, who knew and loved her back, were gone. She had ignored the boy. Turned away and cried. Perhaps she should have stayed with Da, back at the stream. Just as she was considering going back there, if she could even find it, a woman appeared at the front of the house.

She was pretty. Her long blond hair hung out over her coat and she had the prettiest blue eyes that Dani had ever seen. She didn't say a word, just reached down and picked Dani up, her arms warm and strong. The outer door swung open then, the boy inside wasn't the only one there, and Dani ducked her head against the woman, tucking in close, suddenly terrified by all the strange faces.

There was a tall boy, almost a man, and the boy she had already seen, and even a girl not much older than Dani. They stared at her curiously and Dani, suddenly surrounded by warmth, began to shiver uncontrollably. The tears started up again as well.

The next few hours were a blur of being bathed, new clothes, and a hot meal. No matter where she went in the house, Dani saw no evidence of the bad men. The voices weren't the same, and these people were kind. Still, Dani could not seem to make her lips work. No words escaped. She didn't have anything to say, nothing that could compare to the howling loss she felt. The little girl pressed a doll into her arms and Dani thought of her bear, her lovey as Mama had called it, still stuffed in her backpack which lay abandoned by the stream. The food in her belly was more than she had eaten in a long time. She sat there, propped up in the chair, two books wedged under her to raise her to the height of the kitchen table and, despite the staring eyes, found her eyes slipping closed.

She barely noticed when warm, strong arms picked her up, carried her into a room, and tucked her in.

"It's okay, Sweetheart, you're safe now." The man's voice was kind, reassuring.

As she slid deeper into sleep, Dani let go of her fear. The bad men weren't here, and instead, this family was kind. She missed Da, just as much as she missed Mama and her aunties and Grandma. Here she was safe. And she liked her new name. The woman had called her Erin. Da had a sister named Erin, back in Ireland. Maybe someday she would tell her new family about Da and

Mama, the aunties and Grandma. Perhaps she would tell them about the farm that her great-uncle Jaime had in Alaska, or what she and Da had seen and heard outside of town. But for now, she didn't need to talk, and she really didn't particularly want to. She just wanted to sleep in a warm place, eat good food, and not be afraid anymore.

And as the winter snows fell, melted, and gave way to the sunny days of spring, Dani became Erin, a quiet, peaceful child who said nothing aloud but made herself perfectly understood, nonetheless.

Johnathan

At a ramshackle house north of town, Farley met with Wingo. They hadn't had any contact in months, not after Farley had decided that the trade in flesh was simply too dangerous as the Reformation began to solidify. The world was going back to what it had been, or at the very least, it was returning to a shadow of its former self.

Alaska and Hawaii had declared their independence. So had Texas, California, Oregon and Washington. The states that remained, however, were quickly rebuilding and the new capital of the country would be located in North Carolina.

Wingo leaned back in his chair, poking at the charred remains of a fire in the fireplace. "I hear they found the body."

Farley nodded, "Yes, Thurman Banks found it last week."

Wingo said nothing for a moment,

then turned to stare at Farley. His direct gaze, unblinking, made Jonathan Farley more nervous than he had been when word came through the town of the little girl's discovery a few days after the incident. He broke eye contact, stared out the grimy window with its broken panes. Somewhere out there Wingo had buried the body of Cici Baker. Why he hadn't felt it necessary to bury the traveler, Farley had not a whit of an idea, especially now that Wingo had called this meeting.

"And the child survived."

He forced himself to turn back to Wingo, "She's a mute. Hasn't said a word since she showed up on their front stoop right after that storm."

"Mute, huh?"

"I sent one of the men over to check

it out after I heard she'd shown up."

"Not you?" Wingo's eyebrows raised, "Or young James?"

Farley felt a flash of discomfort. He had thought about it, sure. But she'd *seen* him. What if she remembered something, freaked out, or reacted in a way that caused questions?

Kid that young, she'll forget given enough time. She won't remember what it was like anywhere else in a year or two. And Jess and her family are rarely in town with all the kids.

He kept his face as serene as he could manage, "Didn't have time to. There were other things to attend to at the time. Didn't see a reason to follow up once I heard she was mute."

Wingo stared at him silently.

"Look, the kid is no danger to us.

Jess Aaronson says she's young, barely three years old. Kids don't remember stuff that happens when they are that young. If you had kids, you'd know that."

"I have kids. Grown now, but I'm aware. Still, something traumatic like that, seeing her daddy killed, that's gotta stick in there." Wingo said, leaning back even further in his chair.

Farley gazed at the chair. One of the legs was split, maybe it would break if Wingo leaned back far enough. It sure as hell would if he sat in it, but he was nearly three bills to Wingo's lean frame.

"Yeah, well, why don't you go and see her for yourself," Farley snapped, adopting a facade of false bravado. About the last thing in the world he wanted to do was go anywhere near

Jess Aaronson's place and risk getting fingered by the girl. But he also had no interest in having a little girl killed so he'd made his peace with it and figured it was worth the risk. As winter had slid into spring and there had been no rumors or accusations, he'd breathed easier. Trust Wingo to dig it all up.

"Maybe I will." Wingo responded, his tone cool, coated in steel.

"Well, you do that." Farley snapped, wishing, as he had done all the rest of the winter and spring, that he had never had anything to do with James Wingo in the first place. "If there isn't anything else, I'll be going. I've a town to run."

He turned and headed for the door, his heavy frame caused the old wood underneath to groan loudly, bowing beneath the weight. The damn place was falling apart. As his foot crossed the threshold down to the step below, he could hear Wingo speak. What he said was low, deliberate, and insidious.

"There will come a time of reckoning, Farley. It might be tomorrow, next month, or in five years. But these things have a price. Eventually the bill will come due."

Jonathan Farley said nothing in return as he walked away. He said nothing to his son, other than instructing him to stay away from Wingo, and he felt a wash of relief a few months later when Wingo was shot in some deal gone wrong.

A child that small? She won't remember. Who would expect her to? He thought to himself. Nevertheless,

he gave Jess Aaronson's small family
a wide berth in the months and years
that followed.

Author Note

Thanks for reading!

Please take a moment and post a review of this book on the platform you purchased it and/or (preferably AND) Goodreads. Put simply, reviews indicate that someone has a) read the book and b) thought enough of it (either way) to post a review of it. Your opinion does matter.

Follow me on the Facebook group *General Malcontent's Grumbles and Scribbles* for updates on new releases, as well as what I'm currently working on. You might also enjoy visiting my author website to learn more about me, my projects, the Easter eggs you will find in my books, the stories behind the stories, and all-

new content that can only be found
on my website at
www.christineshuck.com.

Acknowledgments

As always, a deep and abiding thanks to Dori, Rachel, and Kate - for tolerating my complaints over boring grammar books and giving me the chance to fly.

Thank you to my husband, David, for supporting my dreams and believing in me no matter how many years it has taken to get these darn books out.

For my children - one likes me, one doesn't, two are honorary, and then there are the Littles who give me something to look forward to in the years to come.

For Dani, who I think must be my best fan ever (she's super cool).

And to all of the others - good and bad -

you have shaped my life, given me fodder for characters that readers love (and hate), and reminded me that my life has always been my own to chart. Thank you for that.

All Published Works

<u>Non-Fiction</u>:

Get Organized, Stay Organized
The War on Drugs: An Old Wives Tale

<u>Fiction Series</u>:

<u>War's End</u>
The Storm
A Brave New World
Tales of the Collapse

<u>Gliese 581g</u>
G581: The Departure
G581: Mars
G581: Earth

<u>Chronicles of Liv Rowan</u>
Fate's Highway a.k.a. Schicksal Turnpike

<u>Benton Security Services</u>
Hired Gun
Smoke and Steel

<u>Children of Ruin</u>
Winter's Child